New York Times and *USA TODAY* bestselling author **Katee Robert** learned to tell her stor... grandpa's knee. H... act was a RITA® Aw... named it 'a comp... with ...dren, driving ... what-if questions and planning ... zombie apocalypse.

New York Times bestselling author **Lauren Hawkeye** never imagined that she'd wind up telling stories for a living…though she's the only one who's surprised. She lives in the Rocky Mountains of Alberta, Canada, with her husband, two young sons, a pitbull and two idiot cats. In her non-existent spare time Lauren partakes in far too many hobbies! She loves to hear from her readers through e-mail, Facebook and Instagram! Sign up for Lauren's newsletter here: eepurl.com/OeF7r.

If you liked *Make Me Need* and *Between the Lines* why not try

His Innocent Seduction by Clare Connelly
One Wicked Week by Nicola Marsh

MAKE ME NEED

KATEE ROBERT

BETWEEN THE LINES

LAUREN HAWKEYE

MILLS & BOON

First Published in Great Britain 2019
by Mills & Boon, an imprint of HarperCollins*Publishers*
1 London Bridge Street, London, SE1 9GF

ISBN : 978-0-263-27383-0

MIX
Paper from
responsible sources
FSC www.fsc.org FSC C007454

This book is produced from independently certified FSC™ paper
to ensure responsible forest management.
For more information visit www.harpercollins.co.uk/green.

Printed and bound in Spain
by CPI, Barcelona

MAKE ME NEED

KATEE ROBERT

MILLS & BOON

To Hilary

CHAPTER ONE

TRISH LIVINGSTON DIDN'T do sad. Life was too short to focus on the negative crap. No matter how bad things got, it could always be worse.

Granted, she wasn't exactly sure how much worse *her* life could get. She was drowning in student loans, living with her wonderfully understanding but ultimately smothering parents and the only job she could get was one with her older brother's cybersecurity company.

Positive, Trish. You could be homeless. Your parents could be awful people—or gone completely. You could have as few job prospects as you did two weeks ago.

She smoothed a shaking hand down her skirt and squared her shoulders. Maybe this wouldn't be so unnerving if Aaron was actually here to introduce her to his partner and walk her through her responsibilities. But his fiancée had had their baby a week earlier than expected, so he was currently playing the doting father. He'd offered to slip away for a few hours, of course. That was what her brother did—took care of everyone around him. She'd declined because that was what *she* did—smoothed waves and gave people what they really wanted.

The elevator shuddered to a stop and the door slid open, removing any chance she had to change her mind. Trish smoothed her hair back as best she could, pasted a bright smile on her face and stepped out.

From what Aaron said, this entire floor was Tandem Security offices, which seemed a little strange since it was the two of them, but who was she to complain? Trish eyed the front office. *Not the most welcoming first impression.* A layer of dust covered the desk and she'd been under the impression that plastic plants couldn't actually die, but the teetering tree in the corner threatened to make a liar of her. Even the chairs were eyesores, a perfectly functional beige…that belonged in a hospital waiting room somewhere.

She walked over and sank into one and grimaced. *Thought so.* Whoever had designed these chairs didn't want the occupants to spend any amount of time in them. She shook her head and muttered under her breath, "Well, this is what Aaron hired you for. Apparently he actually *does* need someone—desperately."

"What do you want?"

She jumped to her feet and teetered in her cotton candy–pink heels. "Sorry, I was just trying out the chairs and…" She trailed off as she caught sight of the guy who'd snarled at her. He wore a pair of faded blue jeans and a white T-shirt that stretched tight across his impressive chest and set off his dark brown skin to perfection. A chiseled jaw and shaved head completed the picture and made her mouth water.

At least right up until she registered who this must be.

Trish turned her smile up to an eleven and stepped forward. "Cameron O'Clery? I'm Trish Livingston. Aaron was understandably occupied, so he said I should just head over here and make myself at home." She held out a hand until it became clear hc had no intention of shaking it. Undeterred, she dropped it and smoothed a nonexistent wrinkle from her skirt. "I know he mentioned this place needed a bit of a face-lift, but I never realized my brother had quite such a gift for understatement."

He stared and finally shook his head. "Info is in the top drawer of the desk. Do what you want."

Cameron turned and stalked down the hallway and out of sight.

Trish frowned. She rounded the desk and pulled open the creaky drawer. The only things in it were a credit card with Tandem Security's name on it and a paper with account names and passwords written out in neat block lettering. A little more snooping found a brand-new laptop tucked in the next drawer down. Trish shot a look down the hall, but since Cameron hadn't made an appearance, she shrugged and booted it up. Typing in the websites listed brought up accounting software, an email address and the company software itself. She scrolled through the list of clients—past and present—and sighed. *This would be a lot easier if I had a little guidance.*

Chin up, Trish. You know how to make the best of any situation. This is no different.

She stood and propped her hands on her hips. Since she had to start somewhere, the waiting room was the way to go. Aaron had hired her to redesign the office space, liaise with incoming clients and provide general support to him and Cameron. She turned in a slow circle again, mentally tallying everything she needed to accomplish her first goal. No reason to pay top dollar for everything. It didn't matter if the company could afford it or not. Even bargain shopping, it would be a chunk of change to do it all at once, so she'd roll up her sleeves and save costs wherever she could.

She palmed the credit card and headed into the back offices. There were no plaques or signs to indicate where anything was, but only one door had light coming from beneath it, so she headed in.

"I'm busy." Cameron didn't even bother to look up from his monitor.

Good grief. If this is his attitude, I can see why Aaron needed someone to handle clients. She didn't let her smile slip, though. "I can see that, so I won't take much of your time." Trish held up the credit card. "Just let me know the budget for the front office and I'll be out of your hair. Or, well, you have a shaved head so..." She smiled harder. "Sorry, I'm wasting time with babbling. Budget, please."

His dark brows drew together and he finally deigned to look directly at her. "What?"

"A budget. For the front office." The urge to keep talking bubbled up, but she pressed her lips together to prevent the words from escaping. Call it a hunch, but Cameron O'Clery didn't seem the type of man to appreciate small talk or meandering conversational threads.

His frown didn't clear. "Spend whatever you want."

Lord, grant me patience. She crossed her arms

over her chest. “With respect, I do better when I have clear guidelines. A budget would be helpful.”

Cameron cursed, as if this two-minute conversation had taxed what little patience he had. “Spend what you need to. If I think you’re out of line, I’ll tell you.”

Of that, she had no doubt.

Recognizing this was a losing battle, Trish edged back out of the office. “I’ll just get started, then.”

“Do that.” He turned back to his monitor, and it was as if he’d forgotten she was in the room.

She’d never been so summarily dismissed in her life, and Trish couldn’t deny that it rankled. She opened her mouth, but common sense got the best of her. As satisfying as it would be to pester one half of her new bosses, it was her first day. Better to set a precedent of doing her job well before she started pressing Sir Crankypants to hold down an actual conversation.

She headed back to her desk and considered. It was Friday, which gave her today and all weekend to get the decorating stuff out of the way. Then she could start bright and early Monday with figuring out the client aspect. Aaron wanted her to deal with new clients’ preliminary meetings to get a baseline for what services they required. From there, either Aaron or Cameron would take the client.

Though I guess Cameron will be taking them all until Aaron is back in the office.

One problem at a time.

She dropped into her desk chair and pulled a dusty notebook out from the second drawer. A list would keep her on track. Trish gave the room one last look and sighed. Her shoulders dropped a fraction of an inch before she caught herself and forcibly straightened them. *None of that, Trish. Think positive.*

Working as a glorified secretary for her brother's company might not be part of her bright plans for the future, but that didn't change anything. She gave 100 percent. It was what she did—who she was. This job would be no different.

She'd be the best damn glorified secretary Aaron and Cameron had ever had.

Cameron finished the last bit of code for his current client's site and sat back. There were still tests to run and scenarios to play out to ensure he'd filled every nook and cranny with the proper protections and hadn't left any back doors accidentally open, but they could wait until tomorrow. He rubbed a hand over his head and then stretched. He was past overdue for a massage—he usually kept regular appointments to prevent the kinks in his back from getting too bad—but Aaron's pending fatherhood had kept his partner out of the office more and more as his woman's pregnancy got further along, and more work had landed on Cameron as a result.

He didn't mind. His friend was happy, and that was enough for Cameron. He liked the work, liked keeping occupied with it. All he had was an empty apartment waiting for him, so it wasn't as if he missed much by spending more time in the office.

As he pushed to his feet and stretched more fully, he frowned. *What's that smell?* Another deep inhale had him checking his watch. It was well after eight in the evening, so who the hell was painting?

Cameron stalked out of his office, already calculating where the vents could be sending the scent from. It was probably the floor below theirs. The woman who ran the consulting business down there liked revamping her office with startling regularity. Saying shit wouldn't accomplish anything, and it *was* after-hours. He was just tired and hungry and overreacting.

He reached the front office and stopped cold. White cloth covered the floor and blue painter's tape marked off both the ceiling and trim. Half the white walls were now a soothing green, but that wasn't what set him back on his heels.

No, that was reserved for the barefoot woman

teetering on the top of a stepladder—*above* the sign set into the step warning not to stand above that point—her curly blond hair tied back in a haphazard knot that looked like a bird's nest. He started forward, belatedly realizing she still wore the outfit she'd had on earlier, a simple black skirt that hugged her hips and ass and a loose pink blouse in the same startling shade as the heels she'd worn.

This is Aaron's little sister. Get your eyes off her ass.

It was a great ass, though. As she went onto her tiptoes, the muscles in her lower half flexed and he had to bite back a groan. At least until she wobbled and overcompensated. Cameron jumped forward and caught her. He was a bastard and a half because he let himself enjoy the feeling of her in his arms for several seconds before he set her back on her feet.

Trish shoved the cloud of curly blond hair that had escaped its knot back and gave him a blindingly bright smile. "Thanks! I thought I could do this without scaffolding, but those nine-foot ceilings are no joke." Her smile wobbled. "Crap, I'm sorry. I got paint on you."

Cameron looked down to the streak of green marking his shoulder and then back at her. "You just took a nosedive off a ladder and you're worried about my shirt?"

"Well…yeah." She shrugged and leaned over to set the paint roller on the tray perched precariously on the ladder. "I fell. You caught me. Thanks again, by the way. But there's no reason to dwell on it."

He stared into those guileless blue eyes. She truly looked more worried about his shirt than any injuries she would have suffered if his timing had been a little off. "What would you have done if I wasn't here and you broke your leg?"

"At that angle, I'm more likely to break an arm." When he just glowered at her, she huffed out a breath. "My phone is right there, within easy reach." She pointed at the ladder. "If I didn't topple the ladder when I fell, and for some reason I wasn't able to stand, I would have kicked it over, retrieved my phone and called for help. Happy?"

Fuck no, he wasn't happy. The woman was obviously crazy, because she didn't seem the least bit concerned with that scenario. Cameron crossed his arms over his chest. "If I leave right now, you're going to climb right back up that ladder and finish painting, aren't you?"

"No?"

He growled. "If you're going to lie, at least try to pretend you're not fishing for the right answer." He gave up his happy thoughts about the pizza place down the block from his apartment. There was no way he could leave this woman unsupervised. He'd spend the rest of the night worried that she'd fallen again and he hadn't been there to catch her, and there would be no rest and a whole lot of indigestion in his future. Cameron stalked around the ladder, testing its stability. *Should be fine as long as no one stands on the top of the damn thing.* He pointed at the untouched brush near the paint can. "You're on edges."

"Actually, I—"

"You're on edges," he repeated, staring her down. "I'll handle this."

Trish opened her mouth, drawing his attention to her pink lipstick. He'd never had a thing for painted lips before, but the bright pigment made the sharp Cupid's bow of her top lip stand out against her skin and… *For fuck's sake, she's got freckles.* She was downright adorable, and that should be enough to banish any thoughts of getting his hands on her perfectly rounded ass or kissing her until she forgot about whatever argument she was obviously debating delivering.

It wasn't.

He wanted her, and hell if that didn't complicate things.

Cameron hadn't bothered to date in longer than

he cared to think about. It was so much goddamn work getting to know another person. Most of them ended up storming off before the second date because he said something wrong. Or he didn't talk enough. Or he talked too much about work because, God forbid, that wasn't a safe subject, either. It was exhausting just thinking about it, and he hadn't met anyone tempting enough to make him want to run that particular gauntlet. Easy enough to scratch the itch in loud bars where talking was the last thing on either his or his prospective partner's mind, but even that had gotten tiresome recently.

If he'd run into Trish on the street, he might have asked her out. Might have let her obvious enthusiasm and sunny attitude wash over him.

But she worked for him. What was more, her big brother was one of the few people in this world who not only put up with Cameron's bullshit without expecting him to change but also was a genuine friend.

He might want Trish, but she was the one woman he couldn't touch.

CHAPTER TWO

TRISH DIDN'T KNOW what to think of Cameron, but after looking like he wanted to give her a blistering lecture, he just picked up the paint roller, glared at her and got to work. She watched him climb the ladder and gave herself a shake. Staring at her boss's shoulders was *not* going to get this room painted before midnight. He obviously wasn't willing to listen to reason or let her do the job she was hired for, so she might as well take advantage of the extra set of hands.

Unsurprisingly, Cameron wasn't much of a chatterbox and every time she tried to talk to him, she only got grunts or one-word answers in response.

She gave up. Not forever. But it was kind of nice to just paint and not have to worry about being chipper. There was no relaxing, though—not with Cameron taking up too much space in the front office. Every time she moved, she caught a glimpse of him out of the corner of her eye. He moved with perfect precision, each roll of the paint even and uniform.

It took two hours to finish up, and part of Trish was almost sad to end the companionable silence. She stood back and pushed her hair away from her face with her forearm. "Oh yeah, this is the right color."

Cameron surveyed it as if he were a color expert. Hell, maybe he was. His brows furrowed. "It's strangely pleasing."

"That's the point." She placed her brush in the paint tray and started gathering up the various supplies scattered around the room. The tape would come off in the morning and then she'd touch up as needed, but she had a feeling there would be little of that necessary. Cameron was too much of a perfectionist to leave drips anywhere, which served her just fine.

She straightened and realized he was still watching her. His dark eyes studied her face as if he could divine her thoughts. Cameron frowned harder. "What are your plans for the front office?"

So now we have questions?

She bit back the sarcastic response and smiled. "This is the first impression clients get when they walk through the doors, so I want it to be welcoming and designed to set them at ease." Trish's main degree was in sales, but she'd gotten a minor in design. Her dream might be to eventually work in corporate fashion, but she knew how to use that skill set to set the tone of a room—and help people choose clothing that would make them happy. Not that she got to use the latter at all these days.

"We usually meet clients off-site."

"Yes, I'm aware. But that wastes time in transit and Aaron mentioned that there's a boardroom perfectly suitable for conducting meetings." Though, considering the state of the front office, she hadn't had the heart to check out that room yet to see what *perfectly suitable* meant. There would no doubt be more painting in her future, but hopefully it at least had furniture that was acceptable.

Cameron seemed to consider that and looked around the room again. "Tell me your plans." A tiny hesitation. "Please."

He's trying. Throw him a bone. Aaron had warned her that Cameron didn't bother with the social niceties, which set most people on edge, but his abruptness had still caught her off guard. If he was going to make an effort, though, she could do the same.

Trish walked over to stand in front of the door to the elevator. "Come here."

He gave her a look like he thought she was trying to put one over on him but joined her in facing the room. His shoulder brushed hers, sending shivers through her body that she couldn't quite control. He was just so *big*. Big and overwhelming and he smelled really good. *He's your boss, Trish. Slow your roll.*

"Okay." She cleared her throat. "Imagine this. You walk in and are instantly put at ease by the soothing green. I can make the desk work, but there will be a grouping of new chairs there." She pointed to one side of the office. "And a smaller one there." On the opposite side. "The window facing the street brings in enough light to justify some kind of plant, but I haven't decided what will be the best fit. Probably one on each side of the window to create balance. A small water fixture on the other side in the corner. Some kind of art on the wall behind my desk, and maybe on another wall or two, though I haven't decided yet."

"Lots of changes."

He sounded neutral enough, but she couldn't help straightening her spine and lifting her chin. "Yes, but that's what I was hired to do—create the best client-facing aspect of this business as possible. That starts with first impressions. You and Aaron have a company that's one of the best in the business, and as silly as it might seem, presentation matters. Meeting in secondary locations is fine, but this is better."

"One condition." He kept going before she had a chance to protest. "No more painting alone."

"Of all the—"

Cameron turned to face her, his chest nearly touching hers with each inhale. The proximity stalled her breath in her lungs and choked off whatever she'd been about to say. Trish swallowed hard, caught between wanting him to kiss her and wanting him to back the hell up and let some of the air back into the room. He didn't touch her, though. Didn't lean down. Didn't cup her jaw or press her back against the wall and ravage her mouth.

Get yourself together.

His voice disturbed the air between them. "No. Painting. Alone." Cameron's dark gaze dropped to her mouth for the briefest of seconds before it snapped back to her eyes. "Do we understand each other, Trish?"

The sound of her name on his lips turned her knees to Jell-O. She swayed toward him, toward the command in his voice, but caught herself at the last moment. *Do not kiss your boss.* Trish took a step back, and then another. She looked at the floor and swallowed hard. "Yeah, we understand each other."

He helped her finish cleaning up in silence, though she stewed a bit when Cameron made a point of taking the ladder and stowing it in the closet without letting her touch it. He walked back into the front office as she slipped on her shoes. "You're staying with Aaron?"

She could have let him believe that, but Trish had already misstepped enough on her first day without adding lying to the list, too. "I was, but I got my own place." Her brother had fronted her the money for the first month's rent, but she didn't think he wanted her underfoot any more than she wanted to *be* underfoot while he and Becka got used to the whole new baby thing.

Cameron gave her another of those dark looks like he wasn't sure what he thought of that. Good Lord, but the man was cranky. He finally sighed. "I'll call you a cab."

It didn't take much to read between the lines. He'd been on his way out of here when he caught her unfortunate fall. She was keeping him from plans of some sort, but his weirdly stubborn chivalrous streak wouldn't let him abandon her. *Chivalry? More like control freakishness.* Either way, he'd helped her out with painting even though he didn't have to, and she wasn't about to impose on him further.

Trish smiled and grabbed her purse. "Actually, I'm walking. It's only a few blocks from here."

"Then I'll walk you." If anything, he sounded *more* grumpy now than he had before.

"Oh, that's totally not necessary. The neighborhood is just fine and it's not particularly late." She gave Cameron an absent smile and headed for the elevator. "Thanks, though." It was edging toward eleven, but that didn't mean anything. She'd checked the street out last week with Becka—apparently walking could induce labor and Becka had been *determined* to make it happen—and there were several bars that would still be open around now, which meant pedestrian traffic. It was one of the pluses of the area when she was picking a place to live—that and the apartment came furnished and was within walking distance to the office. The rent was still astronomical, but Aaron was paying her an astronomical salary.

He'd promised it wasn't a pity job, that he really needed her specifically to do this, but it *felt* like a pity job.

Stop it. Chin up. You're going to help out your brother, save up some money and explore the city while you figure out your next step. Those are all good things.

She'd been so caught up in her thoughts that she hadn't noticed Cameron walking beside her until Trish stepped out onto the street and was hit full in the face with icy wind. She shivered and barely had time to wish that she'd packed a warmer coat before a heavy weight settled on her shoulders.

She blinked and touched the coat Cameron had just draped over her. “You’ll freeze.”

“I’m fine.”

He shoved his hands into his pockets. “Which way?”

She could keep arguing and let them both stand out in the cold or she could just give in and spend next week establishing that she didn’t want Cameron looking after her. She had an older brother. She didn’t need two.

You don’t see this man in a brotherly light and you know it.

Shut up.

And he wouldn’t have stared at your mouth like that if he saw you *like a sister.*

Seriously. Shut. Up.

She picked up her pace and Cameron easily fell into step next to her. Even as she told herself to keep her smile in place and just accept his chaperoning, she couldn’t keep her mouth shut. “You realize I’m an adult, right? I can walk three blocks without having you shadow my steps and glower at anyone who looks at me sideways.” When he didn’t respond, her irritation flared hotter. “I have an older brother. I don’t need another one.” She jerked her thumb toward the door they’d stopped in front of. “This is me.”

“Trish.”

God, the things that man could do with a single syllable. She froze, her feet rooted to the ground as he stepped closer, his big body blocking the wind. This time, she couldn't stop herself from swaying toward him, answering the gravitational pull he exuded. He didn't move, but he didn't have to. Trish went up onto her tiptoes and her mouth found his as if there had never been another destination for her.

The contact shocked her right down her to bones. His lips moved against hers, cautious and then commanding, taking everything she gave and then demanding more. Her knees actually buckled at the slow slide of his tongue against hers, and Cameron caught her easily around the hips.

He lifted his head, breaking the contact between them. All she could do was stare as he took his jacket from around her shoulders and shrugged it on. He nudged her to her door and waited for her to key in the code to get through. Then Cameron stood there until she shut the door firmly behind her.

Trish watched him stalk away. *Did that just happen?*

She'd just kissed her boss.

On her first day.

She pressed her shaking fingers to her lips. "I am in so much trouble."

CHAPTER THREE

CAMERON SPENT ALL weekend cursing himself for kissing Trish back. He should have stepped away and clarified that they had a professional relationship only. Reminded her that she was his best friend's little sister. Done literally anything except coax her mouth open with his tongue.

Now he knew what she tasted like. And that she'd melted so sweetly against him at the first contact. Not to mention the delicious way she'd shivered when he'd grabbed her hips.

Fuck me.

When Monday morning rolled around, he almost decided to work remotely. That was the path of a coward. Better to rip the Band-Aid off now and deal with her hurt feelings and move on. It might make the workplace awkward, but if Aaron's glowing praise of his baby sister was any indication, it wouldn't get her down for long.

It was only a kiss, after all.

The elevator seemed to take twice as long as normal, and he had to concentrate to keep from fidgeting. Cameron had arrived thirty minutes early on purpose. If he was safely camped out in his office, hopefully they could just pretend that misstep on Friday never happened.

The elevator doors opened and he barely made it a single step. If not for the walls being painted the same green he'd been elbow deep in a few days ago, he'd have thought he was in the wrong place. Comfortable-looking chairs—a warm sand color with a stripe of burnt red—were arranged on either side of the room. A leafy tree gracefully rose on either side of the window.

A window that had new curtains to match the chairs.

On the other side of the room, a water feature was arranged in the corner, a geometrical design with round stones and dark wood borders.

There was even fucking art on the walls.

When the hell did she find time to do this? She had to have put in long-ass days to find the pieces and haul them up here. He could comfort himself that they'd been delivered, but from what little he knew about Trish Livingston, he had no doubt that she'd physically carried every single piece up here herself.

Without asking for help.

Without once *considering* that she *should* ask for help.

Irritation flickered closer to true anger. He eyed her desk as he passed, taking in the cheery flower arrangement, the stack of bright Post-it notes and the overflowing mug of equally bright pens.

He clenched his jaw and headed down the hallway, but Cameron only made it three steps when the door to their mostly unused conference room opened and Trish herself appeared. She had a handful of paint color swatches in front of her face, and her brow was furrowed and her lips—red, today—were pursed. She hummed to herself. "This blue is too cold. No red. No yellow. I need a power color that's not in-your-face."

He planted his feet, irritation derailed by sheer curiosity. And the woman, damn her, didn't even notice him standing there. She ran right into him and bounced off his chest, and it was only his cupping her elbows that kept her from landing on her ass.

"Damn!" Trish laughed. "Mom always said to keep my head on the here and now. Guess I should have listened, huh?"

Cameron just stared. They were so fucking

close, if she leaned a little farther in, he would be able to see directly down her flowy purple top. He averted his eyes and released her. "You're here early."

"Lots of work to be done."

It was too fucking early for her to be this chipper. He shot her a look. "How much coffee have you had?"

"Coffee?" She frowned. "I don't drink coffee. It gives me the shakes and that's just not my idea of fun. I stick with chamomile tea when I want something warm and cozy in my hands." Trish's blond hair was in a cloud around her shoulders today, her curls giving her an angelic look that was completely at odds with her fitted skirt.

For fuck's sake, Cameron, stop looking at her. She's being professional. You're being inappropriate.

He cleared his throat and took another step back. "The conference room is fine. You don't need to kill yourself for this job. The front office didn't need to be finished so quickly."

She wilted a little, but then her smile brightened until it was damn near blinding. "I like the work." Trish charged forward, and he had to scramble back to avoid making contact with her again. She glanced at him as if he was being ridiculous. "And, no, the conference room is not fine. You can't expect clients to take your presentations seriously when there are spiderwebs in the corners and all the chair cushions are moth-eaten. I'll take care of it."

That was what he was afraid of.

"Trish."

She stopped in her tracks, and her smile dimmed to something closer to a genuine expression. "I was hoping we didn't have to do this, but obviously you've been chewing on it all weekend." Trish sighed and turned to face him fully. "Look, I'm sorry. I was out of line when I kissed you. I could give half a dozen reasons why it happened, but the truth is that it was inappropriate and I put you in a bad spot. So I'm sorry. Let's pretend it never happened?"

Cameron wanted to know what those half a dozen reasons were, but he couldn't ask. Not when she was so determined to put them back into their respective boxes of employee and employer. There was one thing he couldn't let stand. "If you remember, I kissed you back."

Her blue eyes flared with heat, quickly banked. "I remember." Just like that, she was chipper Trish again, so sweet she made his teeth ache. "Don't let me keep you from your work. I was hoping we could sit down later today and go over your current clients and their needs, but other than that I can get the conference room whipped into shape pretty quickly."

"I have some time this afternoon." Which would hopefully give him the opportunity to put a little distance between whatever the hell was going on between them.

"Perfect. If anything pops up between then and now, I'll let you know."

He shifted, realized he was backing away from her like someone trying to avoid being mauled by a wild animal and forced himself to turn away. "Do that." He could have sworn she laughed a little as he strode away from her, but a quick glance over his shoulder showed her sunny expression firmly in place.

Must have been my imagination.

Trish walked to her desk on shaking legs. She'd had a plan. It was a very good plan. The best plan, considering her insane impulse to kiss Cameron a few short days ago. She'd come into the office and pretend like nothing had changed, like she was a professional who'd made a mistake, like she hadn't used that brief kiss with him to bring herself to orgasm no less than seven times over the weekend.

It wasn't her fault. She'd wanted to get the front

office set up for Monday, but everywhere she looked, she saw evidence of Cameron. That was the spot he'd caught her when she'd fallen off the ladder. Over there in the corner was where she'd spent a solid sixty seconds staring at the line of his back muscles pressing against his shirt every time he'd reached over his head to paint. Right here was where they'd stood shoulder to shoulder as she'd told him her vision for the room.

A man shouldn't be able to imprint himself on her inside of two hours with only a handful of words exchanged, and Trish had managed to convince herself that it was all in her head.

Until she'd collided with him in the hallway. They'd been so close, his big hands clasping her elbows in a way that should most definitely not be erotic, his chest rising and falling in the most tempting way possible.

She'd almost kissed him again.

Trish dropped into her chair and bumped her head against her desk a couple times. Sadly, the contact did nothing to clear the desire from her brain—or her body. *I want my boss. I want to kiss him and do the horizontal tango and a few things that are illegal in half a dozen states.*

What a mess.

A footstep had her opening her eyes, and she turned her head to press her cheek to her desk.

Cameron stood in the middle of the hallway, his body tense and expression unreadable.

Because of course.

She couldn't just have that brilliant little scene where she played it cool and professional and totally unaffected. No, he'd had to come back out here and see her for the mess she really was. *Too late to salvage this. Might as well ride with it.* "Can I help you with something?" She kept her tone even despite the fact she had her head on her desk and was obviously in the middle of a lust-driven breakdown.

Cameron looked like he wanted nothing more than to retreat and pretend this interaction had never happened. *You and me both, man.* He finally cleared his throat. "Is everything okay?"

"Sure. Fine and dandy." Since he obviously had something to say, she sighed and straightened. "You don't have to worry about me."

"Somehow I find that hard to believe." He shook his head and held up a thin file. "I have a web meeting to finish up a contract with an existing client in an hour. Would you like to sit in on it?"

She cautiously took the file and flipped through it. She didn't necessarily need hand-holding, but it would be really useful to see how Cameron conducted business—both to see what he'd expect from her and to verify if it was as bad as Aaron seemed to think. But that also meant being in the same room as Cameron, and in close quarters.

It had to happen at some point.

I'm not ready.

You're never going to be ready.

Wasn't that the damn truth?

She took a careful breath and smiled brightly. "That would be great. I'll go over this so I'm up-to-date." She motioned to the file.

"Great." He turned and walked away without another word.

Great.

She spent the next forty minutes going over the file to familiarize herself with the account and what Tandem Security did for the client. It was all pretty basic. They'd beefed up the client's online security and added in a secondary package that was biannual upkeep for any major changes the client wanted. *Smart. Keep a long-standing relationship so they come back here if they need more done.*

By the time she walked into Cameron's office, she'd managed to get herself under control. At least until she sank gingerly into the chair next to his in front of the monitor. He'd brought it over so she could be in the camera frame once the video call started, and the positioning put them within easy touching distance. It shouldn't matter. It *couldn't* matter.

To distract herself, she focused on his computer setup. It was more advanced than she'd ever had to deal with, dual monitors showing a variety of programs running that might as well have been Greek for all Trish understood them. She was more than decent with technology, but she'd never come close to what Aaron and Cameron did for a living. It blew her mind a little bit. "Fancy."

"It does the job." He hesitated and then tilted the screen so it faced her a little more directly. "This damn client is always late. Every single fucking time."

Before she thought better of it, she laid her hand on his biceps. "You're almost finished with this account. Just keep that in mind during the meeting and everything will go swimmingly."

Cameron's eyes dropped to where she touched him, and his arm flexed slightly beneath her palm. Slowly, oh so slowly, his gaze dragged up to her mouth, hesitated and then settled on her eyes. "You take positivity to a new level."

A simple sentence, but the way he watched her didn't *feel* simple. It made her stomach twist and ignited the desire she was working so damn hard to keep under wraps. It would be the simplest thing in the world to lean in a little bit, to give him a clear signal that she wanted a repeat of the other night—and more.

He'd kiss her until she forgot her own name, until she wasn't worried about the future beyond where he'd touch her next. Until she felt the ground steady beneath her feet even as he made her fly. She'd hitch up her skirt and climb into his lap and…

"Trish?"

She blinked, her heart beating too hard. "Sorry, I didn't hear what you said."

Cameron reached up to touch the side of her face, gently guiding her to look at the monitor instead of him. "Client just logged on. I'm going to start the meeting."

The meeting. Right. She swallowed hard. "Great."

But he didn't move back. His breath brushed the shell of her ear, drawing a shiver from her. "After the meeting, we'll…talk."

Talk? Or *talk*?

She stared blindly at the monitor, reality sinking its claws into her and digging deep. The attraction she felt for Cameron wasn't going away—if anything, it was getting worse. Stronger. And if he meant what she thought—hoped, dreaded—he meant about *talking*, he was getting swept away alongside her.

Oh God, my brother is going to kill me.

Too bad she couldn't bring herself to care. She'd played it safe for so long and she'd missed her dreams by a mile.

Maybe it was time to throw caution to the wind.

What could possibly go wrong?

CHAPTER FOUR

CAMERON MANAGED TO get through the final meeting without letting his disdain for the outgoing client show—because he was so damn distracted by Trish's flowery perfume. No, not perfume. It was too subtle. It was probably lotion or shampoo or something, and the faint scent rose every time she shifted. Her hair brushed his shoulders, and his hands clenched against the need to dig into the thick curls and tilt her head back so he could claim her mouth again.

Focus.

He signed off the meeting and sat back, careful to angle his body away from hers. It didn't help. Cameron had always considered his office obscenely large compared to the amount of space he actually needed to do his job. That was before Trish took up residence in it, filling every inch with her sunny presence. He didn't know how to deal with it, and commanding her to get the hell out wouldn't solve anything—and would only make him look like an asshole in the process.

Rightly so.

Cameron cleared his throat. "Did you decide on a color for the boardroom?"

Trish blinked those big blue eyes at him. "That's what you wanted to talk about?"

No, what he wanted to talk about was how she felt about being spread out on his desk so he could kiss her until she was dizzy. Then he'd inch up that tease of a skirt and taste her there, too. Right here. In his office. While they were both on the clock, so to speak.

He was so out of line, it wasn't fucking funny.

Focusing on work when she was so close he could run his thumb over her full bottom lip was a herculean task, but Cameron didn't have any other option. He nodded, his voice gruffer than it had right to be. "The ceilings are just as high in there as in the front office, and you've already proven you can't be trusted to follow the instructions on stepladders. Since I doubt you're going to hire someone to do it, I'll help you." There. That was reasonable.

Except her eyes had gone wide and her jaw dropped. "That is the most ridiculous, back-handed compliment I've ever heard. I'm not even sure there's a compliment in there. I am more than capable of doing my job."

"I never said you weren't."

"Actually, you did. Thirty seconds ago." She shoved to her feet, which put her breasts directly in his line of sight. Cameron jerked his gaze back to her face, but it wasn't any better for his control. She was gorgeous when she was pissed and trying not to be, her hair moving around like a live thing and her body practically vibrating with repressed fury. She pointed a finger at him, seemed to realize she might be crossing a line and let her hand drop. "Aaron hired me to do this job because he knows I'm capable of handling it. That *includes* managing painting." She stalked out the door without another word.

Cameron stared hard at the doorway, walking back through the conversation to figure out where it went wrong. Choosing not to kiss her again was the right call. *That*, he was sure of. Asking about the boardroom was a reasonable thing to do. Maybe he'd spoken a little harsher than he intended, driven by the need to keep the lust from his tone, but he hadn't yelled at her. Telling her to accept his help was only reasonable because she'd about broken her damn neck when she'd tried to do the front room herself. It was possible he could have worded it more carefully, but he'd hardly called her inept. He'd been more abrupt in other conversations and she hadn't reacted so intensely.

Another replay of the conversation and he thought he had the answer. *I am more than capable of doing my job.* Well, of course she was. Aaron wouldn't have hired her if she wasn't, sister or no. Cameron certainly wouldn't have signed off on it unless she was qualified. She might not be well-balanced when standing on a stepladder, and her college degrees weren't an exact fit, but she obviously had an eye for creating a welcoming environment, and how she'd handled herself in the meeting just now had only reinforced that hiring her was the right call. She was fucking perfect for the job.

He'd told her that…

Cameron frowned. Shit, he hadn't told her that, had he? He'd been so focused on the thought that she might pull another stunt like working after hours to finish the front office—and get hurt in the process—that he'd barked at her over it. He frowned harder. He wasn't wrong about telling her not to paint without him. He *knew* he wasn't.

But…maybe he could have approached it differently?

"Fuck," he breathed. He wasn't equipped to tiptoe around another person's feelings. If he was, he'd have been better at the client-facing part of this business. Trish wasn't a client, though. He couldn't just end a meeting and cease having to deal with her. She'd be in this office, day in and day out.

He had to apologize.

Cameron played through his options a couple times, but there was really only one reality. If she was pissed, it would make the office unlivable. What was more, it made her a whole lot more likely to go ahead and paint the damn boardroom—and potentially hurt herself—when he wasn't around. Since he wasn't a fan of either option, he pushed slowly to his feet and went in search of her.

Unsurprisingly, he found her in said boardroom. The chairs around the old table had disappeared somewhere, and she stood on the table, in the process of changing out the overhead light fixture. Cameron froze, not sure if he should rush over to catch her in the event that she fell or that damn light fixture came undone and crashed down on her head.

Trish glanced over and gave him a brilliant smile. "This thing is so coated with some gross combination of dust and time that I'm calling it a wash and tossing it."

"Okay," he said slowly. A smiling Trish was not

what he expected. Was this a trap? "You seem... not mad."

"Why would I be mad, Cameron?" Her tone was as sweet as honey, but her use of his name might as well have been a hook in the gut.

This was most definitely a trap. He cleared his throat. "Earlier, I didn't mean to—"

"To question my competence? To treat me like I'm a child in need of tending?" Every single word was that blend of sweet and sharp, until it was a wonder he didn't bleed out on the floor at her feet. She turned to face him, the light fixture in her hands, as regal as a queen despite the streak of dust over the shoulder of her shirt and what appeared to be a cobweb clinging to her curls near her face. Trish looked down her nose at him. "If you have a problem with the way I do my job, that's fine. You're my boss. You're more than entitled to correct and/or punish me as you see fit."

He got hung up on the word *punish* and had to force himself back to task.

She wasn't done, though. "That said, if you ever talk to me like that again, I'm out. I took this job as a favor to Aaron and, yeah, I kind of need it, but I don't need it badly enough to put up with that level of disrespect. I get that you don't handle people well, but at some point you're just making excuses for bad behavior that's inexcusable..." She trailed off, her breath coming too fast, and seemed to realize she was yelling at him. Trish clutched the light fixture closer to her chest. “So…there.”

God, she was something else. Fired up and willing to put him in his place, though she had to be truly pissed to have let the peppy sunbeam mask slip. Cameron leaned against the doorjamb. “I’m sorry.”

“Why, you—” Trish blinked. “What?”

“You’re right. I was out of line. I’m sorry.” He stepped farther into the room and held out a hand.

Looking dazed, she took it and allowed him to guide her off the table. He finally managed to relax a little once her feet were both firmly on the floor. Trish gave him a suspicious look. “Why are you being so agreeable?”

“Contrary to what your brother thinks, I can see reason on occasion. I was worried about you falling again, and so I overreacted. But you’re right, I’m your boss.” He almost choked over the words—the reminder—but powered through. “Talking to an employee like that isn’t okay.”

“Exactly.” She still didn’t look convinced this wasn’t some kind of trick.

That made two of them.

Cameron…didn’t do this. He didn’t do interpersonal relationships. *Too damn bad. Going to have to figure it out as you go, and it’s one hell of a learning curve.* He didn't move from his spot. "I respectfully request that you either hire out for the painting or wait until after hours when I can help you."

Trish opened her mouth like she was going to snap back but seemed to consider. "It's an unnecessary expense to hire such a small job out when I'm more than capable of handling it. For that matter, there's no reason for you to take time away from your…whatever it is you do for leisure…to help me. I have it covered."

She had it covered all the way to an ER visit with a broken arm. Or worse.

He met her gaze steadily. "When are you buying the paint?"

Cameron could almost see the gears whirling in her head as she tried to find a way out of this. He could have told her there was no way out. He wouldn't let her paint this room by herself, and her little stunt this weekend had shown her hand—if she thought she could get away with it, she'd do it behind his back to avoid dealing with him.

If she was anyone else, he would have found her independence a relief. It meant he could focus on his job and let her do hers. But Trish wasn't anyone else—she was Trish. He needed to keep her safe, even if that meant keeping her safe from working herself to the bone.

Finally, she sighed. "I'm going to pick it up after work."

"Pick it up tomorrow." He didn't bother to keep the command out of his voice. If she went and got it after hours, she'd be right back here the second he wasn't looking.

She's not a wayward puppy, asshole. She's a person.

Yes, she was. A person who had excellent work ethic and showed every evidence of being just as stubborn as her older brother—the same older brother Cameron would have to answer to if something happened to her. That was all. It was simple, really. Not in the least bit complicated. He certainly didn't have any ulterior motives.

Trish narrowed her eyes. "You can't tell me what to do after hours."

"It concerns this job, so I sure as hell can. We'll take a long lunch tomorrow and paint the damn boardroom. You can pick up the paint late morning beforehand."

For a moment, it seemed like she'd keep arguing, but then she gave him a brilliant smile. "Sure thing, Mr. O'Clery." Trish turned on her heel and marched out of the room.

Okay, that was definitely a trap.

CHAPTER FIVE

TRISH ALMOST SAID to hell with it and bought the paint anyway. She got so far as to leave her apartment and start in the direction of the store… But common sense reared its ugly head. Cameron might have been kind of an ass with his command for her to wait, but he'd also apologized and he wasn't being *completely* unreasonable with wanting to help. It might even be kind of nice for the job to go faster.

Honesty, Trish.

She huffed out a breath and turned in the opposite direction. "The honest truth is that I'm pissed that when he said we'd talk, he meant he'd treat me like a child instead of kissing me again." She shot a look around her, half expecting Cameron to melt out of a nearby shadow and call her on her idiocy. There was only the normal foot traffic at this time in the early evening, and they were obviously all NYC natives, because they didn't so much as blink at her talking to herself like a crazy person.

She grabbed dinner from the little Chinese place a few blocks down and carted it back to her apartment. Behind locked doors, she finally sighed. *Okay, my pride was hurt. I let it get the best of me. We both agreed that the first kiss was a mistake that shouldn't be repeated...but that doesn't stop me from wanting a repeat.*

The trilling of her phone drew her out of her thoughts. When Trish saw it was her mother, she almost deliberately missed the call. It had been a long day and she didn't have the energy to reassure her mother—and through her mother, her father—that she was doing just fine in the big, scary city. She knew for a fact that Aaron hadn't been subjected to these worried phone calls when he moved here.

She took a deep breath and put as much smile into her voice as she was capable of. "Hey, Mom."

"Trish, there you are! I was worried when you didn't pick up."

That was her mother. The eternal worrier. She'd been born and raised in Lake Placid and had always harbored a hope that her daughters would do the same. Trish's older sister, Mary, had followed that path. She'd married her high school sweetheart and settled in after college to become an elementary school teacher. *Mary* was practically perfect in every way. She didn't keep her mother up at night, worrying herself to death.

No, that role had always fallen to Trish.

She kicked her cheerfulness up a notch—the only way to combat her mother's concern when she got like that. "I was just about to sit down to dinner."

"Dinner? Trish, it's after seven. You haven't been working this whole time! Aaron said that partner of his was a good boss, but if he's got you working twelve-hour days, that's abuse!" Her voice took on strident tones.

Trish repressed a sigh. "Mom, you're getting worked up for no reason. I'm eating late because I stopped by Aaron's to see my new niece and got distracted with her adorableness." *There's no need to lead an army down here to haul me back home.* An army of three—her mom, her dad and Mary—but no less fearsome for its numbers. Though her mom hadn't been *happy* about her needing to move back home after college, she hadn't exactly shed a tear to have her youngest daughter under their roof again. Now she was treating this move like Trish had left for college all over again.

And was just as helpless and out of her element as she'd been at eighteen.

"I worry about you. That city—"

"Mom." If she didn't do something drastic, her mother would end up on an hour-long spiel about all the ways she could get mugged or worse in New York. It didn't matter that Trish had found an apartment crazy close to where she worked or that she'd pulled it from a list that Aaron himself had put together. New York City terrified their mother and she would spill that feeling over at every opportunity, whether she meant to or not.

Unless Trish distracted her, she'd be up all night running scenarios—each more terrifying than the last—and her mother would call tomorrow and be a total mess. She cast a longing look at her cooling Chinese food and resigned herself to a reheated meal. "Did Aaron send you the pictures he took of Summer? She was especially cute today. He says she can't really smile yet, but I swear to God she was smiling at me."

The distraction worked. Her mother went on to gush about how Aaron did a video call with her and the baby, and wasn't his fiancée the sweetest thing, though goodness, they should be married by now if they're having babies. Through it all, Trish's mind wandered…right back to Cameron.

She wanted him to kiss her again.

Or, rather, *she* wanted to kiss *him* again. To do more than kiss. To break half a dozen rules and regulations that she wasn't even sure Tandem Security had in place.

Not to mention that Aaron might lose his damn mind if he finds out I'm lusting after his business partner.

She blinked, realizing that her mother had been silent for a beat too long. Trish faked a yawn. "Mom, I have to go. I have a big day tomorrow, and I want a full night's rest."

The silence extended for a beat. Another. Then her mother sniffled. "I just wish you were here."

Oh good Lord. She was going to devolve to sobbing next, and Trish was too tired to be sure she wouldn't snap in response. She was twenty-fucking-four years old. She couldn't live at home forever. She understood that her mother's empty-nest syndrome was in full force, but Trish couldn't form her entire freaking life around making her mother feel fulfilled. Not that her mom wanted her to. Not exactly. She was just emotional and weepy and Trish wasn't capable of stepping back and cutting the cord fully. It would hurt her mom and she didn't deal out pain—only good things.

So she cleared her throat and smiled so hard that her cheeks hurt. "Mom, how am I supposed to find a man to make an honest woman of me and have a bunch of babies for you to spoil if I'm living in the same room I've had since birth? Aaron needs me right now. I can't leave him hanging."

Leveraging Aaron's name got her mom back under control. She gave another sniffle, but the wavering quality of her voice evened out. "You're right. Of course you're right. It's just so hard not seeing you."

"I know, Mom." She touched the side of her Chinese food container and sighed. *Cold.* "I'll talk to you later."

It took another five minutes to actually end the call, and by the time she did, it was all she could do to sink onto her couch. Trish stared at her cold dinner and fought against the burning in her throat. She wasn't overwhelmed. She was capable and positive and could handle anything the world threw at her.

But, God, she was so tired.

"I should eat." Her words barely diminished the growing silence in her apartment. She should turn on the television or do something to get some ambient noise going so she didn't feel quite so alone, but Trish just couldn't work up the energy to reach for the remote.

She closed her eyes. *I'll just rest here for a minute...*

Cameron checked his watch for the sixth time in the last thirty seconds. There was no denying it—

Trish was late. He stalked to the boardroom, half expecting to find her passed out under the table after a long night of ignoring his order, but it was just as drab and empty as it had been yesterday.

She didn't live that far away. How the hell was she late on her third day here?

He paced across the front office and back again and shot a glare at the elevators. Another look at his phone confirmed she hadn't answered his texts or responded to his missed calls. She was too damn excited about painting to have gone out drinking last night…wasn't she?

When it came down to it, he didn't know much about Trish at all. She was Aaron's sister. She was good at her job. She was far too peppy for his comfort. That about summed up his knowledge.

And she doesn't follow safety instructions particularly well.

Cameron stopped short. She was hurt. That had to be it. She wouldn't be late for anything other than a catastrophic reason, and if it involved Aaron and his family, Cameron would have heard about it. Which meant it had happened either in her apartment or somewhere in transit.

She could be injured right now, and he'd wasted time when he could have been helping her.

Not willing to wait for the elevator, he charged down the stairs. Seconds later, he was on the street, nearly running for her place. *Thank God she only lives a few blocks away.* Cameron made it there in record time. He keyed in the code Aaron had given him for safety reasons and then stopped short. He didn't know which apartment was hers.

Cursing under his breath, he yanked his phone out of his pocket and called Aaron. Cameron barely waited for his partner to answer before he cut in. "What's Trish's apartment number?"

Just like that, the sleepiness was gone from his friend's voice. "It's 3b. Why?"

"Call you in a few." He hung up and took the stairs again, nearly sprinting. He had no idea how he'd get into her apartment if she wasn't able to answer the door. *Should have thought that through.* Since he was already there, he pounded on the door and listened closely in case she cried for help.

Instead, footsteps padded on the other side of the door and a sleepy-looking Trish opened it. She yawned and then froze at the sight of him. Her blue eyes went wide. "Uh… What time is it?"

Cameron was too busy casting a worried eye over her to answer. She didn't *look* injured. No blood or protruding bones. Maybe she fell and hit her head? He stepped into the apartment and slipped his fingers through her tangled blond curls, gingerly feeling for a goose egg that might indicate a concussion.

Trish frowned. "What's going on?" She swatted at his hands. "What are you doing?"

"What did you fall from this time?"

She blinked and then backed up a few steps. "What are you talking about?"

She was definitely concussed if she didn't realize what the hell was going on. Cameron pointed at his watch. "It's nine."

Horror dawned across her face. "Oh God, I'm late." She looked down at herself and then at him, which was right around the time he noticed that she wore flannel pajamas with little cats frolicking across the bright blue background. It should have made her look childish, but Trish in pajamas led to thoughts of Trish in bed and Cameron turned to survey the apartment before he could follow *that* to its inevitable conclusion.

Small place, which was to be expected. A little studio apartment with a door on the other side of the room that must lead to the bathroom. Her bed was made—the comforter printed with brightly colored flowers—and she'd managed to imprint herself on the space in a limited amount of time. Flowerpots perched on either side of the kitchen sink, soaking up what little sunlight they could get this time of year. She'd even managed to find time to hang art on the walls—more florals, though they were strangely moody in black-and-white photography instead of bright oil like he would have expected. The only thing out of place was a container of what appeared to be Chinese takeout sitting on the coffee table.

Trish cleared her throat. “Cameron. You’re in my apartment.”

“You were late.” He spoke almost absently, his gaze going back to the paintings. Black-and-white with the faintest hint of color in each. Compelling, though something about the close-ups of the different kinds of flower petals made him a little sad. Or maybe melancholy. One of those less than happy emotions that he wouldn’t have thought to associate with the peppy woman in front of him.

Cameron wouldn’t have said he was without layers—he was human and humans had layers of personality—but he tended to set aside the bullshit and call things like he saw them. It didn’t always work out in his favor, but at least there wasn’t room for misinterpretation or confusion.

The more time he spent around Trish, the more he realized this woman was nothing *but* layers. The bright woman who smiled her way through every situation. The flares of irritation and anger on occasion. The pride. And now this new revelation that he couldn’t quite place within the puzzle that was Trish Livingston.

He cleared his throat. "I thought you'd fallen off something and hurt yourself."

"Cameron." Her exasperation drew his attention back to her. Trish crossed her arms over her chest. "You know I don't actually fall off things often, right? I'm not particularly injury-prone and just because I took a tumble off a ladder and you caught me like some kind of romance hero doesn't mean you need to get all anxious about my health."

She sounded perfectly reasonable, but perfectly reasonable people read the instructions on ladders and didn't step on the top step and lean precariously while painting. He mirrored her pose. "You're an hour late. What else was I supposed to think?"

"Oh, I don't know." She rolled her eyes. "That I fell asleep on my couch and forgot to set my alarm and overslept. That's a very *normal* thing to do." She made a face. "Wait, I take that back. I don't make a habit of being late, and I'm sorry I am, but you're acting like I'm an accident waiting to happen."

He started to argue, but the bottom line was that she was right. He shouldn't be here any more than he should have done half the shit he'd pulled with Trish up to this point. If he was smart, he'd make some excuse to leave and put this whole awkward encounter behind him.

At least until she showed up at the office to work.

Instead, Cameron stalked around her couch and used a single finger to pry open the Chinese-food container. *Full. Not even a bite missing.* "You skipped dinner."

"Not on purpose."

He glanced over, but she'd set her mouth in a firm line that told him no more information would be forthcoming. All evidence pointed to her sitting down to eat dinner and then falling asleep on the couch. Missing dinner. Missing breakfast. If he turned around and left now, no doubt she'd get ready and rush straight to the office and not eat until lunch, which put a full twenty-four hours between meals.

Unacceptable.

He sat on the couch and pointed at the bathroom. "Get ready. We're going to have a late breakfast before we go back to the office." Since there were no paint cans in evidence, she'd actually listened to his order, which was something at least. "We'll get the paint you want on the way. After you eat."

Trish's eyes sparked, but she got it under control almost immediately. She gave him a sweet smile that did nothing to mask the anger written in every line of her body. "Sure thing. I'll do my best not to slip on a bar of soap and bash my head against the tile. You know, because I'm *so* klutzy." She stalked to the bathroom and shut the door with a resounding snick.

Only then did Cameron relax back into the couch. They'd gone past the point of *should* this morning. He'd crossed the line coming here, but he wasn't sorry. Trish was okay, and that was all that mattered. She wouldn't be late again, and even if she wouldn't tell him what really happened last night, he had to be satisfied with that.

In the bathroom, the water turned on and Cameron groaned. Maybe leaving Trish to her own devices was the smarter option. Because, right now, all he could do was imagine her stepping beneath the spray, to mentally follow the cascade of water down her shoulders, her breasts, to her stomach and then lower yet. He wanted to follow that path with his mouth, to taste her and tease her and bring her to thc edge over and over again until he finally tipped her into oblivion.

He just flat-out *wanted* her.

CHAPTER SIX

TRISH REALIZED HER mistake the second she stepped out of the shower. In her huff to get out of the room before she said something *truly* unkind to Cameron, she hadn't grabbed clothes. She wrapped a towel around herself and considered her options. Screaming at Cameron to close his eyes was tempting, but her stubborn streak kicked in and wouldn't let her.

He'd decided to burst into her apartment and then command her to have breakfast with him. Oh, she knew he'd only shown up because he was worried, and he'd decided on breakfast for the same reason. It didn't matter. The man didn't have a subtle bone in his body, but he should damn well try to talk to her like she had a brain in her head.

Or, rather, like she wasn't about to trip over some piece of furniture like she was starring in some old-school slapstick comedy.

Trish wiped down the foggy mirror and stared at her reflection. *You know why you're pissed, and it's not because Cameron was worried about you.* It might even have been kind of nice to bask in his concern if it wasn't attached to so many conflicting emotions.

Cameron saw her as Aaron's little sister. Emphasis on *little.*

He wanted her—she hadn't missed those signals—but he'd just as obviously written her off as untouchable. That should be a good thing. He was her boss, as she had to keep reminding herself. He *was* off-limits.

That didn't stop her from wanting to force him to acknowledge that he wanted her.

You're acting like a crazy person. Get ready in here. Walk to your closet like you totally aren't bothered by a really sexy man sitting on your couch and watching you do it. Retrieve clothes. Retreat to bathroom and get dressed.

It really was that simple.

Trish took a deep breath. She could do this. She'd faked her way out of awkward situations before, and she'd fake it out of this one, too. That settled, she quickly did her makeup and worked some product into her curls. Then there was nothing to do but open the door.

She paused to ensure her towel was wrapped

firmly around her body and straightened her spine. *I can do this. It's ten feet. It'll be fine.*

She opened the door and nearly ran into Cameron. Trish brought herself up short a bare inch from his chest and let loose a squeak of surprise. "Cameron!" Just as quickly, surprise morphed into frustration. She glared at his deep gray tie. "Damn it, Cameron. I didn't fall in the shower. That was a joke. You don't have to kick down the door and rescue me from some magical injury. You really need to relax, you know that? Have a beer, smoke a joint, meditate, do *something* because you jumping up my ass every time I turn around is going to get old fast."

Oh shit, I just said that. Out loud.

Still he didn't respond. She stared harder at his tie, sure that if she looked at his face, she'd see pure fury and then they'd really be fighting. *Think, Trish. Defuse the situation. Do something to distract him from the fact that you're yelling at him in a completely irrational way.* Her mind went blank and she panicked.

Trish dropped the towel.

Cameron's only response was a sharp intake of breath. She'd already gone too far to take it back now, so she lifted her chin and glared at him. Mortification threatened to take hold and drive her back to the bathroom. What was she doing? He had her so twisted up, she was parading naked in front of him, and she wasn't even doing it in a sad seduction attempt. No, this fell firmly into the Panic and Make Poor Choices column. "Don't you dare say anything."

"Freckles."

Her whole body clenched at the way he growled the inconspicuous word. She licked her lips. "What?"

"Freckles," Cameron repeated. He lifted a big hand and hovered a single finger over the center of her chest. "You have freckles everywhere." He traced a pattern over her breasts, connecting them without touching her.

The air disappeared from the room. Hell, the room itself disappeared. There was only Trish and Cameron and that single inch of space that kept him from touching her. Her body warmed beneath his attention, and he just kept tracing freckles, a look of utter concentration in his dark eyes. As if he had nowhere else to be, nothing else to be doing, and he wouldn't stop until he'd connected every single freckle on her body.

This could take hours.

Her nipples went tight at the thought. She actually started to lean forward before she caught herself.

It was already too late.

Cameron took a careful step back, and then another, though his gaze never left her body. Each movement was jerky and filled with barely controlled lust. He wanted her. *That* couldn't have been clearer. It was equally as clear that he had no intention of touching her again. He bumped into the couch and swung around to face the front door. "You should get dressed."

Right. Dressed. Because this thing between them couldn't happen.

Despite the fact he pointedly wasn't watching her, Trish kept her head up and her shoulders squared as she grabbed the first things she got her hands on—a red flare skirt and a white blouse—and retreated into the bathroom to get dressed. She stared at herself in the mirror for the space of a breath. *Yeah, definitely don't need blush if I'm going to be spending time around Cameron. I keep acting like an idiot, so I'm going to walk around with permanently pink cheeks. Wonderful.*

Her life would be so much easier if she could just find another job—preferably in a company run by women so she wouldn't have to deal with falling into lust with her boss.

This isn't just to help Aaron and you know it. You need experience to be able to get in for the jobs you really want instead of an unpaid internship or something entrance level. Because, let's be honest, you couldn't even get one of those *jobs after you graduated. You can't afford to quit.*

She really sucked at pep talks.

Trish found Cameron exactly where she'd left him and she gave a silent sigh. They could be in bed right now, doing fun, filthy things instead of about to have yet another conversation about why he couldn't want her. She got it. She *so* got it.

There was nothing for it. If she didn't do something drastic, he'd sit her down and gruffly reject her over and over again with his words. She'd had quite enough of that for today.

For always, really.

She straightened her shoulders and grabbed her purse from the table. "Shall we?"

"Trish."

Oh no. It wasn't a gruff talk she was going to get—it was a gentle one. *So much worse.* She blasted him with a bright smile. "We've already wasted enough time, don't you think?" She marched out the door and barely waited for him to step into the hall to lock it behind them. Then she was off, charging for the elevator, Cameron's muttered curse in her ears.

It wasn't until the elevators closed—shutting them in—that she realized her tactical mistake.

He shifted to face her, not quite blocking the doors, but ensuring she'd have to slide past him to bolt. Cameron slipped his hands into his pockets. "I'm not rejecting you."

Trish stared hard at the numbers ticking down and silently spit out a few curses of her own. Correct choice or not, it sure felt like rejection. She made a blatant—if panicked—offer. He turned away. End of story.

Except it wasn't the end of the story, because he was still taking up too much space in the previously spacious elevator. Since she couldn't will the machine to move any faster, she smiled at him. "It's irrelevant. Message sent and received. It won't be a problem." She made a face. "Well, it won't be a problem again. I guess I should apologize—again."

"Knock that shit off."

She forced her smile brighter and tried not to hunch her shoulders. "What are you talking about? I'm being professional." *For once, when it comes to Cameron.*

He didn't step back as the doors opened. He just frowned at her like she was a puzzle he didn't have all the pieces necessary to put together. "You don't have to wear the mask with me, Trish."

If Cameron had reached out and slapped her, he couldn't have surprised her more. She jerked back. "Actually, Cameron, I can do whatever I damn well please when it comes to how I arrange my face around you. I am being pleasant and professional and I don't know you well enough to expose an emotional vulnerability just to give you the satisfaction."

"You know me well enough to strip naked."

No way he just went there.

Except he most definitely just went there.

She shouldered past him and into the hall leading to the entrance of her apartment building. Though she could tell herself all sorts of true facts to try to calm down, she didn't much feel like calming down at this point. Cameron might take being blunt to a whole new level, but he was just being a flat-out dick with that statement and she wasn't in the mood to give him the benefit of the doubt.

No, she was more likely to give him a literal kick in the ass.

Into slow-moving traffic.

"Trish," he said as she exited the building.

She ignored him and swung around a group of three guys to head in the direction of Home Depot. It was too far to walk, especially on her way back with paint cans in tow, but if she hailed a cab, either Cameron would climb in with her—which would just piss her off further—or it would be a childish fleeing of the conversation he obviously wanted to have. It didn't seem to matter that she *didn't* want to.

Clear the air. If you don't, it'll fester.

Trish spun on her heel and got a little perverse pleasure at the fact Cameron had to skid to a stop to avoid running into her. She glared pointedly at the distance between them until he backed up a step. They had an audience in the form of people passing by, but she didn't care. "I don't care if you are half owner of Tandem Security or my brother's best friend or richer than sin or anything else. You do *not* get to talk to me like that. Even if we were fucking six ways from Sunday, you still don't get to talk to me like that. You're a cranky asshole. I get it. Everyone gets it. That is no excuse to be a jackass and throw the rejection that's supposedly not a rejection in my face. A good guy would never speak of it again, but I suppose it's too much to hope that you'd know that without me telling you." She pointed at herself. "This is me telling you—do not bring it up again. Do you understand me?"

Cameron narrowed his eyes but seemed to realize that there was only one right answer in that moment. "I understand."

"Good. In that case, I will see you back at the office." She turned and flagged down a cab, sending a silent thank-you to the universe that she didn't have to stand there like an idiot during her dramatic exit.

Even though she knew better, she turned to look

out the back window as the cab pulled away from the curb. Cameron stood there, watching her with an unreadable expression on his gorgeous face. She should have felt, if not peaceful, then at least sure that this was the end of things between them outside of the safe roles of boss and employee. Of Aaron's little sister and Aaron's best friend.

Too bad she couldn't shake the niggling feeling that nothing had been resolved.

That things between them were just beginning.

CHAPTER SEVEN

"NO. ABSOLUTELY FUCKING NOT." Cameron shoved out of his chair and nearly threw his phone across the room. It wouldn't help anything and finding a new phone was a pain in the ass, but that didn't kill the impulse to banish Aaron's voice from his ear.

His partner was, naturally, totally unsympathetic. "I already had Trish book the flights. Concord Inc. is a huge company and if we can impress them, they'll keep us on retainer going forward. That's not the kind of account we can afford to turn away just because you're an asshole who hates people—or because you have a history with the COO."

"I don't hate people." He didn't sound convincing, which was just as well because he and Aaron had had this conversation more times than he could count. "They just waste my time." He growled. "And it's hardly a history."

"For the potential price tag attached to this account, it's the opposite of wasting your precious time. Hell, *I* took time out of paternity leave to talk to Nikki Lancaster. They're not going to wait on this."

Cameron paced another circle around his office but slowed as everything Aaron said finally penetrated his irritation over being commanded to leave the city. "You said 'flights.' Plural."

"Yes. I did. Because Trish is going with you. It's a huge-ass leap to toss her into shark-infested waters by doing this, so you're going to have to buck up and try not to make her job harder than it's already going to be."

"She can't go." The sentence burst out before he could stop it.

For the first time since Aaron called, he paused. A second. Two. Three. "Why can't she go?"

Because I have the picture of her naked imprinted on my brain and I've jacked myself off to the thought of tracing her freckles with my tongue every night since. A truth he would cut out said tongue before admitting aloud. Cameron scrubbed a hand over his face. "She's too new. Nikki Lancaster will eat her alive." Nikki had taken over as COO of Concord Inc. when it was a struggling corporate business and had almost single-handedly turned it into a Fortune 500 company over the last five years. Aaron was right—securing that account would not only be a shit ton of money in the bank, but it would open further doors.

Tandem Security wasn't hurting for cash. They accepted the contracts they wanted, when they wanted, and without having to travel to do it.

"Trish can handle it," Aaron said carefully, as if feeling his way.

"It makes more sense for her to stay here and handle the office while I go and deal with Nikki." There. That was a nice logical solution.

That Aaron shot down without hesitation. "She's too new to be left alone, and having on-site experience negotiating with a new client is an asset." He paused.

"Unless there's some problem neither of you have told me about?"

"No problem." No way to get out of this without setting off Aaron's internal alarms, either. He had no choice but to go forward with this trip. Cameron sat on the edge of his desk and stared hard at his closed door. "We have this covered." He might not like the idea of being in close quarters with her—closer quarters, technically, since they'd been working together for over a week since the morning she overslept. It didn't matter if they were going over notes before a client meeting or painting the boardroom. Trish kept a painfully bright barrier between them and deflected anything that might resemble flirting with a beaming smile and blatant change of subject. There was no sign of the temper she'd flashed before she took off in that cab, and the lack bothered him almost as much as having her tear him a new one had.

"Cameron?"

Shit, he needed to keep his head in the game. "Sorry. I missed that."

"I can tell." If anything, Aaron sounded more concerned. "Do you want me to come in and go over the details with you before you go?"

He clenched his jaw to keep his first response inside. Recent years hadn't been kind to his track record when it came to dealing with clients, so Aaron's offer wasn't completely out of line. Aaron knew him better than anyone. Cameron's patience wore thin with increasing regularity, and he found himself snapping at them before he had a chance to dial it back. So he stopped bothering to dial it back at all.

He and Aaron had met in college, and he knew his friend always assumed there was a deeper backstory to his being a dick. Some tragic past he never talked about. Some defining event that made him wash his hands of all the social niceties.

There wasn't.

Cameron's parents were good people. Nothing outstandingly bad had happened to him growing up, and if being a black man in this country came with its own set of bullshit and headaches, it wasn't exactly a surprise. There were always others who had it worse.

No, the truth was that he preferred machines to dealing with actual humans because machines made sense. There was always a concrete answer, one that wasn't open to interpretation. Every aspect of a computer was clearly defined and had its own set of rules to work around—but those rules were clearly stated from the beginning.

People were nuanced and managed to be multiple things, often at the same time. They said things they didn't mean, and then got pissed when he took those things as truth and acted accordingly. They had masks within masks and motivations they rarely put out in the open. Cameron didn't *get* people, and maneuvering through their needs and emotions, even for surface-level interactions, left him exhausted and feeling like an asshole.

Because he fucked it up. Every single time.

Just like you did with Trish.

I couldn't take what she was offering. It would backfire and she'd have been hurt in the process.

There is no good exit route once we step past the point of no return.

Could have handled it better, though.

Yeah, no shit.

"Cameron, you're not even listening to me."

He scrubbed a hand over his head and mentally made a note to shave his head again soon—before they went to London, for sure. Cameron might not handle people well, but he knew Aaron as well as he knew himself. The man didn't want to come back to work yet. He just needed Cameron to say the right thing to assuage his guilt and let him take the break he'd more than earned.

He cleared his throat. "I have this covered. Go back to doting on your fiancée and baby and stop worrying about us."

Another hesitation, but shorter this time. Aaron loved Tandem Security as much as Cameron did, but he loved his new family more. Which was how it should be. Aaron's relationship with Becka had started unconventionally enough, but they'd found a good balance and their love for their new daughter filled up a room in a way that made even Cameron smile. It didn't hurt that Summer was cute as hell and seemed to like *him* just fine. Babies were simple—simple needs, simple desires. If she cried, it was because she wasn't having some need met, and *that* he understood.

Too bad adults weren't that easy to figure out.

He didn't begrudge his best friend his happiness. He just wished Aaron would stop worrying about the company. He was only gone for a couple months. Cameron could manage to apply a filter to himself for a couple months until his friend was back in the office. He wasn't *that* much of a lost cause.

His partner got a dreamy tone. "Summer smiled at me today. The book says it's probably just gas, but I don't give a fuck. It's the cutest thing I've ever seen."

That, he believed. She was adorable. Cameron managed a smile. "I'm glad you're happy." If anyone deserved that happiness, Aaron did. He was a good guy, and he'd spent too many years putting up with Cameron's shit *not* to have earned a good turn or two.

"Thanks. That means a lot."

Cameron checked his watch. "I'll check in once I have things lined up."

"Talk to you then."

He hung up and checked his email. Sure enough, confirmation for a flight to London had appeared. Since there was one for Trish as well, he assumed she had her passport updated. *You're focusing on minor details to avoid focusing on the fact that you're going to be traveling with her.*

Easier to remember why she was off-limits when in this office. There was no escaping the constant knowing that it was inappropriate to follow through on the look he sometimes saw lingering in her blue eyes, or to submit to the gravitational pull between them that seemed to grow stronger with every day he didn't give in.

Put them in a different country, in a hotel together…

Getting ahead of yourself. Trish might have been interested before, but she's made it pretty fucking clear she's not now.

That was a good point.

Cameron sighed and rounded his desk to sink into his chair. Whether Trish did or didn't want to start something still was irrelevant. They had business to conduct and they'd more than proven they could work together when required. He just had to keep his head in the game and not be the one to fuck it up.

Easy enough. Work comes first—end of story.

He had absolutely nothing to worry about.

Trish paced from one wall to the other and back again. "I can't do this. It's going to blow up in my face."

"It might be helpful if you explain exactly *what* you're not doing."

She glanced at her almost-sister-in-law, Becka Baudin. She sat on the couch with Summer propped carefully on a pillow, nursing away. When Trish pictured her big brother with someone, it was some straitlaced woman who probably thought doing taxes was fun and drank expensive red wine and vacationed to exotic places with topless beaches.

On second thought, Becka probably fits the last one.

She didn't fit much else when it came to expectations. She was a blue-haired beauty who was both a personal trainer and led a bunch of hardcore fitness classes—at least before her pregnancy got too far along. She was also hilarious and nice and loved Aaron to distraction. In short, she was perfect.

Trish wasn't here for perfection, though. She needed advice. "I'm traveling with Cameron. To London. Alone. For as long as it takes to secure this account."

"I know it's not super normal for the guys to travel but…" Becka trailed off and her blue eyes went wide. "Oh. *Oh.* You and Cameron?" She leaned forward and winced. "Sorry, Summer." A quick adjustment and the baby was nursing happily again. Becka frowned. "Why didn't I know about this?"

"Because there's nothing to know about." Nothing except she kept throwing herself at him and he kept setting her gently back and trying to explain why he would never touch her. Nothing except her pride being bruised beyond all repair because of her impulsiveness.

It was the height of insanity to still want him after he'd turned her down—more than once—but apparently her self-control had taken a vacation somewhere along the way. She couldn't be in the same room with Cameron without ogling him, and it didn't help that he kept wearing those fitted faded T-shirts that clung to his body like Trish wanted to.

Oh my God, I'm jealous of a piece of clothing.

"That tone of voice says there's definitely something to know about, but okay. Nothing to know about." Becka shook her head. "If you're worried about doing something to screw up the account, neither Aaron nor Cameron would send you if they thought you weren't capable. So they obviously think you can handle it."

"I've been working there like two weeks. I heard Aaron say that Concord Inc. can boost Tandem Security up to the next level. If I botch this, they won't get to that next level." She'd already failed so many freaking times. There was absolutely nothing in her track record that should cause everyone around her to give her yet another vote of confidence.

Not everyone.

She'd bit the bullet and told her parents last night that she'd be out of the country for a while on work and they'd reacted about as well as she would have expected. Oh, her dad was supportive, if worried about his little girl out in the big world without someone to protect her. She didn't hold it against him—he treated both his daughters like that. Her sister just never gave him cause for worry. It seemed like all Trish did was worry him, even when she tried not to.

And her mom…

She sighed. "My mother had some choice words on the subject." Choice words that ended in tears, and demands to know what she'd done as a mother to drive Trish to cross an ocean to get away from her. It had taken two hours and a promise to visit over the weekend once she got home to calm her mother down and get her back to some semblance of normality.

"Oh." Becka made a face. "Look, I'm hardly the authority on healthy parent-child relationships, and your mom is a nice lady, but she really needs to get a hobby that has nothing to do with her adult children. Knitting. Charity. Pole dancing classes.

Doesn't matter, but it might distract her from the whole empty nester thing she's got going on."

Trish stared. "You did not just list pole dancing classes alongside charity and knitting as activities my mom should try."

"Why not?" Becka gave a wicked grin. "It's great core work."

"I'm going to tell Aaron you said that."

"It's been a couple days since I shocked him, so I'm about due for another one."

Trish burst out laughing, and the sound drained out the anxiety that had been building since Aaron called her with instructions for the trip. She sank onto the chair across from the couch and shook her head. "Thanks. I needed that."

"I know." Becka shifted Summer to the other side and adjusted her clothing. "Here's the deal—you're not going to fuck up. Thinking you might is just going to undermine your confidence and ensure you *do* screw up. So do that brilliant shining thing you do and just power through it—fake it until you make it. They'll be so relieved not to have to deal directly with Cameron, they'll fall all over themselves to give you whatever you ask for. Aaron already negotiated a preliminary contract, so it's just a matter of ensuring the actual contract is laid out to his specifications."

She made it sound so easy when she put it like

that. Nice and simple. Trish ran her hand over the smooth fabric of the chair. "Why is everyone so down on Cameron? He's kind of gruff, but he's not a total asshole like everyone says."

Becka shrugged. "Cameron is a difficult personality. I know because it takes one to know one, though we're different flavors." She shifted back and sighed. "I think the real question is, why are you trying so hard not to jump to his defense?"

She shouldn't talk about it. Positivity was Trish's gig, and there was nothing positive about the shame she'd been carrying around since that first kiss. Maybe she could have recovered if she hadn't dropped the towel and had him turn away in response. Maybe. Either way, it wasn't fair to dump her issues on her brother's baby mama and fiancée.

But under those sympathetic eyes, she found herself speaking. Trish shifted her gaze to the pattern on the rug because it was easier to spill her secrets there than to the woman across from her. "I kissed him. And after he politely—for him—told me that it wasn't going to happen, I faked my way through being totally professional and okay with it. Right up until I forgot to set my alarm, slept in and had him show up on my doorstep. I, uh, panicked and it ended up with me naked and him once again explaining that it most definitely wasn't going to happen."

A muffled snort brought her head up. Trish glared. "Are you laughing at me? I've been rejected twice and even if he's right about it being a bad idea to bang like bunnies, it still stings. And if he'd stop *looking* at me like he does, it would make it a whole lot easier to bear." Sometimes she would turn and catch such heat in Cameron's gaze that it was a wonder she didn't turn into a pillar of lustful flames right there in the office. But he turned away.

Every. Single. Time.

"Oh God, you poor thing." Becka let loose a peal of laughter that filled the room to the brim. "Like running headfirst into a brick wall, isn't it?"

"That's not…inaccurate."

Becka grinned. "I'm familiar with the feeling. You've got freckles all over, right?"

The change in subject made her frown. "Sure. Why?"

"Tell me one thing—actually, tell me two things. How long did it take him to turn away when you dropped the towel?"

"Um…" Trish's skin went hot at the memory. "It wasn't instant, if that's what you mean."

"Mmm-hmm. And when he *looks* at you… Is it

possible he's retracing your freckles all over mentally?"

Now that she mentioned it, his gaze did tend to take a specific path when he thought she wasn't looking. A very similar path to the one he'd traced in the air above her skin that day. She cleared her throat. "It's possible."

"That's what I thought." Another laugh. Becka's smile promised all sorts of wicked things. "Have fun on your work trip, Trish. I sure as hell would in your position."

CHAPTER EIGHT

THE FLIGHT TO London was both heaven and hell. Cameron had never had a problem feeling cramped or caged in when he flew first class. The seats there hadn't fallen victim to the desire to cram more paying passengers into the same amount of space that the rest of the plane had. He usually didn't have to worry about his broad shoulders crowding out the person next to him and could relax and work through however long the flight was.

That was before he sat next to Trish.

Even with the space between them, he couldn't shake his awareness of her. Every shift where she crossed and recrossed her legs. Every time her mass of curly hair brushed his shoulder. Every breath. She fell asleep halfway through the flight and ended up slumped against him, her little body curled in the seat and her head halfway in his lap.

He loved every agonizing second of it.

Though he managed to keep from touching her more than strictly necessary, it was all too easy to imagine they were traveling *together*, jetting off to some exotic island or snowy peak to spend a week tangled up in each other and blind to the rest of the world.

Instead, he went over the preliminary contract for the tenth time since Aaron had sent it over. It didn't matter that the terms were standard with a few small exceptions. They'd handled overseas clients before, but Concord Inc. was unique in the way that they had an independent server for all their internal workings. Something like that wouldn't normally need Tandem Security's expertise—impossible to hack what someone couldn't get to in the first place—but Concord Inc. did need access to public servers for outside communications.

And *that* could be breached.

Cameron kept himself busy mulling over the possible options as the plane finally landed. Trish managed to sleep through the entire thing, so he gently squeezed her shoulder. "We're here."

She opened those big blue eyes and blinked at him a few times as if she couldn't quite place where they were or who he was. Awareness rushed over her expression between one breath and the next and she licked her pretty pink lips.

He went rock-hard, and then silently cursed himself for reacting at all. He couldn't seem to stay in line when it came to this woman, but that wasn't her fault. No, the blame lay squarely on his shoulders, and after his dickhead comment that day at her apartment, he'd been careful navigating the minefield that every conversation between them had become.

His fault.

Trish sat up and pushed her hair back from her face. "Sorry. I didn't mean to take over your space."

Since what he wanted most in that moment was for her to take over his space—and his cock—fully, he gritted out, "No problem."

He managed to get control of himself by the time they deplaned, got through the custom's process and grabbed their luggage. It was still relatively early in local time, but they wouldn't meet with Nikki Lancaster until the next day. "Food?"

"Please." She looked a little…wilted…after all the traveling. Trish's hair was fluffier than he'd ever seen it, and she huddled within her large coat, her eyes seeming larger than normal. It was obvious that, despite her nap, what she needed was food and rest and some time to adjust to their new location.

Cameron got them to their hotel—a little boutique place strategically placed a few short blocks from Concord Inc. They'd ended up with a two-bedroom suite, which was what he and Aaron usually booked when their work required travel, but it took on a new significance with Trish.

They were staying behind the same locked door in this place.

For fuck's sake, get ahold of yourself. This is business. This has only ever been business.

Except nothing when it came to Trish felt like business.

He held the door open for her, angling his body away to avoid her accidentally brushing against him. "Take whatever room you want."

"Generous." Trish shot him an arch look over her shoulder, as if she knew exactly why he was being so generous. She didn't say anything else, though. She just dropped her bag in the middle of the small living space and went investigating.

Cameron forced himself not to follow her, but instead walked to the tiny dining room table and started setting up his computer. "If you want a shower, I can run down and grab us some food."

She poked her head out the first bedroom door. "My kingdom for some genuine fish and chips."

"I'll keep that in mind." He left before he could think too hard about what Trish in the shower would be like. Her showering had almost been their downfall before, and Cameron knew himself well enough to know his self-control wouldn't last through a third time of backing away from her. Better to avoid the temptation altogether by removing himself from the building.

He had no idea how they were supposed to get through the next few days without stepping all over each other. Challenging enough to be closeted in an office with her when they were able to retreat to their respective homes after hours. But being together 24-7 in the same workplace, the same hotel suite?

The odds of keeping his hands off her were not in his favor.

Cameron took his time walking down to the lobby and waylaid the bellhop to get recommendations for places with good fish and chips. The nearest one the guy recommended was more than a few blocks, but after being cramped in the plane for so long, he welcomed the chance to stretch his legs.

And it would ensure Trish had plenty of time to shower and get dressed again before he returned.

Satisfied he'd made the right call, he lengthened

his stride and put some distance between himself and the siren call Trish Livingston represented.

Trish took her time in the shower, washing away the grit of traveling. She'd chosen the room with the smallest bed—Cameron needed more space than she did, after all—and it had the added bonus of the better bathroom. There was a claw-foot tub big enough to hold a party in and the shower wasn't exactly orgy-sized, but it was generous for the square footage.

She shut off the water and wrapped a towel around herself. The fluffy fabric slid luxuriously against her skin, drawing out a shiver. Sitting next to Cameron on the plane had her all pent-up and needy. Even after the shower, she was sure she could smell the evergreen soap he used. Her body responded accordingly, skin going tight, nipples pebbling, the spot between her thighs increasingly achy.

God, she wanted him.

Trish padded to the door to her room and peeked out. The suite was silent and empty. She had no idea how long Cameron had been gone—or when he'd be back. A thrill went through her at the thought. *I shouldn't risk it.* But on the heels of that, her innate stubbornness kicked in. *That only makes it hotter.*

She shut her door and tossed the towel over the low-backed chair situated by the window. Naked, she slipped between the sheets and stretched out. It wouldn't take long. She'd been halfway there since she woke up surrounded by him. It didn't matter that they'd been in separate seats and he'd barely touched her. Trish was so damn primed, all it would take was his breathing on her clit and she'd come screaming.

Her toes curled as she cupped her breasts, pretending it was *his* hands there. Not rough. Certainly not gentle. A firm touch. A freaking perfect touch.

It's not perfect because it's not the real thing.

She didn't care. She'd come too far to go back now.

Trish rolled one nipple between her thumb and forefinger and ran her other hand down her stomach to stroke her clit. A moan slipped free as she pushed a single finger into herself. She arched her back, letting the sheets slide down to reveal her breasts. It didn't matter that no one could see her. She *felt* watched, and that was enough to send her skirting along the edge of a truly great orgasm.

Imagining it was *Cameron's* eyes on her?

She circled her clit once, twice, a third time, and as she came, she moaned his name aloud. "Oh my God, *Cameron*." Her orgasm rolled over her, bowing her back and she could have sworn she heard him murmuring her name. Pleasure-induced hallucination, for sure.

Except when Trish opened her eyes, she wasn't alone in her room.

Cameron stood in the doorway, his hand still raised as it must have been when he knocked. The door hadn't even swung open all the way, but there was no way he'd missed the tail end of that self-love session. Especially not the part where she'd moaned his name as she came.

Shit.

She sat up, thought about clutching the sheet to her chest and gave it up as a lost cause. He'd already seen the goods—more than once at this point. The only person who'd seen her naked so many times without there actually being sex involved was her freaking doctor. And Trish didn't want to sleep with her doctor.

Cameron didn't say anything. Didn't move. Didn't seem to so much as breathe.

There was no brazening her way out of this situation. She didn't know who'd cursed her that she seemed to be destined to perpetually humiliate herself in front of Cameron, but it was time to face the music.

She met his gaze directly. "I don't suppose you missed any of that?"

"You said my name when you came." His voice was deeper than normal, and each word rumbled in the pit of her stomach. Lower. "I've tried to stay away from you, Trish."

"I know."

"You're making it fucking impossible."

Was this… Could this actually be happening?

She couldn't go to him. She'd already thrown herself at him too many times for her pride to survive yet another rejection. Trish licked her lips, half-convinced she could taste him there despite weeks passing since their last kiss. "Maybe it's time to try something new, then." *Try me. Touch me. Fuck me.*

He stepped into her room. He moved slowly, seeming to weigh her every breath as if testing her resolve. Little did he know it took everything she had to keep perfectly still and wait for him to approach the bed instead of flinging herself at him.

"Cameron," she whispered.

"Yeah." He matched her tone.

Her next words would either push them over the edge or yank them back to safety. She knew what the smart choice would be, but Trish had been making the *smart* choice for her entire life and look where it got her—nowhere near the path she'd always thought she'd walk. It was time to try something new. She drew in a shallow breath. "Touch me."

He reached down and grabbed a fistful of the blankets covering the bed. "That's not a good idea."

"I know." No point in arguing. It was the truth. "Do it anyway."

He lifted his gaze to meet hers. "You're sure."

Not a question, but she wanted no chance of miscommunication. If they were sprinting past the point of no return, they would do it together with eyes wide-open. "I'm sure."

He drew the blankets from the bed in an agonizingly slow movement. The sensation of sheets sliding down her body had her biting her bottom lip, but the forbidding look in his dark eyes kept her still and silent, unwilling to do anything to break the spell.

"Show me."

Trish stopped breathing. "What?"

"You were imagining me. Us. Tell me what you pictured." He didn't move from his spot at the end of the bed, just out of reach. "Show me how you touched yourself."

She should be embarrassed. Humiliated. But being on display for him set her aflame. She was so close to having what she wanted…

This is exactly what I wanted.

Cameron's eyes on me.

She shifted until she was on her back and resumed the position she'd been in when this all started. With him watching, she cupped her breasts. "You touched me here. Made my toes curl."

"Mmm." His appreciative growl vibrated through her entire body.

She started to slide one hand down her stomach, but he made a negative sound. "Slow, Trish. I've been thinking about tracing your freckles with my tongue since I saw them. I sure as fuck wouldn't rush this."

The heat beneath her skin flared hotter. She licked her lips. "I can't do that myself."

"I know."

Slowly, oh so slowly that she didn't dare breathe, she spread her thighs, revealing everything to him. "Touch me, Cameron. Please."

The bed dipped beneath his weight and then he was there, covering her with his body. His clothes scraped lightly against her skin, a barrier she wanted gone, but Trish couldn't focus with his weight settling over her like the best kind of promise. This was happening. They were doing this.

She grabbed his hand and pressed it to the center of her chest, directly over the spot he'd almost touched her that day back in her apartment. "Touch me," she repeated. "Make it better than I imagined."

He spread his fingers, nearly covering her chest completely from collarbone to collarbone. Cameron shifted his hand up, dragging his thumb along the front of her throat as he cupped the back of her neck and tilted her face up to meet his. He kissed her slowly, beginning with the softest brushing of his lips against hers and then teasing her mouth open with his tongue. The soft kiss was directly at odds with the way he spread her thighs with his own and ground against her clit, his cock a hard ridge in his pants. "This is what you want."

It wasn't a question, but she refused to allow the slightest hint of blurred lines between them. Trish kissed his neck, his jaw, and finally reclaimed his mouth. "This is what I want, Cameron. Don't stop touching me."

CHAPTER NINE

CAMERON HAD SPENT himself more times than he wanted to count with fantasies of having Trish naked beneath him. It was almost enough for him to believe this was a fever dream caused by jacking himself one time too many to the map of the freckles on her body. But as he stroked her tongue with his, there was no denying that this was happening. He kissed along her jaw and down her neck. "I've wanted to do this since that day in your apartment."

He started with the freckle directly over her left breast. Cameron had always had a damn good memory, and he put it to use now, marking a path from freckle to freckle with his mouth. He lingered on the curves of her small breasts, on her pretty pink nipples, on the soft lines of her stomach, before finally settling between her thighs.

Trish gasped out a breath she'd been holding. "Wow."

"That was only one path. I'll revisit…later." He ran his cheek along one thigh and then the other, enjoying the way her entire body flushed at the contact. He spread her thighs wider. As much as he wanted to drive into her, knowing her orgasm had already primed her, he wanted a taste more. Cameron had pictured doing this so many times. He wouldn't let anyone rush him—not even himself.

He dragged his tongue up the center of her pussy and growled at the way she jumped. As if he'd attached a live wire to his tongue. "Relax, Trish. Enjoy this."

"Relax, Trish," she mimicked breathlessly. "You're asking the impossible."

Despite himself, he grinned against her heated flesh. Cameron pinned her squirming hips and gave himself over to the taste of her on his tongue and the way she cried out every time he circled her clit. She was close. Her hips tried to rise to meet his mouth, but he kept her in place, determined to drive her ruthlessly over the edge, to feel her come on his tongue. He needed it like he'd never needed anything before, and like hell would she deny him.

"Cameron." Trish's back bowed as she orgasmed.

He'd barely managed to lift his head when she

grabbed his arms and yanked. Cameron crawled up her body, but stopped while still on his hands and knees. “Fuck. Condoms.”

“Oh yeah, that.” She rolled from beneath him and teetered over to her suitcase, and he took the opportunity to strip. He glanced over as she returned with a giant box of condoms. Trish caught his incredulous look and gave a sheepish smile. “Hope springs eternal.” She yanked out a condom and tore open the foil packet. One well-placed nudge and he was on his back with her straddling him.

The desire in her blue eyes hadn’t abated, but there was mischief there now, too. She smiled as she slowly rolled the condom onto his cock and gave him a stroke. “Oh yeah. This is happening.”

He barked out a laugh. “Your dirty talk is superb.”

“I don’t need dirty talk.” She shifted up and notched his cock in her entrance. Before he had a chance to brace, she sank down until he was sheathed to the hilt. Trish hissed out a breath. “Lordy, you’re big.”

He cupped her hips, trying to keep her still while her body accustomed itself to him, but she was already moving, rolling her hips a little. With the faint light from the window behind her, she looked like an angel, blond curls in a halo around her head and the soft lines of her body shifting sensuously as she rode his cock. Trish planted her hands on his chest and picked up her pace, sliding almost completely off him and then slamming back down. "God, Cameron, you feel good. Better than good. There aren't proper filthy words to describe how good."

"You're doing a damn good job of describing it." He arched off the bed and caught her mouth, needing to taste her even as she rode him. She followed him back to the bed, her fucking him turning into something slower, deeper, her breasts sliding against his chest with every stroke. *Yes. This.* He squeezed her ass, using the leverage to grind her clit against his pelvis as he thrust up.

"Yes." She gasped. "Do that again. Keep doing that."

He obeyed. He couldn't have stopped if he wanted to. Pleasure danced down his spine, taking up residence in his balls and the base of his cock, but Cameron ruthlessly held it at bay. He wanted to feel her come again, *needed* it. He thrust again and again and again.

Trish came with a cry loud enough to make the windows rattle. She slumped against his chest and he rolled them so he could settle between her thighs. The look of sated pleasure on her face was almost enough to make him blow right then and there, but he gritted his teeth and wrestled himself back under control.

Then, and only then, did he kiss her. Slow and deep and exploring as if he hadn't had his mouth all over her body not too long ago. He kissed her until she seemed to come back to herself, until she wrapped her legs around his waist and writhed beneath him where he had her pinned to the bed.

He pulled out and flipped her onto her stomach. Cameron smoothed a hand down her spine, enjoying the way her muscles flexed beneath his touch and her ass rose in offering. She had freckles smattering her back and the curves of her ass, too, and he reached between her thighs to stroke her pussy as he mentally traced the path he planned on taking. He had the fanciful thought that one day he'd like to paint constellations on her skin.

"Oh God, I don't know if I can go again." She moaned against her pillow. But her hips moved to meet his hand again and again.

Cameron leaned down and set his teeth against the back of her neck. "I'm not through with you, Trish."

"Oh, well, then… Carry on." She laughed helplessly, the sound turning into a moan as he pushed two fingers into her.

"Ride my hand, Trish. Take what you need." He kissed down her spine, straying to one side or the other to trace her freckles with his tongue. Her hips bucked against his hand, but he held steady, needed to feel her come apart again.

She went still with a shudder. “It’s not enough. I need your cock.”

The words made him harder than he’d ever been. He forced himself to give the small of her back the same care and attention he’d spent on the rest of her body, but he was more than ready to meet her need as he nudged her knees farther apart and notched his cock in her entrance. He fed her inch after inch, keeping her still with a hand on her hip until he was sheathed to the hilt. He closed his eyes, but the sight of her was too much to resist.

This time, there would be no holding back. He needed this—her—too much.

Cameron gripped her hips and brought her back as he thrust forward. She cried out, and he almost stopped, but Trish reached back and bracketed his wrist with a hand. “Harder, Cameron. I need more.”

“I need it, too.” He gave himself over to the feel of fucking her, her pussy clamping tight on him with every stroke, her cries and the sound of flesh meeting flesh filling the room. She came with his name on her lips, and he followed her willingly over the edge with a curse of his own.

As Cameron slumped onto the mattress next

to her, he was struck by the thought that he might follow this woman anywhere.

Trish stared at the ceiling and wondered when the hell her life had taken a hard turn into crazy town. Was it when she moved back in with her parents after college? When she'd agreed to take the job working for Aaron? The second she set eyes on Cameron O'Clery?

Wherever the tipping point was, the end result had her naked and breathing hard with the taste of Cameron lingering on her lips.

She'd loved every second of it.

"Aaron can't know."

She closed her eyes and counted silently to five—and then to ten. "Did you think I was going to run straight from being in bed with you to call my brother and tell him we just had sex?"

A pause and, despite not looking at him, she could almost see the gears turning in Cameron's head as he mentally replayed what he'd just said. He cleared his throat. "That wasn't tactful."

"You think?"

His big hand settled on her stomach. "Trish, look at me."

She didn't want to. Opening her eyes meant having to fight to reclaim the mask, and she didn't have the energy right now. Being bright and positive had been her go-to thing for so long, she didn't always notice she was doing it. It barely took effort anymore to smile and make people's days better.

It took effort with Cameron. So much freaking effort. Mostly because he insisted on demanding the truth from her over and over again.

He skated his hand up the center of her chest to cup her jaw. "Trish."

She sighed and opened her eyes. If Cameron O'Clery was devastating in the office while wearing clothes, he was downright heartbreaking naked in bed with her. Something about his expression looked softer here, as if some artist had painted him in gentle golden tones. His dark skin stretched over an impossibly broad chest, drawing her eyes south, ever south, to where the sheets hid the lower half of his body from her view. "You're beautiful."

"Thanks." He huffed out a laugh. He stroked her bottom lip with his thumb. "I've never done anything like this before. It has me all fucked in the head, and I'm even less tactful than normal."

"I didn't think that was possible."

Another of those soft laughs. "That makes two of us." His smile dimmed. "But since we're in an uncomfortable position on two fronts, we have to talk about this."

She knew that. Really, she did. She had just hoped to get to enjoy the afterglow from the glorious sex for a few minutes before they jumped right into talking about the nitty-gritty details. Trish forced herself to smile. "Sure. We can't tell Aaron. I'm aware of that." Her brother didn't usually fall into overprotective jerk mode, but there was a first time for everything. Beyond that, he already had enough to worry about with his new baby and a wedding to plan.

Cameron seemed to weigh his next words. "Our relationship while on the clock can't change. We're already blurring the lines too much as it is. If we let it bleed over into Tandem Security…"

"We won't. It's as simple as that." She glanced at the clock. "What are the odds our food is still warm?"

His laugh rumbled through her body in the most delicious way possible. "Even I can take that hint." Cameron pressed a light kiss to her temple that she felt all the way to her toes. "Let's feed you and then we can go over the next steps."

For a second, she thought he meant they were going to detail the rules and boundaries for sex versus no sex, but as he pulled on his pants and headed for the door, Trish realized he'd already made the jump back to business. She stared after him. *What the hell did I get myself into?*

You know exactly what. This is what you wanted.

It was. She just had to remember that, as she

navigated a new existence where she knew what it felt like to come on Cameron's cock.

Trish touched her hair, but it was a lost cause. She'd need another shower to have any hope of taming it, but since their first meeting was tomorrow, it'd have to do for now. A quick rummage through her suitcase for something comfortable to wear, and she walked out to find Cameron setting out the food on the table.

He glanced at her and went still. "What is that?"

She froze. "What?"

"What are you wearing?"

Oh. That. She glanced down at the oversize shirt she'd bought on a whim. It had Minnie Mouse on it and, now that she thought about it, it was probably something a child would wear. "You have a problem with Minnie?"

"I have a problem with the fact that you need to eat, and I see you in that and all I want to do is toss the food and have *you* on the table instead."

"Oh." Trish blinked. *"Oh."*

Cameron shook his head. "Sit down and eat something."

For the first time in well over a week, she found herself enjoying his abruptness. Trish sank into her seat and grinned. "Is it that the shirt is large enough to fit three of me that gets you going? Or is it a secret Minnie Mouse fetish?"

He set her fish and chips in front of her and dropped into the seat opposite. "You could wear a paper bag and I'd still want to tear the damn thing off you." He picked up a french fry. "It'd be easier to get into than most clothes, so there's something to be said for that."

"You just made a joke."

"I do that on occasion."

"Huh." Trish took a few bites. That seemed to satisfy him that she was going to eat instead of waste away before his eyes, because Cameron set to his food with a single-minded focus she'd only ever seen in athletes and big dudes. When she'd eaten as much as her stomach could handle for the time being, she sat back and found him watching her. "What?"

"I don't get it."

"There's a legion of things you don't get."

He frowned at her, completely undeterred by her attempt at humor. "Aaron is good at making people around him happy, but he's not a people pleaser in the strictest sense of the word. He has no problem telling me to fuck off when the situation calls for it, and he's ended more than a few client relationships when things went south. It didn't tear him up to make that call."

She saw where this train of thought was going, and almost derailed it. Cameron had made abundantly clear that he wanted sex-them and work-them separate, but here in this suite with her body still aching from the wonderful things he'd done to it, the line had already blurred. She took a sip of bottled water. "There wasn't a question in there."

"I'm getting to it." He sat back, the muscles in his chest rippling in a way that made her clench her hands to keep from reaching for him. Cameron gave her another of those searching looks where it almost seemed like he could read her mind. "I've met your parents. They're decent people, and your older sister runs more traditional than either you or Aaron, but she's not a basket case."

"Did you just call me a basket case?"

"So where does the nervous shit come from?" He continued without bothering to answer her question. "You…flicker. I thought you were really sunshine personified, but that's the shield—or the sword, depending on the situation. What happened that you need walls that strong?"

Good Lord, he wasn't just making idle conversation. He'd gone straight past polite small talk and right to her heart of hearts. Trish forced herself not to fidget and met his gaze directly. "Why do you want to know?"

That set him back. "What?"

"It's a pretty simple question."

Cameron seemed to mull that over with the

same intensity he gave everything in life. “I want to know more about you. I don’t understand you.”

It was both an encouraging reason and one that cut her knees right out from beneath her. Curiosity. He was curious about her, like she was a bug he couldn’t quite identify and it would annoy the hell out of him until he had her properly categorized and filed away. Then he’d move on and forget all about her as anything other than a vaguely fond memory.

Isn’t that what you want? This was never supposed to be forever.

That was fine. It was even fair.

But it didn’t mean she had to rip herself open for the sake of his curiosity.

Trish pushed her food away. “If you want to know more about me, you start simple. It’s only the proper way to do things.”

“Simple.” He said the word as if tasting it. “All right. What do you do when you’re not overworking yourself on unpaid time?”

The way he asked the question had her making a mental note to check her direct deposit on payday. She should have known Cameron would be keeping an account of all the time she spent in the office during nonworking hours. Silly of her to think he’d missed it.

Trish almost told him there was nothing simple

about that question, but "What do you do for fun?" was about as baseline as first date questions went. *This isn't a first date. This is a first...*

I don't know what this is.

She took another sip of her water. "I watch horror movies and I crochet."

Cameron sat back and draped his arm over his chair. "The crocheting fits. You have this retro thing going on that is too quirky to be anything but genuine. Explain the horror movies. Why that genre?"

The fact he'd studied her enough to decide that her *retro thing* was genuine and not another mask... Trish pulled at the bottom of her shirt, not sure if she was flattered or flayed wide-open. Maybe this wasn't such a simple question, after all. "I like horror. There are rules and while you get more than your fair share of stupid people doing stupid things, it's usually some offbeat heroine who ends up as the last one standing in the face of whatever evil is killing off nubile teenagers. It's really satisfying to know that, no matter how many sequels you're going to get, good always triumphs over evil—and rarely looks pretty while doing it." She hadn't meant to say that last aloud.

He drummed his fingers on the table. "You'd argue that horror movies are feminist."

She blinked. "Uh, I'm not arguing that one way or another. I enjoy them."

He still had that look on his face, the one like he didn't know what to think of her. "Which are your favorites? Slashers, paranormal or sci-fi?"

"All of the above, though if I have to pick one, it's slashers all the way. They're so…predictable. Usually a dude in a mask with a big pointy object and some sneaky ways."

"Helps if the helpless victim trips a dozen times in the effort to cross her front yard."

Trish laughed. She couldn't help it. "You're not a fan, I take it?"

"It's not that." Cameron's frown cleared and he shrugged. "I don't get them. There seems to be a total lack of common sense required to keep all the victims in one place long enough for the killer to find them and pick them off one by one. Why don't they ever just leave?"

"Because then there wouldn't be a story." She laughed again. Whether on purpose or not, he'd effectively moved them away from the emotional minefield and into something much more mundane. Trish relaxed and crossed her legs. "Though there are a couple movies that actually have a vein of logic through them that might appeal to you. I'll lend them to you sometime, if you're interested."

He met her gaze. "When we get back to New

York, why don't you bring them over yourself and explain to me while we watch?"

Oh shit. He just went there. If she had any doubt about Cameron's intentions—at least outside of work and her brother—he'd just cleared them right up. That was an opening that gave her plenty of room to maneuver without either of them over-reaching. She says no, they both retreat once again and go back to the sexual tension–filled days and lonely nights.

Or maybe Trish was the only one spending lonely nights with her favorite buzzy toy and thinking about the one guy she couldn't have. She had no idea how Cameron spent his time outside of the office. It wasn't her business. Yes, they'd had sex, but that didn't mean…

Fuck it.

She set her bottle of water down. "I'd like that. On one condition."

The light tensing of his shoulders was the only indication of his mood. "I'm listening."

"This might be off the books, but until it runs its course, I would like it to be exclusive."

"Done."

She frowned. "You agreed to that awfully easy."

"You brought it up before I had a chance to." He held out a hand, and she dazedly rounded the table to take it. Cameron tugged her forward to straddle him and ran his hands up the backs of her thighs. "I'm a selfish bastard, Trish. I don't share what's mine, even if it's only mine in part."

"That's very archaic of you." She shivered as his knuckles brushed the curve of her ass. "I'm a person, not a possession."

"Agreed," he said easily. Cameron skated his hands to her hips, taking her shirt with him and baring her from the waist down. His thumb brushed her hip bones. "But that doesn't change the fact that you bring out strong…impulses…in me. You make me crazy." His hands reached her breasts and he leaned down to press a kiss to her stomach. "All I can think about is you, when I should be thinking about work. I've never had a problem with distractions before. I don't know how to deal with it."

"Now I'm a problem *and* a distraction." She lifted her arms over her head and let him drag her shirt off, leaving her naked. "You sweet talker, you."

"If I was better with words, we wouldn't be in this position to begin with."

Trish made a show of looking at where his hands were. "I think I like this position."

That earned her a brief smile. "I'm never going to say the right thing."

"This isn't about saying anything at all." She

leaned down and kissed his shoulder as she unbuttoned his pants. A crinkle had her laughing against his skin. "Is that a condom in your pocket or are you just happy to see me?"

"It would be a shame to put that truly ambitious box to waste, don't you think?"

She sent out a silent thank-you to Becka for giving her the idea in the first place, though Trish would never say as much aloud. She stroked his cock. "I couldn't agree more."

CHAPTER TEN

CAMERON WOULD HAVE spent the entirety of their trip to London without leaving the suite, but the next day dawned with a full schedule. He went over it with Trish while they ate breakfast. "Nikki Lancaster makes me look like I should be winning Miss Congeniality contests."

"You mentioned that. Twice." Trish studied him over the rim of her coffee. "Why are you so nervous?"

"I'm not nervous." Nervous was a strange, prickly sensation, and Cameron had stinging bees swarming in his stomach.

"You're the very definition of *nervous*. If you think I'm not capable—"

"It's not that." He couldn't just leave it at that, no matter how little he wanted to deal with this entire thing. *Damn you, Aaron.* "Nikki and I…

had a short fling a couple years ago. It went sideways pretty fast, and while it shouldn't matter in the grand scheme of things, I can't guarantee that it won't affect how she treats this meeting."

Trish sighed. "That would have been good information to have before we started this whole process. I suppose you said something that pissed her off and she dumped you?"

He couldn't even bristle because it was exactly what had happened, but the exasperation in Trish's tone said she wasn't surprised in the least by this turn of events. "We never got far enough for someone to be dumped. There was a first date and the next morning, one minute we were having a conversation that skirted into work, and the next she was kicking me out in only my underwear."

"Mmm-hmm." She was all false sympathy and smiles. "You didn't happen to tell her that her company's cybersecurity is inferior or something along those lines?"

That was exactly what he'd told her. Cameron poked at his food. "She asked a question and I gave an answer."

"Oh, you poor thing." Trish's laughter pealed through the room. "You wouldn't know tact if it clobbered you over the head in a dark alley. How long ago was this?"

"A couple years. Three…no, four? I think four."

Shit, he couldn't remember. It had been just another failed dating experience and he'd moved on with his life, assuming that Nikki would do the same. He still wasn't sure that she *hadn't* moved on with her life.

Trish gave him wide eyes. "You don't even know. God, what was Aaron thinking, sending you over here? I'm assuming he knows."

"He knows." They hadn't hashed out details, but considering the power Concord Inc. wielded, it wasn't something he could keep to himself.

"That's something at least." She shook her head. "Let me deal with Nikki. You keep your mighty opinions to yourself for the duration of this, unless there's a need for you to offer specific technical information."

Though Cameron wasn't much a fan of being handled, he could admit that he liked the way Trish assumed power without thought. It wasn't until she ordered him about that he realized she'd been… muted. No, not muted, exactly, but she held herself back normally. Toned herself down. He'd recognized that the sunny disposition was a mask, but he hadn't realized the depth of the deception she offered the world.

Did she even know herself?

Not my problem.

You made it your problem the second you laid eyes on her.

"I *can* have a conversation without pissing off everyone in the room."

"Prove it," she fired back. "This account is important, and it would reflect badly on both of us if we botch it. You know as well as I do that the second Aaron heard the bad news, he'd be on a flight over here to rectify the situation, and that would upset both him and Becka. We can handle it—we just need to *handle it*. That starts with you learning when to keep your opinion to yourself."

"You're handling me."

"Damn right I am." Trish pushed to her feet. She wore a simple black pencil skirt with a deep blue blouse that made her eyes almost glow. It was toned down for her, but he could barely look at her without wanting to slip his hand under her skirt and give her a distraction they both needed.

She pointed at him. "Cease and desist this second."

"I don't know what you're talking about." He stood as well and rounded the table to capture her hips. The height of her heels put her mouth kissably close to his and he found he liked being able to look into her eyes without making the muscles in his neck twinge. Cameron skated his hands over her hips to cup her ass and bring her hips flush against his. "You look devastatingly beautiful today, Trish."

"I… What?" Her perfectly painted pink lips parted. "You can't just go and say something like that! I'm in work mode, and you're flustering me with your pheromones."

"We haven't left the suite yet." He pressed a slow kiss to the pulse fluttering in the hollow of her throat. "Ten minutes won't make much difference."

"Oh no you don't." She smacked his hands and ducked out of his grip. "Focus, Cameron. This is important and you wouldn't be making eyes at me if you were thinking with the right head. *Focus.*"

He huffed out a breath and tried to think past the blood rushing to his cock. She was right. He was better than this. The sex might be outstanding, but it was just sex. It had to be. If he couldn't compartmentalize, he had no business climbing into her bed to begin with.

"Sorry." He gave himself a shake. "Give me a minute."

"Take it. I have to get my purse." She ducked into her bedroom, leaving him wrestling for control of his reaction to her.

Cameron never lost control. He sure as fuck never lost sight of a work goal to pursue his own pleasure or interests. This morning, he'd done both. Hell, last night he'd done both, too. He'd crossed lines, and there was no way to take those actions back.

He was a selfish bastard because he didn't *want* to take it back.

Last night had been the first time in as long as he could remember where his brain had shut off entirely and he'd been functioning on feel alone. It felt good to be with Trish. The sex, yes, but he'd had almost as good a time teasing her about her apparent love for horror movies as he had coaxing her orgasms.

She was a joy.

And he couldn't have her. Not in any permanent sense.

If he was smart, he'd cut this thing off before it went further. It would hurt her feelings and he'd be walking around pissy as hell about it for a while, but better a little hurt now than to have the situation blow up in both their faces later on. She might not be happy with him—that reaction was all but guaranteed—but she'd understand.

He stood there and made himself imagine how that conversation would go. The hurt flaring over her face, pooling in her deep blue eyes, the way her bottom lip would quiver for the breath of a second before she got control of herself. The sunny smile she'd give him to cover up…

No.

Fuck no.

He might not have her for keeping, but he had

her for the time being. And she had him. Cameron wasn't going to give up a single second with Trish until he had to. If it meant she dealt a blow unlike he'd ever felt when she left…

So be it.

After Cameron's cryptic words about Nikki Lancaster, Trish hadn't known what to expect. A fire-breathing dragon, maybe. The woman that approached them as they walked through the doors of Concord Inc. didn't fit any of her preconceived notions.

Nikki looked like a warrior goddess. She had her black hair pulled back into a businesslike coif thing and her pantsuit showed off curves for days. It was the glint in her dark eyes that gave Trish the most pause. A fighter scoping out an adversary.

She turned an identical look at Cameron, before she gave him a tight smile. "O'Clery."

"Nikki." He touched the small of Trish's back, urging her a step closer. "This is Trish Livingston, our newest addition."

Nikki took her in with those witchy dark eyes and Trish couldn't shake the feeling that she'd already had judgment passed on her. Whether it was good or bad was anyone's guess at this point. The woman extended her hand. "Aaron said he'd be sending a keeper for you, O'Clery, but he didn't mention the fact that it would be his little sister." No mistaking the emphasis on *little*.

Cameron's hand at the small of her back flexed, but Trish was already moving to defuse the situation. Whatever the situation was. She couldn't get a true read on Nikki. This could all be posturing for the sake of posturing, or it could be exactly what Cameron had feared. Trish smiled sweetly. "I think you'll find I'm more than qualified to get the job done." She glanced at her watch. "Shall we take this to wherever the meeting is being held? I would hate to be late."

Without another word, Nikki turned on her designer heels and led the way to a bank of elevators that took them to the executive floor.

Trish didn't dare exhale the breath she'd been holding on to. They'd managed to get through the first interaction without someone calling the whole thing off or yelling, but they still had the deal to hammer out. Even with Aaron taking care of the preliminary stuff, this whole thing was hardly guaranteed. She very carefully didn't look at Cameron as the elevators opened and they stepped out into a long hallway lined with doors.

Everything about the building was designed to create a modern minimalist look. Though Trish could appreciate the cool gray walls, white tiles marbled with black and stainless steel everything, the whole thing left her cold and edgy. As they headed into a small boardroom where three other people were assembled, she found herself longing for the cozy front office she'd created back in New York.

That's not your place any more than this one is. Forgetting that would be a mistake.

Nikki introduced the CEO of the company and their respective assistants. Once everyone had coffee, they got down to work outlining what they needed from Tandem Security. Cameron answered the questions directed at him, but there was a wariness she'd never seen in him before. Trish couldn't tell if it was brought on by dealing with his ex or dealing with people in general, and it wasn't like she could ask.

Not at the moment, anyway.

Through it all, she couldn't help watching the other woman. *This* was Cameron's type? She couldn't be more different from Trish. She was confident and bold and seemed perfectly at home in her skin. Not to mention that Nikki had almost single-handedly made Concord Inc. what it was today. She'd come in as COO, looked around and seen the potential of the company. And then she made it happen.

To say it was impressive and more than a little intimidating was a vast understatement.

They broke for a quick lunch and Trish found herself alone in the room with Nikki. She moved to make a quick exit, but the other woman stalled her. "Sit, sit. You're exhausting me with all your nervous energy."

Trish hesitantly sank back into the chair she'd just tried to abandon. "Something I can help you with?"

Nikki raised a perfect black brow. "How long have you been sleeping with O'Clery?"

Her jaw dropped. "I don't... What... I'm not—"

"You are, and I'd wager that Aaron doesn't know. He loves O'Clery like a brother, but he's not blind to the man's faults." She laughed. "Get that look off your face, honey. I'm not going to go for your throat over some guy I hooked up with half a million years ago."

It sounded totally reasonable, but Trish couldn't make herself relax. She stilled her hands in her lap, doing her best not to give herself away with any nervous movement. "You have a reason for bringing it up."

"I do." Nikki sat back. "I've known O'Clery and Livingston for nearly a decade in one capacity or another, and I've never seen him like this before. He's a grumpy asshole, but he's got a shitty poker face. Every time he looks at you, he goes all soft and gooey."

Yeah, right. This had to be some sort of weird mind game, though she couldn't figure out what the point was. "If you'll forgive me for being blunt, I don't see what my theoretical relationship with Camcron has to do with this deal."

"Nothing at all." Nikki's red lips curved, just a little. "It's a purely selfish curiosity to get a better look at the kind of woman who could manage to have *him* tripping all over his feet like an eager puppy. I'll admit that I don't see it. You're beautiful, of course, but the peppy cheerleader thing doesn't seem like it's a solid match for O'Clery." She lifted a single shoulder. "Then again, what do I know? Good for him. And good for you, too. He's got a heart of gold if you can get past the dumbass shit he says and the pissy attitude."

She still couldn't get a read on Nikki, couldn't tell if this conversation was exactly what it presented to be on the surface or if the woman was trying to undermine something. She couldn't help comparing herself to the other woman. Thcy weren't even on the same planet, and she couldn't be more opposite if Cameron had intentionally picked her for that reason. Rationally, she *knew* it didn't matter. He and Nikki were ancient history—and a brief one at that—but Trish looked at her and saw everything Trish would never be.

Someone completely at ease in their skin and

confident enough to handle any and every situation life threw at them without breaking her powerful stride. Someone who'd perfectly executed their plan for life, despite any hurdles thrown in their way.

No, Trish was just Trish. She let her smile drop. "Frankly, I don't see how that's any of your business."

"So you do have some backbone. Good."

The door opened and the men filed back in. She couldn't shake the suspicion that they'd been hiding out in the hallway while this conversation went down and, as happy as she was that Cameron had managed to keep his temper through the first half of the day, she still wanted to kick him under the table for abandoning her with Nikki.

It shouldn't have mattered anyway. Nikki had never been a girlfriend, and Trish certainly wasn't. They were both flavors of the week... *Maybe we should get T-shirts or something.* Her joke fell flat, even in her own head, and she tried to set the whole uncomfortable feeling aside. It shouldn't matter what Cameron and Nikki's past was, because the woman obviously had no intention of letting said past get in the way of this business deal.

Would he expect the same from Trish when this was all over?

The rest of the meeting passed without incident.

Concord Inc. signed the contract, which extended the trip to London since Cameron had to be on-site to set up the security requirements.

And Trish would go home.

Guess things are ending quicker than I could have anticipated.

CHAPTER ELEVEN

CAMERON MIGHT NOT be entirely in tune with other people's emotions, but he would have had to be particularly dense not to notice something was wrong with Trish. After their lunch break, she'd been subdued, her light dimmed. He'd tried to catch her eye a few times, but she resolutely refused to look his way. He could explain it away as her focusing on the deal…

Right up until she tried that same shit as they walked back to the suite.

He noticed a sign for a pub and hooked her waist. "Dinner."

"I'm not hungry."

Oh yeah, Trish was pissed. Cameron ignored her protest and guided her into the low light of the pub. He took a quick look around and headed for a table far enough into the room that she wouldn't get a chill when the door was opened to let a draft in. He held out a chair for her, his irritation battling with amusement as she huffed and dropped into it.

Once he was settled on the other side, he leaned forward and lowered his voice. "Now you're going to tell me what crawled up your ass back there. I played the good boy and kept my mouth shut, and the deal went off without a hitch. Which means something else happened to make you mad. Tell me."

Trish shrugged out of her coat and let it drape over her chair. Then she started shredding the paper napkin in front of her. Her anger disappeared, replaced by…embarrassment? She finally sighed. "I'll book my return ticket to New York as soon as we get back to our rooms."

He sat back. "I know you're pissed, but running back to the city seems a little dramatic, don't you think?"

"Dramatic?" Her light brows slammed together. "Are you kidding me? I'm not being dramatic. I'm being reasonable. You don't get to call me dramatic."

He knew better than to point out that her tirade was nothing if not dramatic. "Something upset you. If you need to yell at me to get around to telling me what it was, fine. But you *will* tell me."

She drew a breath for what seemed like a solid

dressing-down, but deflated on the exhale. "This is going to end."

Cameron went still. "If you want—"

"No, no, it has nothing to do with want. It has to do with reality. And the reality is that this is going to end." She gave a sad smile. "Every relationship either ends or results in marriage. Even this one." Before he had a chance to process *that*, she was off to the races again. "I mean, it's whatever. We knew this was coming. It's just showing up a little earlier than I thought and it surprised me and sometimes I react poorly to surprises. I know it's not your fault. Of course it's not your fault. It's just the way things are."

He caught the bartender's eye. "Two shots of whiskey, please."

If anything, Trish frowned harder. "I don't see how whiskey is going to help anything."

"A little bit of whiskey helps everything." When she stared, he shrugged. "It's when you tip into too much whiskey that the trouble starts. This conversation calls for a single shot."

When said shot was delivered to their table, he slid one over to rest in front of her. Cameron raised his glass and waited. With a put-upon sigh, Trish did the same. They took them smoothly and the soft clink of glass hitting the wood table was soothing in its own way. He leaned forward again. "Now, down to business."

"If you're going to—"

"Why the fuck do you think this is ending?"

She stopped. Stared. "What?"

Cameron spoke softly and clearly. "Do you want this thing between us to end?"

"It doesn't matter what I want."

"If it didn't matter, then I wouldn't ask you. But I am asking, Trish—do you want this to end?"

She narrowed her eyes. "No. Of course not. I'm enjoying being with you."

Damning him with faint praise, wasn't she? It didn't matter. He'd take it if it meant she didn't call the whole thing off. He hadn't put much thought into the *after* that would come when reality intruded on their little oasis of pleasure. That was Cameron's mistake, because Trish sure as fuck had been thinking about long-term implications. He reached out and took her hands in his. "I'm not ready to let you go."

He wasn't sure he'd *ever* be ready to let her go, but now was hardly the time to broach the subject, with her on the verge of panicking. Cameron had to find a way to ease her into the idea. First, though, they had to navigate through the current issue.

Her pink lips moved but no sound came out. Finally Trish shook her head. “I don’t get it. I don’t get *you*. A fling is one thing, but a long-distance fling is more than a little ridiculous…”

What was she talking about? “What’s long-distance?”

Her hands tensed beneath his. “The contract is finalized. That’s all I was here for.”

Realization dawned, and he almost laughed in relief. This, at least, had a simple fix. “Woman, you aren’t going back to New York without me. You’re staying until we get their preliminary security set up.”

“What are you talking about? Why would I stay?”

“If Aaron was in the office, it would be a different story, but for the time being, *I* am Tandem Security. That means I need you with me to do your job wherever I am. Most of the time that’s in the office, but I can work remotely as required, which is what’s going to happen while I’m needed here for Concord Inc. That means you’re here, too.”

That means we don’t have to have a conversation about this ending yet.

“You’re serious.”

“Yes.” He met her gaze steadily. “Unless you want to leave. Aside from client meetings—which we won’t be having until I’m back in the States, there technically isn’t anything that requires your physical presence. It will make things more challenging, but it's doable."

Trish tilted her head to the side. "Do you want me to leave?"

Now was the time to retreat, to allow her to make the choice for herself without him appearing to pressure her. But… Cameron only had one answer to that question and he was incapable of lying. Not to her. Not when it would endanger what little chance they had. "No." He said the word on an exhale, but once it broke the stillness emerging between them, it was easier to let the honesty flow. "I don't want you to leave. I don't want this to end."

She gave him a look like she wasn't sure if he meant their trip or *them*, but Cameron left her to draw her own conclusions. He never would have pegged Trish as skittish—not when she was a one-woman wrecking ball—but there were definite nerves showing around her too-wide eyes.

The bartender saved them when he tossed two menus onto the table. "You going to eat?"

"Fish and chips?" When Trish nodded, Cameron looked at the bartender. "Fish and chips for both of us."

"All right, then." He snatched up the menus and walked off as quickly as he'd approached.

Trish cleared her throat. "So, this is getting super awkward super fast and I don't know how to deal with it, and I don't know how I want to deal with it, so I'm just going to ignore it for the time being."

Her penchant for talking in run-on sentences when she was nervous shouldn't be endearing, but Cameron had given up trying to reason away his attraction to the woman. Even when she was driving him up the wall, he still found himself drawn to her.

But he could give her a reprieve for the time being. She obviously wasn't ready to make a decision about staying or going—both on a plane and in his bed—so Cameron scooted his chair back the slightest bit to give her space. "How do you feel about ghosts?"

Trish blinked. "Ghosts?"

"Yeah, you know...ghosts. Whether you believe they're energy or memories or literal souls doesn't matter."

Another slow blink. "I think I'm hallucinating because nothing coming out of your mouth makes a lick of sense."

"We're in London. There's half a dozen haunted tours within easy walking distance. There's one starting in an hour or so. It's entertaining, to say the least."

"But...ghosts. That doesn't seem like something you'd be into."

It wasn't, but she'd confessed her love of scary movies, so he'd looked it up this morning while she was in the shower. Logic said that sort of thing would go hand in hand, and as much as Cameron wanted to toss her over his shoulder and haul her back to bed until they were required somewhere, Trish had never been to London before. It was entirely possible she'd like to explore a bit.

He shifted, not sure how to deal with how closely she watched him. "I thought you might be interested in it."

Trish must have hit her head. It was the only explanation that made sense. She studied her water, trying to reconcile the man sitting across from her, shifting like a schoolboy who'd done something wrong and didn't want to admit it, with the confident boss she'd come to expect. "You want to go on a haunted tour," she said again, as if repeating it enough times would transfer the meaning of the words.

"We don't have to." There it was again—Cameron's almost-guilt.

Because he doesn't care about ghost tours. He looked up the schedule because you *do.*

She took a hasty sip of her water and set the glass back on the table. "I would love to do a haunted tour." She noted the almost imperceptible relaxing of his shoulders. It wasn't guilt she read from Cameron—it was nerves.

The realization almost made her laugh. She'd spent so much time tripping over her own feet in front of him, it had never occurred to her that he might be in over his head, too. The ground centered a bit below her feet, her perverse nature liking that he didn't have a playbook he was pulling from. Not that she'd believed that, exactly. Cameron was many things, but a playboy didn't make the list. That said, he obviously wasn't the settling-down type or he would have done it by now.

Unless he hasn't found the right person to settle down with...

Stop that.

You don't even know where you're going to land yet. You can't make choices one way or another when it comes to being with another person. Even without all the stuff stacked against you, it would never work.

She didn't want to think about that right now. Reality seemed very far away with them sitting in a darkened pub in the middle of freaking London. Trish cautiously reached out and touched his forearm. "Could we…" She swallowed hard, gathering her courage around her. "Could we table any conversations about the future for now? At least until we get back?"

“We’re only going to be here about a week.”

Such a short time and yet longer than she would have dared when she let herself imagine what it would be like if Cameron gave in to the pull between them. *It will have to be enough.* “The question stands.”

His dark eyes searched her face. “That’s what you want? Not to talk about anything too scary for the time we’re here.”

“Well, any haunted tour worth its salt is a little bit scary.” Her joke fell flat as the bartender appeared and set food on the table in front of them. Her mouth watered as she took in the crispy fish and chips. *Oh yeah, I love London.*

“Trish.”

She reluctantly dragged her gaze away from her food and back to his face. “Yeah?”

“You can have this week. After that, we’re having a conversation.”

A conversation destined to be the death knell of their fling. The writing couldn’t have been clearer on *that* particular wall. All she had to do was open her mouth and tell him she wanted to call the whole thing off—that it was wiser for her to leave things as they were and get the hell out of the UK and back to New York, where she could at least pretend she had her head on straight. They’d had sex a few times, but easy enough to chalk it up to temporary insanity and hope a week apart would be enough to cool their chemistry.

Leaving was the *smart* thing to do, and Trish always did the smart thing.

But she found herself smiling at Cameron. "Tell me about this haunted tour."

CHAPTER TWELVE

"THAT WAS THE biggest load of shit."

Trish laughed and slipped her hand into the crook of Cameron's arm. The wind had kicked up during the last half hour, and it cut through her thin jacket as if it wasn't there. She was self-aware enough to admit that craving warmth wasn't the only reason she wanted to touch him. He might be a human-shaped furnace, but being this close to him just felt *good* in general.

He absently rearranged her, tucking her against his body and wrapping an arm around her shoulders as he turned so his big body took the brunt of the wind chill. Cameron shook his head. "He wooed at one point." His voice kicked up a register as he mimicked their hapless guide. *"Wooooooo."*

"Oh stop." She playfully smacked his chest. "He knew his history. It was very educational." Her heart felt like it was two sizes too big after seeing places she'd only read about. The extra flavor from having a haunted tour only made the whole experience that much better.

That, and being with Cameron.

"The information was good. The delivery was off." He turned and guided them in the direction of their rooms, still grumbling about the guide. He cut himself off and shot her a look. "I had fun."

"I can tell."

"No, I'm serious. It was nice spending time with you."

Warmth blossomed in her chest, and no amount of reasoning could dispel it. She'd had fun with Cameron this evening, too. And last night. And this morning. Reminding herself that it was going to end—and probably end poorly—didn't make a difference. This runaway train was out of her control and it would keep going until they ran out of tracks. It didn't matter that she wouldn't be staying with Tandem indefinitely, or that Aaron would be furious when he found out how they'd crossed the line. Nothing mattered but how much she enjoyed being with Cameron. "What's your story?"

"What do you mean?"

She shot him a look. "Well, you didn't just pop into existence in your current form. I'm assuming you were a child at some point, probably had a parent or two in one form or another. Siblings? I mean, let's just start with the basics."

"I think I can do that." He squeezed her shoulders and nudged her to turn right at the street corner. "My parents live in California. My mother is a teacher, and my dad is military—retired now. No siblings to speak of. Apparently I was a difficult child, and—"

"Imagine that."

He continued without missing a beat. "They decided I was enough and didn't have any more kids. We weren't in one place for more than a few years, but they were a solid foundation while I was growing up. They're good people."

Trish had been born and raised in the same place as a long line of Livingstons had. Their roots went core deep in town, and she'd grown up knowing exactly what her place was, whether she wanted it or not. She couldn't imagine switching schools every few years and having to face dealing with figuring out her place in the pecking order… *Makes a lot more sense why he can be so damn standoffish. Easier not to play the game or get close to people when he'd just inevitably move on.* "You met my brother in college."

"More like he adopted me as his pet project in college," Cameron grumbled. "We were lab partners and he decided I just needed a little more structure in my life. Look where that got him."

"Mmm, yeah, terrible life you're both living." She laughed. "You're rich as sin and running a successful company together, and for all of both of your bitching, you never actually fight. Must be terrible." In truth, she envied them their friendship a bit. Trish had friends, but when it became clear she wasn't going to follow the ascending path to her dream career within the corporate fashion industry like she'd always planned, she withdrew more and more. One friend had scored an internship with her dream clothing designer, a position destined to shoot her into greatness if she survived it. Another had secured a junior position in a prestigious law firm.

Trish?

Trish had failed to find even an entrance-level job in her field of choice, and mounting student loan bills had forced her to move back into her parents' place to try to stem the hemorrhaging of her minuscule bank account. It turned out that her chosen field didn't have much in the way of entrance-level jobs, and securing one in their competitive industry had turned into an impossible task.

"Where are you headed?"

She started, belatedly realizing she had dropped her sunny persona and he'd picked up on it. Damn it, she kept doing that more and more as time went on. She wished she could blame it on Cameron's grumpiness rubbing off on her, but it wasn't the truth. Life weighed her down. Or, rather, the truth about life weighed her down.

Not everyone got a happy ending, no matter how many stars they wished on.

Some people had to settle on the mediocre instead of aspiring for greatness.

She just never thought she'd be part of either group.

With a sigh, she tried to focus on Cameron. "I'm sorry, I missed that last bit."

"In life." They turned another corner, and she started to recognize shops from the next street up from their hotel. "I had reservations when Aaron decided to bring you in, but you're good at handling people and situations."

"Yeah, I'm a great glorified secretary." Managing her mother's moods had given her plenty of people skills, though they mostly meant she gave excellent customer service no matter what her personal level of frustration was.

"Trish."

Oh no. She knew that tone of voice. It meant nothing good for the conversation. Cameron obviously wasn't pleased with her blasé comment, and he just as obviously intended to sit her down and…

Well, she didn't know what. A come-to-Jesus talk about knowing her worth? Or maybe one where he pointed out that she wasn't a glorified *anything*—she was literally their secretary.

No matter which way he was headed, she wanted no part of it. They would have their talk when they got back to New York. It could sure as hell wait until then. If this was an escape, she wanted to get her money's worth, so to speak.

Trish turned into him, grabbing the front of his jacket and leveraging herself up to take his mouth. His surprise only lasted a second, and then his hands were on her hips and he guided her several steps until her back hit the wall. Cameron dug his big hands into her hair and tilted her head back to get a better angle. He moved away long enough to say, "I know you're trying to distract me."

Of course he did. He wasn't stupid. She forced an impish grin. "Are you complaining?"

"Not especially." He reclaimed her mouth, but this time the pace slowed down. Cameron teased her with soft, barely there kisses until she growled in frustration, and only then did he set his teeth against her bottom lip and slip his tongue into her mouth.

The man kissed like a dream.

A really naughty one.

Give and take, advance and retreat. Over and

over and over again, until she lost all comprehension of the other people on the street or the fact that they were most definitely in a public place with an audience.

Trish had only meant to keep him from his questions, from pulling her apart at the seams to satisfy his curiosity, from creating a foundation of trust that neither of them could follow through on.

It didn't matter what she'd intended, only the end result.

And the result was that she wanted his hands all over her body, wanted him to stroke her just so, to send her hurtling over the edge. She wanted to take him into her body and ride him until they stopped worrying about the future, because the future was just a distant dream and they were *here* and *now*. That was the only thing that mattered.

He tore his mouth from hers. "Upstairs. Now."

Incapable of words, she nodded. Cameron gave her a look like he wanted to throw her over his shoulder because she wouldn't move fast enough on her own, but he settled with grabbing her hand and towing her behind him. The half a block back to the hotel passed in a blur, and she caught sight of the startled face of the front desk lady before the elevator doors closed between them and the lobby.

Cameron turned to her, but she was already moving. She hopped and he caught her just like she'd known he would. Her legs went around his waist and her back hit the wall as he took her mouth again.

Yes, this.

Yes, more.

He didn't let her down as the elevator doors rattled open. Instead, Cameron walked them down the hallway. His dark eyes looked just as wild as she felt, as if he might take her right there in the hallway if they didn't get through the door fast enough. Trying to anticipate, she dug into her purse for the hotel room key, barely getting it out before they reached the door. "Got it!"

He grabbed it out of her hand and then they were in the room. Cameron strode into the bedroom. "I need you."

"Yes. Now. Hurry." Making out on the street like a couple of teenagers had her so primed, she practically vibrated with it. He kept her pinned in place as she reached between them. Cameron used one hand to grab a condom and undid his pants. It didn't take much to work them down his hips to free his cock, but even the two-second delay was too long without him inside her. "Hurry, hurry, hurry."

He knocked her hand aside so he could roll on the condom and then he thrust, filling her completely, assuaging her empty ache. They froze, both breathing hard. Cameron leaned back enough to check her expression. "You good?"

As if she hadn't been right there with him this whole time. Trish rolled her hips, taking him deeper yet. "Don't stop."

His grin made something in her chest twinge in a way that would have terrified her if not for the pleasure building with every beat of her heart. A tempo that reduced itself to one word. *Yes, yes, yes, yes, yes.*

Cameron lowered her to the bed and shoved her shirt up to bare her breasts. "I like you like this, Trish. It's fucking indecent and I'm never going to be able to look at you in a pencil skirt without thinking about that skirt around your hips and my cock buried deep inside you."

"Good," she gasped. Something to remember her by, even after it was over.

The wildness trying to escape her seemed to translate to him, because there was no teasing, no driving her to distraction before taking what he wanted. No, there was just Cameron moving over her, driving into her again and again in the most delicious way possible. Every stroke hit the end of her, the pleasure-pain building to a desperation unlike anything she'd ever known.

She ran her hands down his strong back and

grabbed his ass, pulling him closer yet. Deeper. Harder. "I never want this to end."

His words were slightly muffled against her temple, but she could have sworn he said, "It doesn't have to."

Trish came between the space of one breath and the next. She could feel Cameron trying to pull back, to get enough distance to keep his own orgasm at bay, but she was having none of it. "Come with me, Cam. Come for me."

He cursed and she knew she'd won. His strokes became rougher yet, driving them both up the bed until his entire body went tense and he clutched her to him as he came. He had the presence of mind to roll to the side, but he didn't release her, so she ended up with one leg sprawled over his hip and his cock still buried inside her. Trish kissed the center of his chest and allowed herself to enjoy the feel of him holding her close.

So good...

So better than good...

She instinctively went tense, sure that he'd say something or she'd let her fear get away from her. But nothing happened. He just stroked a hand over her hair again and again until she finally relaxed. "What kind of movies do you like, Cam?"

"I'm more of a reader."

She smiled sleepily against his chest. "Let me guess—John Grisham?"

"Occasionally, but I'm more of a fantasy fan."

That got her attention. "Really? Like the farm boy is really the chosen one who has to save the universe and he's probably really a king but he doesn't know it… That sort of thing?"

His laugh rumbled through her. "Sometimes. Though there are a lot more stories within the genre than just that type."

"Oh yeah?" She snuggled closer. "Tell me about them." And she listened as he spun out teasers for tales that she'd never heard of. Cameron had a natural storytelling gift, yet she never would have guessed it before now. His low voice soothed the last of her fear away.

It would be okay.

They could have this week, and she could keep her issues at bay long enough to enjoy her time with him to its fullest. The only person standing in the way of that was Trish herself, and she didn't want to do it anymore.

It helped that, for the first time in a very long time, she was well and truly happy and willing to take things one day at a time instead of looking years ahead and seeing only failure.

CHAPTER THIRTEEN

THE NEXT DAY couldn't go fast enough. Cameron had never resented his work before, but it had never kept him from something he wanted before. Some*one*. Trish had set up shop back in their suite, while he was left to make the trek to Concord Inc. on his own. It had seemed reasonable at the time, but he swore he could actually feel the distance between them growing.

Not to mention the seconds ticking away from their time left together.

He didn't know how to fix that. She'd been ready to call the whole thing off before he'd distracted her with an offer for a reprieve. He wasn't delusional to think that more time spent in his presence would endear him to her. His cock? Fuck yeah. But it had been too long since he'd tried to tiptoe around someone else's emotions.

Just from the law of averages alone, he would say something to piss her off and screw things up before the week ran out.

Unless we just keep having sex until we're too tired to talk.

As appealing as that option was, he wanted more. The haunted tour last night *had* been goofy, but Trish's excitement had rubbed off on him, and seeing the tour through her eyes meant he enjoyed the hell out of it. He wanted to watch her favorite horror movies to have her prove him wrong about the genre. He wanted to share his favorite books with her. He wanted to know everything about her, where she'd been, where she was headed.

Cameron could count on one hand how many people he'd actually wanted to spend more time with…and still have fingers left over if he wasn't including family. Trish was so refreshing and amazing, and she never seemed to take it personally when he said the wrong thing. Set him straight? Without a doubt. But she didn't huff and walk away from him and leave him wondering where the hell he'd gone wrong.

Over the years, he'd picked up bits and pieces from Aaron about his two sisters, but Cameron had never paid much attention because he never expected to actually meet them.

He didn't give a damn what Aaron had to say about Trish. He wanted to hear her history for himself.

Moving too fast.

Was he, though? He'd dated enough to know that something like this didn't come around often. It didn't come around *at all* for him. He'd be a fool to let her go, no matter how unfathomable he found this new territory.

Besides, it was hard to move too fast when she was already planning her exit strategy.

He forced thoughts of Trish from his head as he got to work on the security system Concord Inc. had commissioned. It was relatively straightforward as such things went, for all the nondisclosure agreements and secrecy, but setting it up required time. He could put together the appropriate firewalls and systems in his sleep, but Cameron hadn't gotten to where he was by half-assing anything.

No matter how much he wanted to do just that today.

He made himself keep working until five, and then packed up and headed back to the hotel. With each step that brought him closer, excitement thrummed in his chest. He'd drag Trish into the shower with him to ease their thirst for each other, and then they'd head out for food and a little more sightseeing.

He barely made it through the door.

Trish appeared as if by magic—as if she'd been waiting—and gave him a quick kiss even as she started unbuttoning his shirt. She wore a different one of his shirts, and she should have looked absurd in the oversize clothing with her bare legs. Instead, she looked downright delicious. "You've been gone all day."

Surprise kept his feet planted and his hands off her as he watched her finish with his shirt. "That was the plan."

"I know. It was a stupid plan." She shoved his shirt and jacket off his shoulders and gave a little hum of satisfaction. "Do you know how many times I ended up in our bed with my hand between my legs, thinking about you while I worked myself into a frenzy?" Trish had his pants undone and shoved them down before he had a chance to speak. She stroked his cock and gave him a sweet little smile. "We can talk in a minute, okay?"

Cameron leaned back against the wall next to the door and sifted his fingers through her curls. "You're crazy if you think I'm going to stop you. I've been thinking about you all day."

She pressed a kiss to his jaw. "Good. I'd hate to suffer alone."

"Perish the thought," he murmured. He forced himself to keep his eyes open, to watch her kiss her way down his chest until she was on her knees. Cameron used his hold on her hair to push it back from her face and ensure an unobstructed view. He didn't want to miss a moment of this.

She stroked him once, twice, and then took him into her mouth. How many times had Cameron jacked himself to the image of her brightly painted lips wrapped around his cock? Pink, red, and on one memorable day, she'd worn purple. Today her lips were a pink bright enough to be seen from space, and the sight of his cock disappearing between them was almost as good as the feel of her mouth sucking him deep. She went after him with the same desperation he had churning up inside him every time he thought about what would happen once they boarded the plane back to New York.

His cock bumped the back of Trish's throat and it was too much. Cameron hauled her up his body. "I need more than your mouth right now."

"No fair." She wrapped her legs around his waist as he walked them toward what had become their bedroom. "You go down on me all the freaking time. I want my turn."

"Later."

"Why do I think later means never?" She laughed as he dropped her onto the mattress and yanked off the shirt. She wore absolutely nothing beneath it. Her laugh was like nothing he'd ever heard before. Joyfully filling up the room until all he could focus on was this woman in this moment.

As if he'd want to be anywhere else.

Cameron bracketed her hips and dragged her to the edge of the mattress. "If later meant never, then I'd say never. Later means later." He pushed a single finger into her and cursed when he found her wet and tight. "Were you fucking yourself with your fingers while I was walking here?"

Her grin turned evil. "Maybe."

"What am I going to do with you, Trish?"

Her laugh turned into a moan as he pushed a second finger into her. "I have a few ideas."

"I'm all ears." He kept slowly fucking her with his fingers, ensuring he hit that spot inside her that made her eyes damn near cross with every stroke. He circled her clit with his thumb. "Hmm?"

"You're unbelievable." She reached up and hooked the back of his neck, towing herself up to kiss him. "You want it spelled out? I want you. Hands. Mouth. Cock. All of it. Every position. Over and over again."

His stomach dropped, and even though Cameron knew better, he still said, "Your list of my attributes leaves a lot to be desired."

Trish rolled her eyes and flopped back onto the

mattress. "What do you want me to say? That I am having fun with you? That I like how much thought you put into the haunted tour and making sure we eat somewhere that has fish and chips because you know I'm a little obsessed? That I really dig your kind of closet nerdy thing with the fantasy novels? Or maybe that I think it's really sexy how smart you are, and your inability to filter yourself has become charming instead of infuriating? That's the lamest dirty talk out there."

"You like me."

"No, really? Of course I like you—sometimes in spite of yourself." Something akin to vulnerability crept into her blue eyes. "If you haven't noticed, I'm not exactly great at this stuff."

She'd just thrown out a revelation he thought he'd never hear. Oh, he knew Trish enjoyed their time together, but there was a vast difference between enjoying how he made her come and enjoying *him*.

Cameron started to reach for the nightstand where they'd stashed the giant box of condoms, but Trish burrowed her hands under the pillows and came up with one. She tore it open. "Pays to be prepared."

"Words after my own heart." He spread her wetness over her clit as she rolled the condom onto his cock. He pushed into her and they both went still at the sheer perfection of how good it felt. Not enough, though. It was never enough, because it always ended. He hooked her thighs and lifted her legs as he thrust forward, bending her in half and allowing him as deep inside her as he'd ever been.

"Oh, *Cam*." She clutched at his shoulders. "God, that's good. Don't stop."

The same thing she said every time they had sex. *Don't stop.* And he answered just as he always did. "I'll never stop, Trish. Not as long as you want it."

Cameron kept his strokes steady and reached down to stroke her clit how he knew she liked it. He'd had Trish at night and in the morning, but late afternoon Trish might be his favorite. The clouds that had lingered all morning finally parted and golden sunlight bathed her skin, making her damn near glow beneath him. Her expression went ecstatic and her pussy clenched around him as she came. He couldn't hold out longer. He didn't want to. With her milking his cock so sweetly, he let go and came hard enough to see stars.

Never want to let you go, Trish.

He managed to keep the words inside, if only barely. It was time to change how he approached this. Trish had admitted she liked him, and it was a small step from liking to falling for him.

He wasn't going to give her up without a fight.

* * *

After a detour into the shower, Trish finally allowed Cameron to haul her out of the hotel for some exploring. Night had long since fallen, but the city hadn't slowed down in the least. It felt different from New York, though. Less frenetic, maybe. Cameron tucked her under his arm and pulled her close as if they'd walked down the street together a thousand times before.

As if they'd walk down a thousand more streets in the future.

Knock it off. You told him you didn't want to talk about that until you're back in New York, and so there's no point in obsessing over it.

No point, but that had never stopped her before.

She was enjoying this far too much to successfully categorize it as a fling. Not that Trish had much experience with that sort of thing, but it just seemed wrong to enjoy her time out of bed with Cameron as much as she enjoyed her time *in* bed.

"Hungry?"

She glanced at him and smiled. "Always."

He led her into a tiny restaurant. "This place comes highly recommended."

They took a little table near the window so they could see the street. It was so…normal. She fiddled with her fork. Talking about work seemed like a cop-out at this point. They were past that.

She *wanted* them to be past that. *Maybe it's time I stop fighting it and admit the truth?* Trish opened her mouth to break all their rules and broach the subject of *them*, but the distracted look on his face had her chickening out. "Have you been to London before?"

"A few times." He refocused on her and nudged over the menu. "How'd the day go?"

Guess we're talking about work, after all. "It was good. The time difference means a slight lag in emails, but nothing too dramatic has hit since we've been gone. I set up two meetings with potential new clients for the week after next. I figured a little cushion time wasn't a bad idea in case complications arose with the current job."

"Trish."

She dragged her gaze up to his. God, he was gorgeous. The square jaw that she'd spent plenty of time dragging her mouth along, and the sensuous lips and deep, dark eyes. She pressed her own lips together, sure she could still taste him there if she concentrated. "Yeah?"

"I didn't ask how work went. I asked how *your* day went. Did you manage to get out and see anything or were you locked up with a computer the entire time I was gone?"

"It's my job to be locked up with a computer during the day." When he just stared, she sighed and relented. "I took an extra-long lunch break and went to see the Tower of London. The weather was kind of dreary, but it just set the tone." She smiled a little.

Cameron leaned forward, a small smile tugging at his lips. "For someone who's the personification of a ray of sunshine, you sure as hell have a lot of obsessions with dark shit."

"I like it. It's good to try and focus on the positive in life, but that doesn't mean you ignore all the stuff that goes bump in the night. It's entirely possible that Richard III had his nephews murdered in that tower. If that's not a horror story for the ages, I don't know what is." She made a face. "Though, to be honest, a lot of the Tudors could have starred in their own horror show. They were pretty freaking terrible." And she loved it. If ever there was a family that acted as a cautionary tale for the corruption of power, it was *that* one.

"It's a shame we don't have time to visit Amsterdam after we're finished here. There's all sorts of macabre museums and things to see there." He picked up his menu. "Maybe next time."

Next time.

The two innocent little words rang through her like a gong. He'd thrown them out so casually, too. As if they were a given, as if they wouldn't rock her right down to her core. "Cameron." She waited for him to set the menu down and give her his full attention. "What are we doing?"

"Trying to get dinner." He frowned. "Ah, I see. You mean what are *we* doing." The slightest of hesitations, so slight she wouldn't have seen it if she wasn't watching him so closely. "I thought you didn't want to talk about that yet."

"I changed my mind." She'd gone too far to backtrack now. *They'd* gone too far. "I like you," she blurted out. "I know that's inconvenient and you were very clear about boundaries and limits, but I've never been all that good about following the rules, and I like you, okay? I can't help it."

"There are more than a few people who'd think you were crazy for that."

She glared. "Can you be serious, please?"

"I am being serious. Are you sure it's not the intimacy of sex that's clouding your judgment?"

For the love of God. She sat back and crossed her arms over her chest. "Are you seriously trying to talk me out of liking you? Who does that?" But she knew who did that—Cameron O'Clery. The man was nothing if not obstinate.

"No. Definitely not." He reached out and grabbed her hand. "I'm saying this wrong... Which shouldn't surprise you. I'm simply trying to understand the change of heart."

It would be so easy to retreat, to agree that,

yeah, she'd let the sex go to her head, and no, she wasn't *really* falling for him. It wouldn't be the truth, though. The truth was that she liked Cameron despite the fact she couldn't see an outcome where this wouldn't blow up in their faces. One way or another, it would end in tears. She wouldn't stay with Tandem forever, and if she pursued the job she'd gotten a degree for, she'd be traveling. Between that kind of work and the number of hours Cameron put into the company, she didn't see how it could possibly work.

If he even wanted it to work.

He still hadn't said anything in response.

Maybe because he still waited for an explanation from *her*.

She cleared her throat. "I have always had a very clear idea of where I want my life to go and what I want it to look like. It hasn't worked out. Not once. This is the first time where the plan falling apart might not be the end of the world. I didn't plan on enjoying spending time with you so much, but I do. I don't know if I can go back to not being with you once we go home."

CHAPTER FOURTEEN

CAMERON WATCHED TRISH try and fail to dredge up her sunny smile. "Why do you do that?"

"Do what?"

"Fake it." She *was* sunny normally, but she also used it to retreat when she felt awkward or exposed. The fact that it was sometimes genuine had confused him at first, but now he had a better read on her. He wouldn't let her take back what she'd just put out there between them. Cameron squeezed her hand and ran his thumb over her knuckles. "You don't have to hide from me."

"You've said something like that to me before."

"It was true then. It's true now." He had to release her when the waitress finally approached, all apologies for the wait. They ordered food and drinks and as soon as the woman headed to plug the order in, Cameron turned back to Trish. "I like you, too." *More than like you.* He knew her well enough to know he couldn't push harder than he already had. "We're in this together."

"How is this even going to work?"

She always had a plan, and her plans didn't always work out. He reclaimed her hand, wanting to touch her as much as he wanted to offer her a physical touchstone to back up his verbal one. "Occasionally, it's okay to play things by ear."

She snorted. "You don't believe that any more than I do."

It wasn't how he normally lived his life—winging it. Cameron liked a plan as much as Trish seemed to. A plan created boundaries and expectations and efficient measuring sticks for progress. Plans worked great for school and co-running his own business.

One area he'd learned plans didn't work for shit? Relationships.

He brought her hand up and pressed a kiss to her knuckles. "I enjoy the time I spend with you."

She frowned. "I enjoy the time I spend with you, too."

"There's no reason to overthink it, then. We keep spending time together. We keep spending our nights together. We handle each new challenge as it develops, real time." He ignored the unease that slithered through his stomach at the thought of no reassurances for a future with Trish. It didn't matter if it made sense—if it was *logical*. He wanted guarantees that she'd be in his life for the long-term.

Demanding that would mean he'd lose her. She was barely considering extending their fling into something longer. Telling her he wanted something serious, something permanent, would spook her.

She pursed pink lips. "That sounds stressful."

"And trying to plan every development of this thing between us down to the smallest detail sounds like a lesson in insanity." He turned her hand in his grip and kissed her wrist.

"You *do* make me crazy." But something in her relaxed a little and she gave him a genuine—if small—smile.

"Tell me about your parents."

Instantly, the smile was gone. "You already know about my parents. You've known Aaron for ages."

"Sure," he agreed easily. "But his relationship with them is different from yours."

"There's nothing more to add. My dad is a good old boy who has lived his entire life knowing where his place is and being comfortable in it. He loves all of us, but he works a lot, even still. My mom…" She tensed slightly. "My mom is a worrier. I don't know how much Aaron sees it, but she can work herself up into a panic attack over things outside her control. And no one worries her as much as I do."

"Why's that?" From what Aaron had said about his youngest sister, she was never anything that could be termed a problem child, and all evidence supported that reality.

A shrug, this one too tight to be as nonchalant as she pretended. "I didn't have the same sense as my older sister to find a nice boy, get married and start a family close to home. First I went to college out of state, and now I'm working in the big, scary city—both things my mom is sure are choices I made solely to give her a heart attack. I don't think she was *happy* to see me fail to land a job after I graduated, but she definitely liked having me home again while I figured out where I was going to land."

Cameron considered that new information with what he already knew about Trish. The pieces fell into place with a satisfying *click*. "That's how you learned to manage people so well."

"Clients are no big deal when it comes to un-ruffling feathers. Really, compared to my mom, no one is that big of a deal." She made a face. "I'm not being fair. She's a good mom. She loves all of us to distraction, and she was one hell of a support system growing up. Something just…went a little strange when I graduated high school."

Having her youngest leave the nest had to have been challenging, especially considering that her mother's entire identity seemed to be wrapped up in her children. Or at least that was the impression Cameron got from Aaron. "She tried to clip your wings."

"What? No. No way." Trish used her free hand to take a sip of water. "It's more like she didn't exactly cry when I had setbacks that brought me home."

Which was as good as clipping someone's wings. Cameron's parents had shown him nothing but support from the time he could remember. Even when they didn't really understand his fascination with online security systems, they still sacrificed to ensure he could go to the school of his choosing. "I'm sorry."

"Don't be." She set her glass down. "Your parents sound pretty great."

He let her change the subject without pressing the issue. Her feelings about her mother might be conflicting a bit, but it wasn't something that Cameron could solve in a single conversation. He wasn't sure he could solve it at all—or if he should even try. So he gave her a reprieve and more details about his own parents. "They are. They made sure I never went without while growing up, and they sacrificed a whole hell of a lot to ensure I got to attend my first choice college." He'd known exactly the price required to give him that opportunity. They never doubted that he'd succeed, and he'd never doubted himself as a result. "I don't get to see them as much as I'd like, but I fly over there a few weekends a year, and I fly them over here for Christmas and usually at least once more when they have some free time."

"Aaron mentioned a vacation."

He smiled. "Yeah, they won't take money from me, so I take them on some ridiculously fancy vacation every July. My mom is too damn proud to pick the places she really wants to go, so my dad slips me a wish list every few years and I make sure we get there." She had a strange look on her face and he glanced down. "What? Do I have something on my face?"

"No." Trish shook her head. "That's just…really, really sweet that you do that for them."

"Don't get any funny ideas. I'm still an asshole most of the time. I'm just not an ungrateful asshole. Every opportunity I've had in life is because they helped ensure I was in a place to take advantage of it. It's right that I can take care of them now that I'm in a good place." He was still working on his mom about moving them out to the East Coast when she retired, but that was a long argument that would be years before it reached completion. Cameron got his stubbornness from her, and she wasn't going to agree to move their life without him pulling some serious moves. After moving so much when his father was still in the army, his parents had embraced living in one place and weren't eager to uproot again.

Grandkids might help sway her.

He shut down that thought *real* fast. Too much, too soon.

Trish sat back as the waitress appeared with their food. "Cameron O'Clery, you don't fool me. For all your snarling, you're a good man."

I want to be your *man.*

Trish turned the conversation to lighter topics as they ate, but she kept thinking about the look on Cameron's face when he talked about his parents. *Love.* He loved them without reservation, without caveats, without complications. She wished things were that simple with her parents. There was plenty of blame for that to go around, though. They might have held too tightly to her, but she'd been so damn determined to put miles between herself and her childhood home. To be free.

She still wanted that.

The thought soured her stomach and she pushed

her food around on her plate, conscious of the way Cameron watched her. Faking her way out of her melancholy mood wouldn't work with him—he'd more than proven that—and she didn't have any backup plan. A sweet smile and soft tone had always worked as deflection up to this point.

She was stripped bare for this man, and it wasn't comfortable in the least. How could she have barriers in place to keep herself safe when he saw through every defensive measure she took? "Stop that."

"Stop what?"

"Stop looking at me like you want to crawl around inside my brain."

Cameron didn't look away. "Would you like to fight with me over nothing? Or would you rather talk about what's bothering you?"

Lord, even in this, he somehow managed to cut through all the bullshit she'd thrown in his way, right to the heart of her.

Maybe… Maybe it would be a good thing to talk about the soul-crushing realities she carried around with her. If that wasn't enough to scare him off, maybe this could actually work. The thought made her snort.

"Trish?"

"Okay, fine. I was just thinking about how all I

want is freedom—and how it's the one thing that I seem to miss by a mile no matter what I do."

Cameron leaned back, giving her his full attention. "Explain."

"I'd like to pretend I'm free right now. I have my own apartment. I have a job I actually enjoy. I'm in London."

"You're saying you don't feel free."

It was as if his words opened the floodgates. She couldn't hold back the barrage of words that poured from her lips. "Because I'm *not* free. My awesome apartment? My brother paid for me to get into it, because my bank account was dangerously close to red before I got this job. The same job that Aaron set up for me, despite my qualifications being totally not up to par. Am I really any freer now than when I was living in my old bedroom in my parent's house?"

"Yes." Cameron frowned. "Aaron must know you well enough that you've set up some kind of payment plan to repay him for the money he fronted you."

"Well…yeah. He did do that. But—"

Except Cameron wasn't done. "And I'll admit I had my doubts when he suggested you for the position, but you've proven to be *more* qualified than I could have dreamed. You're an asset, Trish.

It strikes me that everyone around you can see it, even if you can't."

He meant it. Sincerity practically radiated from him, and even if it hadn't, Cameron wasn't in a habit of saying things he didn't mean.

She just wished she could believe it, too. Trish had run so far and so fast, but she kept falling back on the safety net her family represented. She hadn't truly stood on her own two feet…ever.

Cameron might not understand that, but *she* did.

Trish took a hasty sip of her water. Better to change the subject than keep trying to convince him she was a continuous disappointment. And, truth be told, it felt kind of nice to have one person look at her like she was this amazingly accomplished woman…even if she hadn't actually accomplished any of her goals.

Focus. Subject change. You can do this. She leaned forward. "If you're so into fantasy, have you thought about traveling to New Zealand and seeing *The Lord of the Rings* stuff they have set up there?"

"You're trying to change the subject."

"Correction, I *am* changing the subject." When a stubborn look settled over his features, she sighed. "Look, I'm feeling raw and angsty, and I would greatly appreciate it if you'd throw me this bone and talk about your geeky love of all things hobbits and wizards and dwarves." She met his gaze. "Please, Cameron."

"Okay." He gave a surprisingly soft smile. "And yeah, I've thought about visiting New Zealand. My mom is a fan of the series, too, so the summer after this one, we're going. I'll probably strong-arm them into a longer vacation for that one so we can visit Australia as well."

When she met Cameron, she never would have guessed he was too good to be true. She still wasn't sure he was—not when his flaws were readily apparent. But the longer she spent with him, the more the brusque attitude and the painfully truthful comments stopped feeling like flaws and just became part of the man as a whole. "That's really sweet."

"I guess." He got a strange look on his face but masked it almost as soon as it had come. "You do much traveling?"

"Only Stateside. A couple of spring breaks down in Florida. One very memorable road trip to see a Green Bay game with a friend who was a huge fan. Nothing fancy." She looked around at the restaurant they sat in. It wasn't fancy, exactly, but it was in *London*. "Thank you. For bringing me here. To London, I mean. This trip has been surreal in the extreme, but in a good way, and I just… Thank you."

"You don't have to thank me. I needed you to ensure I didn't fuck up this contract."

He said that, but she was no longer sure it was the truth. Nikki Lancaster might be standoffish to a criminal degree, but she obviously put her professional goals before any personal slight she might feel after how things fell out with Cameron. And she had the advantage of knowing how he operated, so she would have been prepared to handle him as needed to close the deal. Trish had been mostly ornamental to the whole situation. "You would have done fine."

"No, Trish. You can claim that now that it's all said and done, but it's not the fucking truth." He shook his head sharply. "There were half a dozen times during that meeting when I started to say something and looked at you—and realized I needed to keep my damn mouth shut. I wouldn't have bothered to show restraint if you weren't there. That might not seem like a big deal to you, but it is to me. I value your presence on this trip—and not just because you're in my bed."

"But I *am* in your bed, and that changes things."

"Yes, it does. And we'll negotiate as needed when we're home."

God, she loved him a little in that moment for not pussyfooting around the truth. No matter how long she stayed on in her current job, there *would* be an adjustment to how they handled themselves in the office, and if he were anyone else, he would have glossed right over that truth. "Okay."

He eyed her mostly full plate. “You’re not going to eat, are you?”

“I’m not really hungry,” she admitted.

“We’ll get something on the way back so you can snack as needed.” He twisted and motioned the waitress to bring their check. “Are you tired?”

She blinked. “Not especially.”

“Good. There’s something I want to show you. I think you’ll like it.” He made a face. “Though it has nothing to do with untimely death, so maybe we should just go back to the hotel.”

“Cameron O’Clery, was that an actual joke?” She playfully smacked his forearm. “I don’t just like untimely death, you know. I like flowers and bright colors and telling other people what to do. I’m a well-rounded woman.”

“I’m aware.” His gaze dropped to her breasts where they pressed against her T-shirt.

She gave a mock gasp. “You’re terrible.”

“You like it.”

She’d had so many different emotions with him—frustration and irritation and lust and enjoyment. Playing fun only made her like him more. She was up to her neck and sinking fast, and she couldn’t bring herself to care. “I do. Now, let’s go so you can show me your surprise.”

CHAPTER FIFTEEN

CAMERON ALMOST CHANGED his mind half a dozen times on the drive. His idea had felt like the right call when he'd first come up with it, but the closer they got to the waterfront, the more he felt like he'd made the wrong call.

Right up until the point Trish leaned against the door of the taxi and gasped. "The London Eye?"

"It's rather touristy but—"

"No, I love it." She barely waited for the taxi to pull to a stop before she opened the door and climbed out. Cameron paid the fare and followed her onto the street. Her captivated expression made her look even younger, and much less world-weary than she'd been since he'd met her. She spun to grab his arm and tugged him toward the giant Ferris wheel. "How did you know? I've wanted to ride this since I was a kid. It seemed like the most magical thing in the world to be able to see a nighttime London from so far up."

"Aaron may have mentioned that you enjoy Ferris wheels." He allowed himself to be towed along like some well-loved toy. It was only after the words escaped that he realized she might find them creepy.

"It gives you a different perspective of the world, and if that isn't magic, I don't know what qualifies." She shot him a look. "I'd say I'm surprised you remembered what had to have been a passing comment, but I'm not."

With her setting the pace, they reached their destination in short order. Cameron gave his information and they were directed to the priority boarding. As they stepped into their capsule, Trish gasped. *"Cameron."* She took in the champagne and chocolates and turned to him, her eyes wide. "When you pull out all the stops, you pull out all the stops."

He started to tell her that it was a normal package offered and nothing fancy, but he managed to filter himself at the last moment. This was important to her, and he *had* done what he could to make it special. "I'm glad you like it."

"*Like* doesn't even begin to cover it." She explored the capsule, taking in the seats and the clear walls that would give a full 360-degree view of

London once they got moving again. The package was for thirty minutes of uninterrupted time, but Cameron wished he'd booked more, considering Trish's enthusiasm.

"This is amazing." She gripped the railing and leaned out as far as the domed glass would allow. "I can't wait to see it from the top."

He made himself join her close to the edge, wrapped his arms around her and pressed himself against her back, letting the floral scent of her shampoo center him. Even though he'd braced for the movement, his stomach still took a dizzying dip when the wheel started up again. By the time they hit the top point of the Ferris wheel on the first rotation, his palms were sweating and he had to close his eyes in an effort to maintain control.

She turned in his arms. "You're afraid of heights."

"Not afraid. I just don't like them."

"Right. Not afraid at all." She nudged him away from the railing and walked them to the chairs with the champagne. "I don't think the bubbles will do well with your stomach, but maybe it's worth a shot?"

"Sure." With a little distance between him and the sheer drop to inevitable death, he managed to pull in half a breath. "Don't let me ruin the experience."

"You aren't." She poured them both a glass and

passed his over. Trish gave him a surprisingly sweet smile. "You booked yourself a ride on one of the tallest Ferris wheels in the world for me—even though you're not a fan of heights."

"I didn't want you to miss this opportunity." Though he'd bring her back to London sometime in the future when they didn't have work taking up so much time. She had such a unique view on so many things, and Cameron wanted to explore the city and see it through her perspective.

Preferably on the ground level.

She leaned in and pressed a soft kiss to his mouth. "Thank you."

He almost reached for her then and there, to hell with any potential audience, but Cameron didn't want her to miss a second of this ride. He nudged her back toward the railing. "You're going to miss the magic."

"There's absolutely no chance of that." She kissed him again, longer this time, but finally rose and went to lean against the railing.

He watched her watch the city, and something irreversible shifted in his chest. This woman was nothing like he'd pictured for himself in the rare times when he imagined a future where work wasn't his one true love. She was fanciful and stubborn and sunny despite her shadows.

Trish was magic.

Fuck me, I love her.

His world rose and fell with that realization, turning to ash at his feet and rearranging itself into something entirely new. Oblivious to the turmoil going on inside Cameron, Trish took a sip of her champagne and hummed in what could only be described as pure happiness.

He wanted her to look at him the way she looked at London. To feel about him the way she felt about fucking Ferris wheels. He wanted to be her magic.

Cameron couldn't tell her.

Every time they talked about the future, she got a little wild around the eyes. It couldn't be clearer, despite her saying she was willing to give them a shot, that she had no intention of landing with him permanently.

He didn't know how to fix that. People weren't computers. Problems didn't have a guaranteed solution if he just looked hard enough. Trish felt that every plan of hers ended badly. It stood to reason that, no matter how much she enjoyed him, how much she *liked* him, she would view being with him as settling because he had never been part of her plan.

There was a solution here. There had to be. Cameron wasn't romantic enough to believe in soul mates or destiny, but he and Trish *fit*. That sort of thing didn't happen often enough in life to throw it away just because it wasn't part of the plan.

He just needed her to see that, too.

The lights of the city played across her body as the Ferris wheel went round, a slow slide that he ached to re-create with his mouth. If he couldn't tell her how he felt, he'd damn well show her. There was plenty they did right. He just needed her to admit that it *was* right and wasn't yet another of what she considered her life's failures.

Cameron had never had to be convincing before. He usually just powered through any obstacles that life threw in his path.

But for Trish, he'd do whatever it took.

Trish could barely keep from bouncing as they made their way through the hotel lobby and up to their room. "That was amazing, Cameron. Seriously. Beyond amazing."

"It was enchanting," he said as he unlocked their door and stepped aside to let her through.

"I know you're making fun of me, but it *was*." She shrugged out of her jacket and tossed it onto the couch, still riding high.

No one understood her love of Ferris wheels, though Aaron indulged her as only older brothers were able to do. Her sister and their parents mostly rolled their eyes every time she demanded another ride or announced she was going to the fair. It was just another way Trish was a little peculiar, a little too square for the round-shaped hole they expected her to fit into.

Cameron had done more than indulge her. He'd planned a special event solely to give her a private Ferris wheel ride, despite the fact that he was *clearly* afraid of heights.

No one had ever done anything like that for her before. Not at the expense of their own comfort.

She turned to thank him for the hundredth time, and nearly ran into his chest. Trish looked up, her breath stalling in her lungs at the intensity of his dark eyes. "Uh, hi."

"Hey." He slipped his hands over her shoulders and up to cup her jaw, pausing there as if he meant to say something. She found herself holding her breath, waiting for… She wasn't sure what.

But the moment passed. Cameron sifted his fingers through her curls and tilted her head back farther so he could kiss the sensitive spot beneath her ear. "What am I going to do with you, Trish?"

She cleared her suddenly dry throat. "I can think of a few ideas."

"I imagine you can." His dark chuckle curled her toes in her boots. "I'm going to start by taking you to bed."

That sounded like the best kind of plan to her.

She nodded, but he was already moving, scooping her into his arms and heading for their bedroom. Trish couldn't help her breathless laugh. "I can walk, you know."

"I know." He kicked the bedroom door shut. "But why walk when I enjoy carrying you so much?"

Since she didn't have a witty response to that, she kissed him. Cameron let her slide down his body without losing contact with her mouth. He teased her lips open and delved inside, kissing her as if *this* was the main event and he'd be happy kissing her forever.

It wasn't enough.

Unwilling to break the kiss, she undid his pants and shoved them down. Cameron kicked out of his shoes and the pants and walked her back to the bed, working on getting her jeans off in the process. It wasn't smooth or suave, and she ended up giggling as he wrestled the offending denim off, but they finished stripping quickly, until they stood before each other naked.

She stepped closer and pressed her hand over his heart. "This might sound corny, but you're seriously beautiful."

"You're stealing my lines." He pulled her closer, spreading one hand across the small of her back as he fit their hips together. "You know, the first time we had sex, I knew I wanted to someday trace constellations of your freckles."

She'd always liked her freckles—aside from the middle school years where everyone hated everything about themselves—but she'd never considered that someday she'd be with a man who spoke about them like *that*. As if they were as attractive as her breasts or ass. "That sounds unbearably hot." She grinned. "One second."

Trish hurried into the bathroom and dug through her makeup bag. She headed back into the bedroom a few seconds later, wielding her lip liner. "Do it."

If anything, the heat in Cameron's gaze flared hotter. "On the bed."

She scrambled to obey, so turned on she could barely drag in a steady breath. The way he looked at her in that moment would fuel masturbation sessions for the rest of her damn life.

He joined her on the bed and coasted his hand just above her skin, tracing a pattern only he could see. His brows drew together in concentration as he uncapped her bright pink lip liner and carefully connected a series of freckles on her stomach. It tickled, but laughing was the last thing on Trish's mind. "Oh God."

"Mmm." He leaned down and pressed a light kiss to the space in the center of the new constellation. "Hold still."

And so it went. Cameron drew another half-dozen constellations on the front of her body. Her chest. Under her right breast. Just above her pussy. On the inside of her left thigh. The top of each foot.

He knelt between her spread thighs and took in his work. "Fuck."

"Take a picture."

His gaze slammed into her own. "Trish—"

"Do it. I want to remember this always." *Because I won't have it forever. It's something we'll share no matter what happens.* She swallowed past her dry throat. "I trust you."

Another hesitation, longer this time, but he finally nodded and rose to get his phone. Cameron seemed to take the photography as seriously as he took everything in life. He adjusted her position to his satisfaction and snapped a few pictures.

By the time he was finished, her entire body practically vibrated with need. "Touch me."

He rejoined her on the bed and handed her the phone. "Passcode is five-five-six-three."

She realized he'd stuck her photos in a passcode protected folder and typed it in. As Trish swiped through the photos, each sexier than the next, Cameron settled next to her and ran his hand down her stomach—avoiding smudging his work—and cupped her pussy. "You're the beautiful one, Trish." He kissed her neck as he fucked her slowly, thoroughly, with his fingers. He shifted to see the pictures. "That one's my favorite."

In the photo, she had her arms over her head and her legs spread as if she'd just been fucked within an inch of her life. From the angle, she could just make out the slightest glistening of her pussy where she was so wet, she ached for him. The bright pink constellations stood out against her pale skin, turning it from just another sexy-dirty photo into something closer to art.

She lifted her hips to take his fingers deeper. "It's my favorite, too." Driven by the knowledge that this might be one of the few things he kept to remember her by once everything was said and done, she flipped back to the camera and took a picture of where his fingers speared her. *Don't forget me, Cam. Don't forget* this.

"Trish—"

"Not yet." She wasn't even sure what she denied him, only that nothing good came from Cameron saying her name in that rough tone of voice. A tone that spoke of truths she wasn't ready to hear.

She pushed him onto his back and straddled his hips. A few seconds later, she had his cock sheathed in a condom, and Trish wasted no time sinking onto him, taking him as deep as she possibly could, until she wasn't sure where she ended and he began.

She rode him slowly, determined to make this last, to hold out as long as possible. Pleasure built between them, as inexorable as their next heartbeats. The expression on his face was so stark, so possessive, so goddamn *hot*, she had to close her eyes to keep from coming on the spot.

"Don't close your eyes, Trish. Don't shut me out."

Immediately, she opened them again. Cameron pulled her down to claim her mouth as he rolled them and leveraged her legs wider. He lifted her hips a little as he thrust into her, the new angle bowing her back and drawing a cry from her lips. "Oh God, Cameron." She gripped his thighs and wrapped her legs around his waist and he leaned back, and he thrust again, hitting the same spot. Her mind went blank and words sprang from her lips, words she had no control over. *"OhGoddontstoppleasedontstop. IlovethisIlovethisIlovethisIloveyou. Yesyesyesyesyes."* Another stroke and she was lost. Trish came hard enough that she damn near vibrated out of her skin. *"Cameron!"*

CHAPTER SIXTEEN

FOREBODING TOOK UP residence in Cameron's stomach as the plane's wheels touched down in New York. Their week in London had been as idyllic as possible with Trish, but even at its best, he couldn't shake the feeling that a sword hung over his neck.

It didn't help that Trish didn't seem to realize she'd told him she loved him in a fit of passion—or that she hadn't repeated the sentiment since.

He gently shook her awake. "We're here."

"Already?" She pushed her hair away from her face, but it immediately sprang back into place. "I didn't expect to sleep so long."

"You were worn-out." The truth was, *he* was worn-out, too. Cameron needed a solid meal and eight hours of sleep and a couple days' reset before he got his head on straight.

Yeah. Sure. As if that is all it would take.

The ground wouldn't be solid beneath his feet as long as he stood in the shadow of a future without Trish. They'd promised to talk more specifically about what that might look like once they were back in the city, but as much as he wanted a clear conversation, he couldn't bring himself to rush it.

Not when he suspected which way it would go.

So he reached out and laced his fingers through hers. "Let's get dinner."

She glanced at her phone. "It's nine in the morning."

"Breakfast, then. We're not due back in the office until Monday. Come home with me." He formed it as a command rather than a request because he had a feeling if Trish thought too hard about it, she'd try to put some distance between them.

Sure enough, she hesitated. "I don't know… I think my own bed is calling my name."

"If you fall asleep now, you're going to have a wicked case of jet lag and you'll be worthless on Monday."

She made a face. "I know you're right, but a contrary part of me wants to dig in my heels just because of how you phrased it."

"You're too smart to cut off your nose to spite your face." He lifted up their entwined hands and kissed her knuckles. "I have an obscenely large tub. I imagine it would feel wonderful to soak out any kinks."

"Now you're just not playing fair." She gave him a mock frown. "Fine. You've convinced me—on the condition that you don't get weird about me doing laundry at your place."

"Deal."

She smiled a little. "It's weird being back, right? All that time in London felt like a dream, and now it's back to reality."

"Not yet. Not until Monday."

Trish hesitated again, but finally nodded. "I seem to remember my boss—he's kind of a jerk, but he means well—telling me that under no circumstances was I to work on the weekends."

"Sounds like a smart guy." It might be a lost cause to hold on to the dream for a couple more days, but Cameron couldn't bring himself to care. There was no damn reason for his certainty that things would blow up in his face the second they got back into the office. She'd told him she liked him. Fuck, she'd told him she *loved* him, even if it didn't really count because of the timing. Surely that meant more than some plan he wasn't even sure she'd put into motion.

But because he couldn't be certain, he wasn't willing to sacrifice any further time with her. "No work on the weekends—for either of us. No email. No work calls."

"That's a tall order."

He couldn't remember the last time he'd gone more than twenty-four hours in between email checks. It likely hadn't happened since starting up Tandem Security. "A mini vacation."

"I think it's what normal people call weekends?"

He laughed and helped her stand so they could exit the plane. "I don't know these normal people you speak of."

"There it is again—that sneaky sense of humor you have." She looped her arm through his as they walked through the gate and into the airport. "I'll admit—a part of the reason I'm agreeing to this is so I can see your lair."

"Lair? I'm hardly a vampire."

"Well, no, not a vampire." She shot him a look. "Not a werewolf, either. Definitely not a zombie. You're more likely to like the Highlander or one of those other immortals with a quest for vengeance. Loner-ish. Obscenely rich. Doesn't bother with social niceties." She brightened. "Since we're doing a real-life weekend, that means a movie marathon. I'm sure that's in the fine print somewhere."

Her enthusiasm diminished some of the dread eating a hole in his stomach. Maybe Trish wanted this fantasy state to last a little longer, too. "I draw the line at three movies. And there will be breaks in between."

"Breaks for… *Oh.*" She grinned. "I think I can handle that. We'll rent a few from my list. I'll make you a horror fan yet—just watch."

"You're welcome to try."

They collected their bags and hailed a cab back to his place. It wasn't until they climbed out onto the sidewalk and headed into his building that he thought about how Trish might react to his suite. He punched the elevator button and turned to her, and sure enough, her blue eyes were wide. "Fancy place."

He tried to see the lobby through her eyes. It was decorated in a modern chic style—whatever the fuck that meant—and was big on stainless steel and minimalism. He'd never put much thought into it before. It was a lobby, and he never spent more than a few seconds crossing it to get to the elevator. It wasn't as if he lingered there. "If you say so."

"Good Lord, you're hilarious. I don't have to say so, because it's the truth." She followed him into the elevator and they took the ride up to the top floor. Trish shot him another look. "You're afraid of heights."

"I don't like heights," he corrected.

"Sure. You don't like heights. And you live in the top-floor penthouse suite?"

"The windows are reinforced," he said stiffly. "And it's not like I spend a lot of time looking out them."

She nodded. "That doesn't make any sense, but I'm going to pretend it does." Trish wandered around his suite and, once again, he tried to see things from her point of view. Cameron hadn't bothered to decorate the place himself. He'd hired a designer to outfit it after he bought it, and the man had done well enough. All the essentials were there—furniture, television, bed, various kitchen tools despite his rarely having time to cook. Everything was nice and neutral but, looking at it through the lens of what he knew of Trish, it seemed…boring.

She propped her hands on her hips. "You didn't pick out a single thing in this place, did you?"

"How do you know that?"

"If you ever sat on that couch, you'd know it was wickedly uncomfortable and it isn't nearly big enough." She peered into the kitchen, hummed under her breath and turned back to him. "The only thing that really feels lived in, aside from the bedroom where you probably spend most of your time when you're home, is the bookshelf." She pointed at the inset bookshelf that he'd filled with first editions over the years. It was one of Cameron's few extravagances, and he forced himself to limit how many he bought a year for the sole purpose of keeping it under control.

Trish drifted closer to the bookshelf. "This case is pretty impressive."

"Some of those books are worth obscene amounts of money." When she raised her eyebrows, he flushed. "I like to see them displayed like this. They make me happy."

"You're such a nerd. I like it." She cupped the side of his face, gave an absent smile and wandered through the door to his bedroom. He followed her into the bathroom and laughed at her expression. "I did say the tub was large."

"It's humongous." Trish fiddled with the faucets until they turned on, sending steaming water cascading out. She sat on the edge of the tub. "You just need a little color in this place, that's all. Nothing too outrageous because it would drive you crazy. Just some soft tones to warm up the place and a few key pieces to bring it all together." She frowned. "Maybe a plant or two. You have someone who cleans?"

"Once a week." He didn't spend enough time at home to truly make a mess, but he liked how fresh the place felt after his cleaning lady had been in.

"Often enough to keep certain plants alive as

long as it's not too fussy." She nodded to herself. "Maybe a fern or something. I'll have to think about it."

Despite his determination to hold on to the promised reprieve, he couldn't help speaking. "Have you ever thought of doing this?"

"We are doing this, Cameron." She waggled her eyebrows at him.

He snorted. "Get your mind out of the gutter. I mean this—the interior designing thing. You've been in here five minutes and already have a better bead on things than the original guy I hired. You totally changed the feel of both the front office and the boardroom in a way I would have said was impossible before I saw it done. With the ability to work both in commercial spaces and private residences, you could make a killing."

Something like interest flared in her blue eyes before she shook her head. "I have degrees in sales and design. That's barely in the same realm."

"Because it's not part of your precious plan." Bitterness soaked into his words, turning them ugly.

Trish crossed her arms over her chest. "There's nothing wrong with having a plan. You wouldn't have gotten to the place you're in now without a plan."

"Plans are nothing if you can't adapt them,

Trish. They're not meant to be set in stone. Life changes things." He could keep going, but every line of her body screamed a resistance to talking about this. "Take your bath. I'm going to order food." He turned on his heel and stalked out of the bathroom.

When he'd realized he loved her, he'd truly thought there was some solution to the way she clung to plans as if they were the word of God. He *still* thought there were options moving forward… but she had to meet him halfway.

Not today.

Nothing would happen today.

He chafed at the restraint, hated the fact that things remained up in the air because of his own doing, but hell if Cameron saw a way around it. *Lose her now, or lose her in a few days.*

I know which one I choose.

The weekend wasn't the relaxing oasis Trish had hoped. Tension strummed between her and Cameron, a cord growing tighter with each passing hour, filled with things neither of them said. The sex remained better than amazing, but after every time, she lay in Cameron's arms, feeling like they were saying goodbye without words.

Worse, she didn't know how to stop it.

He'd thrown out the interior design thing so

casually, as if it was the easiest thing in the world to change her life course. She wasn't flighty. She didn't jump ship just because things got hard and the future didn't look like she thought it would. Just because she was good at colors and getting a feel for a room didn't mean that her dream of being in corporate fashion wasn't valid.

You're talking yourself in circles.

It was all she seemed capable of doing.

To distract herself while Cameron was in the shower, she checked her email on her phone. A small break of their rules for the weekend, but justified. Mostly. She scrolled absently, deleting junk mail to whittle down the number she'd have to handle on Monday, but stopped when she recognized a name. *Mandy?* Trish clicked on the email and nearly dropped her phone.

Hey girl,
So I'm sure you remember my brother, Tom. He's working for Barton Fashion and they're looking for a corporate buyer. I was a total brat and sent your résumé along without mentioning it, but they want an interview! Below is the contact information, so just give them a call and set it up.

Fingers crossed for you!
XOXO, Mandy

Trish read the forwarded email, her heart beating harder with every word. It wasn't just *any* fashion retailer company. It was Barton Fashion. They were in her top three dream companies to work for when she'd first compiled her list back in college. Getting a job there…

Except she was already committed.

Damn it.

She closed her eyes, took several deep breaths and tried to focus. An interview wasn't a job offer. Surely Cameron could do fine without her for a day once they scheduled it. It wouldn't be the end of the world.

What if you get the job?

The thought was almost enough to make her laugh. What if she got the job? Her life plan hadn't worked out once in the two years since she graduated college. There was no reason to think her cursed streak would end *now*, when she was finally starting to come to terms with the fact that maybe her plan wasn't her be-all and end-all. She forwarded the email to Aaron as a courtesy and set her phone back down.

What would happen to her and Cameron if she got the job?

Barton Fashion was based out of San Francisco, which was about as far away from New York as someone could get and still remain in the continental United States. That was part of the attraction when she'd first put the company on her list. She'd wanted distance and enough time to figure out who she was without her family hovering. Without a safety net firmly in place should she fail. If she got the job, it would be a chance to see if she could actually stand on her own two feet without someone there ready to catch her.

Long-distance relationships happened, but she wasn't sure if she and Cameron had a strong enough foundation to pull it off. Yes, she liked him. Yes, she kind of more than liked him. But without the amazing sex cementing them together? With work pulling them both in different directions?

She just didn't know.

Trish picked up her phone again and emailed Barton Fashion to arrange an interview. There was no point in borrowing trouble.

She had enough as it was.

CHAPTER SEVENTEEN

CAMERON STALKED AROUND his office. Something was off, but he couldn't put his finger on the source. It could be all in his head…but he didn't think so. Instead of the weekend bringing them closer together, Trish had become more and more withdrawn as it went on.

He stared hard at his door, but he'd effectively trapped himself in here. He told her he would respect the work boundaries between them, which meant he couldn't haul her in here and demand an explanation. And after the day was done, she'd go back to her apartment and…

And what?

Nothing had changed. There was no reason for the dread curdling his stomach. Tomorrow she would be back in the office, and the next day, and the next. They didn't have to spend every night together, despite the fact that he wasn't keen on the idea of more distance between them.

You hold her too close, and you're going to suffocate her.

Fuck, he didn't know how to do this. Relationships were iceberg-scattered waters under the best of circumstances, and this was hardly that. It didn't help that Trish wouldn't *talk* to him.

Footsteps sounded down the hallway, and Cameron's chest got light. She was coming to talk to him. This weirdness had to bother her as much as it bothered him, and she wasn't too conflicted to put it all out in the open here and now. Trish had never been afraid of anything, so there was no reason to think she'd start now.

Except it doesn't fit in with her plan.

He opened the door and froze. "What the hell are you doing here?"

Aaron raised his eyebrows. "I know I've been gone a few weeks, but last time I checked, I'm still the other owner of Tandem Security."

Suspicion flared. "You're on paternity leave for another month."

"Technically, yes, but with the way things are falling out, I thought it'd be prudent to come back on a part-time basis for the rest of my leave. I'll mostly be working remotely, but I'm officially back."

Nothing short of a catastrophic event would drag Aaron away from his new family earlier than planned. "What happened?"

His friend's smile faltered. "Nothing happened, not yet. But since Trish has an interview for a job in California later this week, things might be moving for her, and I don't want to hold her back. We can find someone else to work the front desk if she needs to quit, but I'm not going to put everything on you while we figure that out. It's really not that big a deal. Becka and I have found a good rhythm, so cutting out a few hours while they nap to work from home is doable."

Cameron picked apart everything Aaron had said and focused on the single most important statement. "Trish has an interview."

"Yeah, she just found out this weekend."

It struck him that his friend had no idea about the change in their relationship. Cameron sure as hell hadn't told him and Trish obviously chose not to as well. They'd more or less agreed on keeping things to themselves, but the knowledge stung unexpectedly. Aaron had no clue that his casual mention of Trish making life plans without Cameron would be an issue at all. And why would he?

She didn't tell me.

If she found out this weekend, she had plenty of opportunity to share that information with him. While they were watching her favorite horror movies. While they were walking down to the restaurants he liked to frequent on the weekends. While they were lying in bed and talking about nothing.

Trish hadn't said a word.

He knew Aaron was looking at him strangely, but he couldn't get his reaction under control. "Excuse me." He shouldered past his friend and stalked down the hall to the front office. Trish looked up as he crossed the threshold and if he hadn't already known that she kept something from him, her guilty look would have made it clear. "Why didn't you tell me?"

"There was nothing to tell."

It shouldn't be possible for five little words to bring his hopes for the future crashing to the ground. "You don't think taking an interview for a position across the country is worth mentioning to me? I was under the impression we were on the same page." Every word got colder and more remote, but his mouth was a runaway train, and Cameron had never been that good at filtering himself to begin with. "It appears I was mistaken."

"It's an *interview*." She pushed to her feet and gave him a pleading look. "We talked about this. Every single thing that's happened to me after graduation has been one step forward and seven steps back. This could be the thing that finally puts my plan back in action. This could be the thing that finally gives me my freedom."

"Your freedom." He clipped out the words. Cameron felt Aaron come up behind him, but they'd gone too far to pretend like everything was all right now. "And your fucking *plan*. You love that damn plan more than you can ever love another person. I understand wanting to get out from beneath your mother's presence, but fuck, Trish. Did this thing between us really mean so little to you that you're not even willing to reconsider that plan you worship so much?"

Her guilt disappeared, replaced by anger. "Easy for you to say. You are living your dream job in your dream city, and you'll eventually succeed in convincing your parents to move out to this side of the country and won't have to compromise on *that*, either. What the hell do you know about constantly reaching for something and being constantly told that you're not good enough?"

"I'm a black man in America, Trish. I think I know a thing or two."

She stopped, pressed her lips together, but charged on. "Point conceded. But the fact remains that working for Barton Fashion is one of my dream jobs and prematurely saying no to an interview with them because of a guy I'm sleeping with is the height of stupidity."

"The guy you're sleeping with," Aaron muttered behind him.

The guy you're sleeping with.

That was all this was to her. He'd known. Damn it, he'd been the one to set the terms to begin with. Stupid of him to think that just because things had changed for him that meant they'd changed for her, too. He couldn't tell her he loved her now. She'd accuse him of trying to keep her from taking the interview—from potentially taking the job—and she'd be right.

He had to let her go.

The realization nearly took him out at the knees. He couldn't ask her to stay. He might love her, but he had no right to ask her to give up her dreams just because those same dreams would take her away from him. Damn it, he had to end it. "You're right."

Trish blinked. "I'm sorry, I thought you just said that I'm right."

"Because I did. You have to take the interview—and the job, if they offer it. It would be idiotic not to." *Even if you made that choice for me.* If she did, she'd spend the rest of their time together resenting him for clipping her wings the same way she felt her mother wanted to, and it would spell the end of them before they had a chance to begin.

Cameron drew himself up, cloaking himself in the coldness he was so often known for. He'd never had to fake it before, though. "Good luck on your interview, Trish. I'll start looking for your replacement this week."

Trish barely saw Cameron the rest of the day, and when she did, he was colder to her than he'd ever been—even when she'd first started working for Tandem Security. She hadn't wanted him to yell at her or to… God, she didn't even know *how* she had wanted him to respond to the news that she had an interview elsewhere.

Not like this, though.

And dealing with Aaron hadn't been any better. When she'd made it clear that her personal life wasn't any of his business, he'd announced he was working from home and abandoned her in the office alone with Cameron.

She went over their fight—if someone could call it that—over and over again as the day wound down. Every single point she made still stood. She was sleeping with Cameron, but that didn't mean she should make life choices based on that fact. She would be worse than an idiot *not* to take the interview because of a relationship, let alone a relationship that had started barely a week previous. That kind of decision-making was the height of madness. If things with her and Cameron exploded or fizzled out, he'd still have his company… and she'd be back to square one. He was his own safety net.

She needed to be her own, too.

But that didn't change the truth. She felt utterly terrible. Her chest was one aching hole of despair and her stomach hadn't stopped twisting itself into knots. Half a dozen times during the day, she rose to walk back to Cameron's office, but she never made that first step. What was there to say? She *had* to take this opportunity. Begging him not to be mad at her wasn't fair to him, not when she'd seen the hurt written on his face before it fell into his distant cold mask. Hurt *she* had caused. Forcing him to rehash it when she knew they'd both come to the same conclusion was just cruel.

Knowing that didn't make her feel the least bit better.

Five o'clock rolled around, and she reluctantly clocked out. Trish turned to the elevator, but she couldn't leave things how they were. She *couldn't*. She walked into Cameron's office. "You would make the same call if our situations were reversed."

"Undoubtedly." He didn't look up from his computer. "I already gave you my blessing, which you already pointed out that you don't need. I'm just some guy you're sleeping with, remember?"

Hurt lodged in her throat, and knowing she was the one who'd caused this mess only made it worse. "I don't see any other option available to me, Cam. I don't know what you want me to do."

He sighed in irritation and turned to face her. "This is the only option available to you. But since you're obviously obsessing over it, let's play this out. You turn down the interview for some guy you're fucking, and two options are available as an outcome. Option one—you end up developing a relationship with him, but you resent him because you turned down what could have been your dream job. Things end badly. Option two—the fling fizzles out as flings are wont to do. You can't deal with working with the guy you were fucking and now aren't, so you quit and end up moving back in with your parents. Things end badly." He recited the potential outcome for them as if reading from some report that had nothing to do with him.

As if he didn't care.

Her throat was too tight, and she tried to swallow past it. "That's not fair."

His composure cracked. "What do you want from me?" Cameron slid his chair back, as if even with the desk between them, he couldn't stand to be that close to her. "Seriously, Trish. What the fuck do you want from me? Do you want me to rail at you and tell you not to go because I love you? Do you really think I'm that selfish? You've spent the entire time we've known each other talking about your plan, and now you have a chance at achieving it. Good for you. I wish you well. But give me the fucking courtesy of not forcing me to rehash this over and over again until you get the job offer because you feel guilty and want me to grant forgiveness or whatever the hell you want. We had fun while it lasted. It's over now. The end."

"You love me?" If anything, the pit in her chest got wider and deeper at the truth he'd spit, a swirling sensation inside her threatening to swallow her whole.

"It. Doesn't. Matter." He stood slowly. "Like I said—it's over now. Get out of my office. Please."

The *please* sent her spinning into motion, hurtling out of his office as if the hounds of hell were on her heels. He loved her and it didn't matter because he'd put his feelings aside so she could accomplish what she'd always wanted to do. She couldn't stay and keep hurting him just because she didn't know what the hell she was feeling. She didn't know what she wanted him to say, but every word had just made it hurt worse.

If they offered her the job, Trish would take it.

Cameron will be okay. He's too strong to let something like a little heartbreak get him down for long. He'd recover and get back to his normal brilliant, cranky self. It would be okay. They would both be okay.

At the end of the day, that was the only thing that mattered.

Not her broken heart. Not her guilt.

Her plan.

She just had to remember that, because it would be the only thing that got her through the coming months.

CHAPTER EIGHTEEN

"ENOUGH IS ENOUGH. Stop moping."

Cameron almost ignored Aaron looming in his doorway, but he'd been avoiding his friend for the week since Trish took the interview—and got the job. Even though he'd suspected she'd nail the interview, he still hadn't come to terms with just how comfortable he'd gotten with her in the office. The new girl was always underfoot and, though she didn't exactly curl up in a ball and cry when he snarled at her, she was no Trish.

That was the problem, though.

After Trish, no one else would do.

Not just for the job. For his fucking life.

"Cameron."

"I'm not moping. I'm working." He closed the window and shut down his computer. He wasn't going to get anything else accomplished today, so there was no point in sticking around.

Especially if Aaron was going to corner him for some kind of misguided intervention. He pushed to his feet, but his friend hadn't moved from his spot blocking the doorway. Cameron stopped short. "We're not having this conversation."

"Wrong. The fact that I've waited this long is only because we're friends and I was waiting for you to pull your head out of your ass and fix things. Since you're showing no signs of doing so, I'm stepping in." Aaron walked into his office and closed the door. He leaned back against it. "When were you going to tell me you're in love with my sister?"

He should have known Aaron would pick up on that. He'd overheard their conversation, after all, and he wasn't an idiot. "I wasn't going to tell you. It's a moot point. She left."

"No shit, she left. She got a job with one of her dream companies. You can't actually have expected her to stay."

Why did people keep speaking the obvious to him? Of course he didn't expect her to stay. Hoping that she would was akin to hoping her dreams would be dashed yet again, and Cameron wasn't monstrous enough to wish for something that would hurt her.

No matter how much her leaving felt like she'd ripped his heart out of his chest and taken it with her.

Since Aaron obviously had more to say, he crossed his arms and leaned against his desk. "I want her to be happy. I wasn't going to hold her back."

Aaron stared at him hard, a flinty look in his blue eyes. He shared similar coloring as Trish, though where she seemed soft and almost innocent in some ways with her curls and freckles, Aaron's looks were carved of ice when he wasn't in the mood to deal with people's bullshit. Much like he seemed to be in that moment. He finally shook his head. "How long have we known each other?"

Was that a trick question? "Going on fifteen years now."

"Yeah. Fourteen years and some change. In all that time, I've never seen you hesitate—not even when you *should* hesitate. If you really love her… Fuck, Cameron, is *now* going to be the moment you decide to break your streak? You're better than this."

"What the fuck do you want from me?" he roared. "I didn't hold her back. I stepped out of the way so she could do what she needed to do without feeling guilty. Why the hell am I being asked for more? I'm not a fucking magician to perform a trick and suddenly make this all okay."

Aaron didn't so much as blink. "This is a problem, and you fix problems."

"I fix problems with computers—*not* with people."

"Figure it the fuck out, Cameron. If you don't, you're going to lose her. The clock started running down the second you let her walk out that door without offering a solution, a compromise, a single goddamn *word*." He pulled an envelope out of his suit jacket and tossed it onto Cameron's desk. "She's miserable, in case you were wondering. This is the happiest she should ever be, and she's so sad, she can barely pull together a fake smile for our parents. She hasn't even bothered trying with me and Becka."

He didn't want to hear that. If he was falling on his sword for her, he wanted her to be happy. More than happy. He wanted her to be walking on air and untouchable. "Why the hell are we doing this if we're both miserable?"

"*That* is the question you should be asking—and answering." Aaron pushed off the door, opened it and walked out without looking back. "Let me know when you have an answer."

Cameron slumped down onto his desk and stared at the plain white envelope. It was smaller than standard, half the width and length of a normal envelope, and the only thing written on it was his name. Even after such a short time together, he recognized the rounded letters of Trish's handwriting.

What else could she possibly have left to say?

He shut and locked his door and sat behind his desk once more to carefully open the letter. It was a torn piece of paper that looked like she'd written on as an afterthought.

Or written on in a flurry before she could second-guess herself about the wisdom of writing in the first place.

He took a second to wish he kept whiskey stashed in a drawer, then began to read.

Cam,

God, I don't even know what to say. You're right. This is what I wanted…except it's not what I wanted. I never expected to fall in love with you. I never wanted it. It hurts, Cam. A lot. I know love is complicated and not as easy as in the movies, but this is just ridiculous. How am I supposed to choose between the career I've spent most of my life wanting and you? It's not fair, and I know that's a child's plea, but I'm feeling suitably dramatic.

You're probably gritting your teeth about now and wondering what the hell my point is.

It goes like this—you hurt me when you didn't try to stop me from leaving. Stupid, right? I know it is, so you don't have to tell me so. I had this moment of surety that if you turned that indomitable will to us, if you loved me, too, then maybe we could figure things out.

You were pretty clear about where you stood, and I'm trying to respect that. I'm sorry if I hurt you at any point, because that really wasn't my intention. But you know what they say about good intentions…

All this is just a long way of saying goodbye. And I'm a selfish ass, because I'm doing it in a letter that you won't have a chance to respond to because I'm afraid if you say a single word, then I won't go. You were right about that, too—I have to go. If I don't, I'll always wonder what my life would have been like, and that's not fair to either one of us.

I hope you end up happy, Cam. I really do. Maybe not right now, or next week, but at some point in the future.

—Trish

He let the letter drift to his desk. "The *fuck* you think you get to have the last word, Trish. Goddamn it." She loved him, and she was going to send him a goddamn *letter* instead of giving him a chance to fix this. She was going to *wish him well*, as if that wasn't the height of insanity.

He stared blindly at his blank computer screen. There was a solution to this. Aaron was right on that count, though there'd be no living with him once Cameron admitted it. He just had to figure it out. The old saying about not being able to have your cake and eat it, too, was bullshit. He wanted his fucking cake.

He wanted Trish.

He'd find a way for them to be together.

There was no longer an option where he sat back and let her ride into the sunset without him.

Not when he knew she loved him, too.

Trish clicked Play for the third time in a row and waited for the credits to play out to restart *The Proposal*. She wasn't sure if she'd even liked this movie before this weekend, but it was on demand on the hotel TV and after the first time watching it, she'd cried and cried and started it over from the beginning.

She pulled her comforter tighter around her shoulders. She only had one more day to get this out of her system before she had to show up for work on Monday. Barton Fashion hadn't hired brokenhearted and can't-stop-crying Trish, they'd hired bright and peppy and *sunny* Trish. She didn't know how she was going to pull it off, but she'd figure it out sometime in the next twenty-four hours.

Plenty of time.

Just like the rest of her life, stretching out before her in a uniform without-Cameron road.

She shouldn't have left that letter with Aaron. It was cowardly and stupid, and begging Cameron to fix things after *she* made this choice wasn't fair. Trish used a tissue to wipe at her eyes, wishing the tears would just *stop.* What if Cameron had already read the letter? What if he was… God, she didn't even know, but dread cloaked her in an unrelenting wave with the suspicion that she'd just somehow made everything so much worse.

She dialed her phone before she could talk herself out of it. *It's just to fix things. It's definitely not so I can hear his voice again.* She didn't really expect him to answer. He had to hate her now, which meant he'd let the call go through and she'd leave a stammering voice mail begging him not to read any absurd letter that Aaron gave him, and that would be that. Simple.

Liar.

"Trish?"

Her heart tried to beat its way out of her chest. *Oh God, he answered.* "Cam?"

"Is everything okay?"

How could he sound so calm and put together when she'd cried her way through a jumbo box of tissues and eaten her weight in chocolate chip cookies? *My fault. Not fair to ask him to react the same when I made this call.* She cleared her throat. "I, uh, wanted to apologize." He didn't immediately say anything, so she kept talking, needing to get it out before she lost her last connection to him, however small. "I did a selfish thing and wrote you a letter, and if Aaron hasn't given it to you, I would really appreciate if you burn the damn thing once he does. And if he has—"

"He has."

Oh shit. "Oh. Ah… Okay. Maybe we can pretend it never happened and move on with our lives?" She looked around the hotel room and her gaze settled on the hot mess the mirror reflected at her. Eyes red from crying, hair in a permanent case of bedhead, still wearing the same pajamas she'd changed into when she'd left her training on Friday.

"Is that what you really want?"

She didn't have an answer to that. Not one that had any kind of solution. Did she want to move on with her life without Cameron? Hell no. But she didn't see a way forward for them, no matter how hard she'd tried. "I don't—"

"Honesty, Trish."

She could do this. She could be honest with him. Trish clutched the phone to her ear. "No, I don't want to move on with my life."

"What do you want?"

"I want you."

He exhaled harshly. "Thank fuck for that."

A knock sounded at her hotel door. She froze, half-sure that she was imagining things, but it came again almost immediately. "Just, uh, one second." She climbed off the bed and padded to the door. Maybe it was the maid service? Though it should be too late in the day… Trish opened the door and stared. "Cameron."

"Hey, Trish." His voice echoed in her ear where she still held the phone. She gave herself a shake and ended the call. "I don't… What are you doing here?"

He glanced past her into the hotel room and raised his brows. "Can I come in?"

"Oh. Yeah. Of course." She skittered back and wrapped her arms around herself. He was here. Why was he *here*?

He only moved into the room enough to shut the door. "I read your letter." He pinned her with a look. "What the fuck kind of cowardly shit was that? You wrote me a letter, Trish. A phone call would have been a hell of a lot better, if only because it would have given me a chance to respond."

"I'm sorry," she whispered. Had he come all this way to yell at her about the stupid letter?

"I'm not." Still, he didn't approach her. "I found a solution, though your brother thinks I've lost my damn mind. I don't care. I watched you walk out of my life once, and I'll be damned if I sit back in New York knowing that you love me and I love you. Fuck that. I choose you, Trish."

What was he saying? Hope fluttered cautious wings in her throat. "A long-distance relationship—"

"I split the company. It's past time we had a West Coast base of operations, and Aaron is more than capable of handling anything that pops up in New York by himself with his new assistant. We're going to each build a little at a time and expand Tandem Security accordingly. Right now, I'm working remote until I figure out where we're landing, but that's the deal—I land where you land, Trish." He hesitated, something vulnerable creeping past his customary confidence. "That is, if you still want me to find a solution. If you still want *me*. I know I was a dick before and—"

"Shut up." She threw herself into his arms and kissed him with everything she had. By the time she came up for air, she was shaking. "You're serious. You moved across the country for me."

"I haven't actually moved yet. But the plans are in place." He gave a soft smile. "I wanted to be sure you hadn't changed your mind before I chased you down and branded myself a stalker."

She peppered his jaw with kisses. "Of course I didn't change my mind, you crazy man. How could I? I love you. I love you so much, and I'm sorry I never told you. That stupid letter—"

"I'm framing it."

"What?"

"The letter." He lifted her into his arms and started for the bed. It took Cameron all of three steps to reach it in the small hotel room. "I'm keeping it forever. I'm keeping *you* forever." He tumbled her back onto the bed and settled beside her. His gaze snagged on the television and he frowned. "Sandra Bullock?"

"The movie makes me think of you. She's this cranky boss who overworks her hapless assistant and they end up falling in love." She leaned up and kissed him. "You're cuter than she is, though."

"Thanks." Cameron pushed her curls back from her face. "I'd like to take you to meet my parents next weekend."

"I'd like that." She cupped his jaw. "I bet they'll

be happy to know that you're in the same state as they are."

"Probably." He gave her a wicked grin. "But, mark my words, my mom is going to start in on when we're going to give her grandchildren."

Trish laughed. She couldn't help it. She hadn't dared think there might be a way for her and Cameron to be together, yet here he was, in her bed again and offering her the solution to everything. She snuggled closer to him. "It'll be at least a few years."

"No doubt." He sounded a little choked, as if the thought of kids panicked him, which only made her laugh harder.

She wrapped her leg over his waist and pulled him closer. "But there's no reason we can't practice in the meantime. Lots and lots of practice."

"I love you, woman."

"Say it again."

His lips brushed her ear. "I love you," he whispered. "And I'm never letting you go."

"Good," she breathed. "Now take off your clothes."

* * * * *

BETWEEN THE LINES

LAUREN HAWKEYE

MILLS & BOON

To Patience, for her patience.

CHAPTER ONE

Then

He always got what he wanted…except when it came to this woman.

Theo Lawrence groaned with something akin to pain as she arched her hips into him, her soft, heated flesh rubbing against his aching cock. He fisted his hands in the front of her thin, ribbed tank top, yanking the fabric up to expose her small breasts, the nipples rosy red from his fingers.

"Don't stop." Pressing her lips into the corded muscle of his neck, Jo Marchande dug her fingers into his shoulders until it hurt, sparking deeper need to life inside him. All the while, her hips rocked restlessly, teasing the rock-solid erection that was straining at the stiff denim of his jeans. "Please don't stop."

"You're killing me." He didn't want to stop—oh fuck, how he didn't want to stop. He'd never loved anyone in his life the way he loved her, and not being able to be inside her was exquisite agony.

The one decent thing he'd done in his life, however, was to keep his hands off his underage girlfriend. He loved her—loved her family—far too much than to disrespect them by taking her before she could possibly be ready.

It was the hardest thing he'd ever done. Especially when she was dead set on making him change his mind.

"You don't have to hold back." Hand sliding down between them, she rubbed her palm over his arousal. His erection jerked in response, angry at being confined to its denim prison. "You know you don't. I want this. Want you."

"Not while you're still seventeen." His words were strained. He tugged her shirt higher still, and she took the opportunity to rub her breasts against his chest, heating his skin to a feverish pitch. "It's not right."

"You're only two years older than me." Her voice was stubborn. This was nothing new—his girl was nothing if not determined. Single-minded. He admired it in every aspect of her life.

Except for this one.

"And two years won't be a big deal when you're

eighteen," Theo growled against the top of her head. He inhaled the scent of her shampoo, straight spicy mint, something he'd never be able to smell again in his life without being aroused. "Tomorrow. We can wait one more day."

In Massachusetts, the age of consent was sixteen. It damn near killed him to do it, but he was making them wait until eighteen. It just seemed like the right thing to do.

"No." That stubborn streak in her voice thickened, and she dipped a finger inside his waistband. She swiped over the swollen head of his cock, and he groaned when a droplet of liquid leaked out in response.

"Jo." Drawing on every last ounce of strength that he had, he forced himself to take a deep breath, pulling back and putting a single precious inch of strength between them. It wasn't much, but it allowed him to inhale without the smell of her skin sinking into the very cells of his being. "It's not happening. You know me well enough to know that I don't change my mind."

"I'm not asking you to." He looked down into her face, the one he'd known since they were kids. Mischief was sparkling in her storm-gray eyes, bubbling up through the thick haze of lust.

"You're going to have to use smaller words." Dipping his head, he pressed a soft kiss to her forehead, then trailed his lips down over her cheekbone. “All of my blood has flooded south of my brain. Far south.”

She laughed breathlessly, and he felt the exhalation, warm as it teased over his chest. “I’m not asking you to change your mind. But I *am* asking you to…to fuck me.”

His mouth went instantly dry, his cock surging forward, cheering at her words. Her dirty words, her innocent tone belying them, were rapidly bringing him to the absolute edge of no return.

“I’m not sure you know what it does to me, hearing that sweet little mouth of yours talking about such filthy things.” Releasing her tank top with one hand, he dragged it up, up until he could rub his thumb over her kiss-swollen lips. In response, she swiped her tongue over it, then sucked it into her mouth, showing what she wanted to do to another part of him.

What they both wanted her to do.

“I’m going to do more than talk about it,” she insisted. Slowly, slowly, she started to work at his belt, the sound of metal on metal one of the most erotic things he’d ever heard. “Haven’t you figured it out yet?”

“Jojo,” he exhaled, running the tip of his tongue over the seam of her lips. She parted them beneath him, and he licked inside. "No more teasing. What are you talking about?"

"I'm not seventeen anymore." She grinned up at him triumphantly. Blood suffused her pale, creamy skin, camouflaging the golden freckles that he knew were there. "It's after midnight, Theo. And I know exactly what I want for my birthday."

Holy shit. Releasing her long enough to look at his watch, he watched as the numbers turned over from 12:02 to 12:03.

She was right. She was eighteen now. And with that knowledge, his noble intentions melted like sugar in a hot pan, becoming something even better.

He growled in response. He'd made it. And now there was nothing holding him back from sinking between those pale, pretty thighs that had taunted him for so incredibly long.

"Put your arms around my neck," he demanded. She cried out when he palmed her ass, lifting her so that she could wrap her legs around his waist. Again, the heat of her sweet core taunted his cock, but it was different now.

Now it just spurred him on because finally, *finally*, he could touch her the way they'd both wanted him to for the last year—the longest year of his life.

"I can't believe we're finally doing this," she

gasped as he carried her to the foot of the bed. Sliding her down his body, he set her down on her feet, then again fisted his hands in the front of her thin cotton tank top.

"I can." He grinned wickedly as he tugged. Jo exhaled harshly as her shirt ripped down the front. For a split second he felt bad—he'd ruined her shirt, and her family didn't have a lot of money.

But when she looked up at him, there was no judgment in her eyes, just raw need.

He'd buy her a new shirt—he'd buy her anything she wanted, if she'd let him. Heaven knew he could afford it. Right now, though, the last thing he wanted was for her to start thinking about the differences between their lives—the one point of contention between them.

Right now he didn't want her thinking of anything. He just wanted her to feel.

"Hold still." He whispered the words into her ear, savored the resultant shiver. She was nervous, and he didn't mind that.

By the time they were done, she'd be too lost in sensation to worry about anything.

He palmed her breasts, running his thumbs roughly over her distended nipples. She rarely wore a bra. She claimed that her breasts were too small to need the support. He didn't care what size they were, because to him they were just perfect.

And the lack of bra gave him easier access to heaven. Who would complain about that?

Her breath hitched when his fingers worked at the button of her low-slung jeans. The denim was worn, the fastening giving way easily. Hooking his thumbs in the waistband, he worked the garment down her slim hips until it fell to the floor. She was left in nothing but a pair of flimsy blue cotton briefs, hardly a barrier to the sweet heat between her legs.

"Lie down on the bed." She did as he told her, scooting back until her head was cushioned on the pillows of his bed. Her slim, pale figure stood out in stark contrast to the deep sapphire-blue of his linen duvet, and he knew that he'd never look at his bed the same way again.

He watched as she propped herself up on her elbows, her avid stare fixed on him. Her lips, swollen from his kisses, parted unconsciously as he undid the buttons on his expensive dress shirt, leaving it hanging open as he pulled his leather belt from his jeans. He was so hard that it was nearly painful, and yet he savored the bite of discomfort before popping the button and allowing the heavy length of his cock to breathe, his swollen length clearly outlined against his underwear.

"Oh." On the bed, Jo's entire body flushed. She ran her tongue over her lips, and he barely suppressed a groan as he imagined those lips swallowing him deep.

"You've felt me before." He'd stuck to his rule, no sex until she was eighteen, but that didn't mean they hadn't touched. But this was the first time she'd seen him naked, and he felt a strange surge of pride at her hungry gaze.

He wasn't a virgin, but nothing turned him on like knowing that she'd chosen him to introduce her to this kind of pleasure. It was a heavy responsibility, but he knew he was up to the task.

"I know," she whispered, her words rasping against the still air of his room. "But I've never really thought about…you know…how it's going to fit."

Theo closed his eyes, his head falling back. What had he done in his life to deserve her?

He hadn't done anything, but he wasn't that noble.

"It'll fit," he promised, shoving his jeans down his hips. He stepped out when they fell to the floor, then rubbed a hand over his erection, which tented the front of his black briefs.

Jo groaned, shifting restlessly on the bed. The sight of her arousal dampening the tender skin of her inner thighs was nearly his undoing.

Quickly, he shed his shirt, then let his briefs fall to the floor. He stood before her naked, and though he wanted to pounce on her and bury his face between her thighs, he forced himself to hold still, letting her look her fill.

He knew what she saw when those inquisitive gray eyes looked him over. He was tall, a good half a foot taller than her five foot six. He was also more than a little vain, and he started every day in the gym on the third floor of the house he shared with his father. He may not have had the drive for school or business that his dad had hoped to see in his offspring, but he never missed a session with his weights.

Because of that, his body was chiseled and solid as a rock, and he'd shared that body with more than a few girls before he'd finally convinced Jo to date him. He knew that girls liked his abs, his cock, and even the fact that his skin was dark gold and his hair nearly black, his coloring thanks to the Brazilian mother who had died when he was a baby.

Yeah, he knew he was a good-looking guy. And that plus his family money meant that he'd never been hard up for someone to warm his bed.

But he'd never, ever wanted anything more than what he had right now—Jo Marchande in his bed, wanting him.

He had to make this good.

"Spread your legs." He clasped her ankles in long fingers, rubbing his thumb over the tender skin at the inside of each. She shuddered, then gasped when he tugged, pulling her to the edge of the bed. Kneeling on the plush carpet that covered his bedroom floor, he hooked her legs over each of his shoulders, opening her wide. Exposing that part of her that he craved.

"Theo… I've never…" Jo squirmed, her heels digging into his back. "I don't know how to do this."

"You don't have to do anything except take what I give you." Beneath his avid stare, the thin cotton of those panties grew wet. He traced it with a finger, circling the hard bud of her clit, and she shuddered in response.

He pressed his lips to the supple skin on the inside of her thigh, just above the curve of her knee. Her quick exhale told him that she was trying desperately to hold her breath. That she was nervous.

Knowing that the nerves would only help to heighten her pleasure, he slid his lips up only the barest inch, determined to draw out the sensations for her. She shifted, and he could feel her heat, smell her arousal.

Trailing his lips farther up her thigh, he teased them both by trailing his tongue over the crease that divided her leg from her abdomen. She jerked beneath his mouth with a breathless laugh.

"Liked that, did you?" He repeated the motion,

and she groaned. He slid his mouth up even more, closer to his goal, savoring the salt on her skin.

"Theo," she breathed as he brushed his lips over the soaked fabric of her panties. "Oh God. I can't—"

"Oh yes, you can." He flicked his tongue over the cotton, and her hips lifted off the bed.

"I've waited so long for this." Nuzzling his nose against her heat, he hooked his fingers into the waistband of her simple underwear. Not wanting to take the time to pull them all the way off, he pulled hard and grinned when they ripped, allowing him to toss them aside.

She didn't give him hell for destroying a second item of her clothing, just rocked from side to side on the cool sheets of his bed. He took a moment to simply look at the glistening pink of her center, hot and wet and all for him.

Jo groaned. This was the only time she got quiet, his girl—when she was aroused. It made him want to drive her so crazy that she got loud again.

It made him want to make her scream his name.

Inhaling her scent, which reminded him of some kind of exotic cinnamon, he leaned forward and swiped his tongue through her folds.

"Oh my God," she breathed, arching up off the bed. He licked again, and she tried to close her legs against the onslaught of sensation, but he was there, the width of his shoulders holding her wide-open.

With long, slow swipes of his tongue, he licked her from bottom to top, brushing the flat of his tongue over the hard nub of her clit every time. She tasted so sweet, and he wanted more.

Using his thumbs, he parted her lips, focusing his attention on the swollen bud. Her heels began to drum into his back, her breath coming in gasps.

"Theo. I can't. It's too much." He could tell that her arousal was spiking hard and high. She didn't have much experience—hell, *any* experience—and he knew that it wouldn't take much to send her over.

That was good. He was going to make her come now, and then again. He was going to make sure that she was so ready for him that when it came to the part that might hurt, she would simply melt around him like ice cream left in the hot, hot sun.

CHAPTER TWO

"THAT'S IT, BABY GIRL." Using one finger, he traced around her slick opening, barely dipping inside. She groaned, arching her back, pressing herself against his mouth greedily. "Let go. I've got you."

"Theo!" She bucked against his mouth as he increased the flicks of his tongue against her clit. Her thighs started to shake, and then her entire body tightened as her pleasure overtook her.

He buried his face between her legs as she came, kissing her now with broad swipes of his tongue. Her words were unintelligible, and when he looked up the slim column of her body, he saw her face flushed the prettiest shade of pink, her eyes closed, her mouth parted for the breathy little pants she didn't seem able to help.

Before the waves stopped battering at her, he pressed a kiss to her inner thigh, then gently moved her legs from where they were clenched around his ears. She lay panting on the bed as he crawled up beside her, placing one hand on the dip of her impossibly slender waist.

He watched as she opened her eyes, fascinated by the glints of auburn in the mink-colored lengths of her lashes. Beneath them, those stormy gray eyes were glittering with need, and he knew, he just knew, that his dirty girl already wanted more.

"Did you like that?" He brushed his lips over the shell of her ear, nipping at the lobe. She nodded frantically but remained silent.

Squeezing her hip, he splayed his palm over the flat, quivering plane of her belly.

"What was that?" Chuckling as she garbled something in response, he slid his hand down, dipping between her legs. "I didn't understand. I guess I'll just have to check for myself."

Her hands fisted in the quilt as he used his fingers to do what his tongue just had. Pinching her clit lightly, quickly, he waited until she moaned, then slid a finger into her waiting heat.

She was wet, and tight, and if she felt like fucking heaven on his finger, then what would she feel like around his cock?

"More," Jo whispered, and he realized that she'd gone still. She was waiting, he realized, for it to hurt.

He didn't want it to hurt.

"Are you sure?" She nodded, so he worked his finger out slowly, then in and then out.

She hissed when he added a second, scissoring them the slightest bit to stretch her. He kept his gaze on her face, searching for any sign of discomfort. Instead, he saw raw, unadulterated need.

He would make this good for her.

Returning his attention to her clit, he caught it between his fingers and rubbed. Wetness slicked her folds, and within moments another keening cry slipped from between those pretty lips. He let her ride the wave of her second orgasm before reaching over her to his mahogany bedside table, removing a small foil packet from the drawer.

Her eyes widened a bit when she saw what he'd retrieved, and he watched the slim column of her throat as she swallowed thickly.

"Are you sure about this?" It just might kill him to stop right now, with her taste on his lips and her slickness on his fingers, but he would. He'd do pretty much anything for her.

"Don't you dare stop!" Rising up on her elbows, Jo caught his chin in her fingers and pulled him down for a kiss. She sucked in a surprised breath, and he knew that she was tasting herself on his lips.

The greedy noise that slipped from her mouth was the hottest fucking thing he'd ever heard.

With hands that were far less steady than any

other time he'd done this, he tore open the foil packet. Her curious eyes watched avidly as he removed the ring of latex, smoothing the sheath down over the length of his erection.

He hissed when she reached down and danced her fingers over his cock. God, he'd dreamed of this, of her hand on him, stroking him just like this.

Pleasure began to gather all the way down in the soles of his feet, and he jerked back with a rueful laugh.

"Did I do something wrong?" She sat up, eyebrows raised in alarm.

"Not at all." Catching her hand in his—the one that had just been stroking him—he pressed his lips to it in a kiss. "It was a little too good, actually."

"Oh." She drew out the word, understanding dawning. "Duly noted."

She smirked. What choice did he have but to kiss her?

They fell back down to the bed, the covers tangling around them. Rolling on top of her, he braced his weight on his arms on either side of her head, looking down into that face that he knew like he knew his own.

Jo Marchande wasn't classically pretty. Her face was a bit too square, her features too angular. Her milky-white skin stayed pale year-round, except for the times she got so absorbed in a book she was reading out in the sun that she didn't realize she was burning. The smattering of golden freckles stayed year-round, too, and he took a moment now to brush a kiss over them on each cheek.

It was her eyes that made people look at her twice. They were huge, a stunning gray that shifted with her mood, surrounded by lashes that she never bothered to tint with mascara. She never bothered with makeup at all, something he loved because it was so different from all of the other women he knew.

Her hair spread out around her head on the pillow as she returned his gaze steadily, the chestnut color adding warmth to that pale skin. No, she wasn't classically beautiful, but he wouldn't have changed a damn thing.

She was his.

"I love you." The words slipped from his lips before he could even think about what he was saying. Her mouth parted in surprise, but then he was burying his face in that long mane of hair, tucking his hand between her legs. She rocked up against him as he tested one more time that she was ready.

His fingers came away soaked.

"Theo, I—" The words got caught in her throat as he reached between them and lined the head of his cock up with the sweet, sweet heat of her center.

She gasped as he slid just the head of his erection into her slickness. He sank his teeth into his lower lip as nerves fired to life. It was everything he could do to hold still, letting her adjust to the feeling of him inside her.

He wasn't expecting her to grab onto his hips and rock herself up.

"Fuck," he cursed as he slid deeper into her soaking-wet channel. He wanted so badly to be in deep, to claim her from the inside out, but when the head of his cock met resistance, he had to force himself to still.

His limbs shaking with the exertion of holding back, he pressed his damp forehead against hers, looking right into her eyes. Their breath mingled, fanning out over their faces, and he kissed her again, their first kiss with him inside her.

"Are you ready?" He rocked back and forth the slightest bit, testing. She whimpered, but it was a sound of pleasure, not of pain.

"Hurry up." Her voice was greedy, her fingers eager as they dug into his ass. She pulled him closer, and he resisted for just one more minute before he pressed forward, the cock that was swollen past the point of pain pushing deeper.

Beneath him she winced, sinking her teeth

into her lower lip. He automatically stilled, but she urged him on with an impatient hiss.

Her body resisted him, clenching tightly until finally something gave way, allowing him to slide home. He grunted as he sheathed himself fully inside her, the sensation causing his eyes to roll back in his head.

"Holy shit," Jo whispered beneath him, looking up at him with eyes that were bright.

"It will only hurt for a minute. I promise." Theo rocked inside her, just a bit to test, and she moaned.

"It hurts, but not the kind you mean." Her hands moved from his ass to his hips, and she shifted impatiently beneath him. "It hurts because I don't even know what this is, but I want it so bad. Please, Theo. Please. *Move.*"

The last strings of his self-control snapped. With small rocking motions, he pulled back, then worked his way back in. He'd never had anything so tight, so hot around his cock, and if he wasn't careful, he was going to lose it before he could make her feel good again.

She wouldn't let him be careful. She rocked beneath him, urging him to go faster and faster. Her tight sheath was swollen, pulling him back in again and again. The pleasure rose hot and fast, and sweat beaded on his forehead as he strained to hold back.

Slipping one hand between their bodies, he located her clit and focused his attention on it. At the same time, he dipped his head and sucked one of her puckered nipples into his mouth.

Beneath him she went taut as a bow. Her cleft tightened as her eyes went wild with pleasure yet again, and he felt his own release start, fire licking along every inch of his skin. Closing his eyes, he finally allowed himself to let go, to let himself revel in the fact that Jo Marchande, the strong, proud girl that he'd loved since the day they met, had given herself to him.

After, he pressed a kiss to her brow. Pulling out, he disposed of the condom, then slid back into the bed, tucking them both under his soft, expensive sheets. She was already drowsy when he tugged her against him, fitting his chest to her back.

"You okay?" He tucked a ribbon of hair behind her ear. She sighed, a small murmur of contentment that made his stomach do a small flip.

How was it possible that she was his? He'd never done anything to deserve having someone so wonderful in his life.

According to his father, he was lazy. He had no drive, no direction, no purpose in life. He was squandering the opportunities that he had. This, of course, was in direct contrast to Theodore Lawrence Sr., who owned a huge import-export company. His mother, famous in her native Brazil before her death, had been a world-renowned concert pianist.

He'd never live up to either of them, so he didn't bother to try. He knew what he was worth, and it wasn't much. So the fact that Jo Marchande, the woman who had imprinted herself into his very DNA, had deemed him worthy?

It wasn't something that he would ever take for granted.

"I've never been better." Casting a sleepy smile over her shoulder at him, she snuggled back into his arms. "Can I stay?"

His heart skipped a beat, sending his pulse skittering to catch up.

"You can stay." If he had his way, she'd stay forever.

"You just couldn't control yourself, could you?"

Theo stiffened, a steel rod snapping into place in his spine. Slowly, he turned, doing his best to look nonchalant as he leaned back against the endless expanse of marble countertop in the rarely used kitchen of the house he shared with his father.

"What am I lacking control in this time, exactly?" His voice was cold when he spoke, every trace of the warmth he'd had for Jo frozen into daggers of ice, meant to maim or at the very least protect. "You have such a long list, you'll forgive me for not immediately understanding what it is that you're referring to, this time."

"You know exactly." His father stepped out of the shadows and into the dim kitchen, leaning against the breakfast bar, his stance mirroring Theo's own. He lifted his heavy crystal snifter of expensive scotch for a small sip. His gaze slid over the matching one in his son's hand, but as per usual, he said nothing about the fact that Theo was drinking, even though he wasn't yet twenty-one.

Theo knew that, at the end of the day, Theodore Sr. just didn't care.

"I assume you're referring to Jo." The words were sour in his mouth. He hated even saying her name right now, not wanting to cast shadows on something that, to him, was so perfect. So theirs.

"Of course I'm referring to Jo." His father's voice was layered heavily with impatience. "They are family friends. They are our neighbors. They are good people."

Theo said nothing. What was there to say?

"You have nothing to offer any of them," his father continued. The utter contempt in his voice was clear. "You've disappointed me time and again, Theodore, but I thought that you at least had the morals to stay away from those girls. Shame on you."

It shouldn't have hurt, but it did. Theo took a hefty swallow of his drink, focusing on the fire that it left as it traveled down to his gut. Taking a moment to study his father—the man he'd come from—he wondered how a person could seem to detest someone who had come from them so very much.

Ha. Why was he even questioning that? He knew exactly what his father saw—he saw his lost wife. Theo had inherited his golden skin, his exotic features, his glossy black hair, even the charm that he used regularly, from his mother.

Theo knew that, if given a choice, his father would rather have his mother here in his place.

"Did you hear what I said, boy?" Theodore Sr. set his glass down on the polished countertop with a sharp crack. The hand not holding Theo's own glass fisted in the thick velvet of his robe, kneading at it like a stress ball.

"Jo and I have been dating for over a year." Theo tried to rein in his temper. "It's not like I plan on sleeping with her and leaving the next day."

"You shouldn't be sleeping with her at all," his father snorted with derision, shaking his head. "What if you got her pregnant? You really think you could make a go of it? You'd run right out the door, and then where would she be?"

Theo expected nothing less from his dad, but

hearing the harsh words was still a lash from a whip. *He* knew he'd do no such thing, but hearing out loud what his own flesh and blood really thought of him reminded him of the worst hangover he'd ever had. Try as he might, he just couldn't ever outrun the nagging pain.

"Have a nice night, Dad." Draining the last of his scotch in one giant swallow, he left the kitchen through the servants' door, preferring the longer route back to his room to going anywhere near his father.

The conversation they'd just had was nothing new. Often he was able to completely deflect the criticism, keeping the barbs from landing and piercing his skin.

Tonight, though? Some of those words had landed.

He loved Jo more than anything. But what if his father was right?

CHAPTER THREE

"HAPPY BIRTHDAY, DEAR JOOOO, happy birthday to you."

"Cake! Gimme." Standing up in her seat, Jo reached for the tower of cupcakes that Mamesie had so painstakingly arranged on the antique silver platter. Grabbing the one with the most frosting, she sank her teeth into the decadent chocolate cake, shuddering with pleasure when the sweetness of the icing hit her tongue.

"I'm hurt." Warm breath misted over her ear, and she made a sound low in her throat. "I thought I was the only one who could pull that sound out of you. Yet here you are, cheating on me with a cupcake."

"Sorry, babe." Turning in his arms, she tuned out the chatter of her mother and three sisters as she focused in on Theo. Thinking about what they'd done last night had a fizzy feeling bubbling up inside her, making her feel like she'd drunk a giant glass of champagne too fast. "The cupcake offers instant gratification. Unlike someone I can think of, who made me wait an entire year."

"It was worth waiting for, though, wasn't it?" His voice was a low rumble against her ear. And even though she was still sore, she felt molten heat gather between her thighs. "At least, you seemed to think so this morning when you were moaning my name."

She uttered another small moan at that. Putting space between them before she shoved the cupcakes off the table and pulled him down for another round, she tucked another bite of cupcake in her mouth as a distraction.

"I know you're trying to change the topic, but I don't think it's working the way you hoped." Jo sucked in a sharp breath as Theo's stare tracked the way her tongue was licking sprinkles off the top of the cupcake. "I can think of a lot of places that would look awfully pretty with a bit of white icing on them."

"Stop it!" Elbowing him, Jo took another deliberate step away, conscious of the fact that her family was right there. But when she looked around, Mamesie had gone into the kitchen for plates, and her sisters Beth and Amy were fully occupied by their own pieces of cake, still being young enough to have their attention fully commanded by the promise of sugar.

Her older sister, Meg, though, cast her a wink before handing her a napkin. Even if she hadn't heard what was said, it was obvious that she knew that something had changed with her little sister. In response, Jo felt her cheeks heat.

"I need to use the bathroom." Giving Theo's hand a little squeeze, she swallowed the last bite of her cupcake and excused herself. She headed upstairs to the bathroom she shared with Amy rather than the small powder room on the main floor.

She splashed icy-cold water on her face, which felt good but did nothing to fade the flush on her cheeks. How was it possible that she wanted Theo again already? Did that *wanting* ever stop?

Wanting to give her telltale blush time to fade before she returned downstairs—Mamesie was no idiot, but Jo still wasn't keen on the idea of flaunting her newfound sexuality in front of her mother—Jo wandered down the hall to her bedroom. Her laptop sat open on the slab of plywood and two sawhorses she used as a desk, flashing a retro screen saver of different shapes made of neon lines, undulating around the screen. Yellow legal pads clumped in haphazard piles around the computer, most covered in her messy scrawl.

The keyboard beckoned. She still had a thousand words to go on her latest story. It was just a little article for the local paper, something she submitted every couple of weeks, but for every article that they published, she received a check for a hundred dollars. It wasn't much, but she loved the process of sealing that check in the crisp white envelope, of feeding it into the bank machine to deposit it into her account.

Mamesie had raised her, Meg, Beth and Amy by herself, and while they certainly no longer had access to some of the finer things that they'd had when her dad had been alive, she knew that Mamesie would never accept money from her girls—not unless the situation were truly dire. So Jo tucked away what she could. She didn't dare to dream too big, but maybe one day she could take some journalism courses. Learn a way to apply her writing to a career, when she'd saved enough.

She reread what she'd written earlier while she waited for her body to calm the hell down. Pulling out the creaky desk chair that she was pretty sure bore a permanent imprint of her butt, she rolled up to her laptop and started clicking through.

"What are you doing up here?" She had no idea how long it had been when Theo spoke from the doorway, scaring the shit out of her. She jolted, her elbow sliding over the keys of her keyboard.

Swearing, she hurriedly pressed the back arrows to restore her work.

"I came up to cool off a bit after you got me all hot and bothered," she replied, her gaze veering back to her screen. She was almost at the end. She was pretty sure she only needed a couple more sentences, and they were right there, fresh in her head…

"It's your birthday party." Theo frowned at her computer as he entered her room, closing the door behind him with the heel of his shoe—his fancy, hand-tooled, Italian leather shoe. Jo didn't pay any attention to fashion, none at all, but her sister Meg did, and she was forever sighing over the gorgeous things that the Lawrences had.

Things the Lawrences had. Things the Marchandes did not. Neither family talked about it, but the difference in their positions in life was always there, the elephant in any room in which members of both families had gathered.

At least, it was always there for Jo. It hadn't been, not always—back when her dad had been alive, they'd enjoyed a lot of the same privileges that the Lawrences had. She knew that Theo and his dad couldn't have cared less that there was now a class difference between their families, but it also meant that when it came to certain things, like money, Theo especially just didn't understand.

"Are you working?" Hastily Jo tried to close out of her document, but when she looked up and saw the puzzled expression on his face, she knew that he'd seen. "Why are you hiding up here working when everyone is downstairs waiting for you?"

"I told you. I came up here to cool off a bit." She could hear the defensiveness in her voice and pulled in a deep breath. "I read a few lines of my article and got sucked in."

"Well, come back down." He reached for her hand. "It's present time. Amy's about to pee herself, she's so excited."

Jo started to rise, but something about the way he was being so insistent had her hackles rising. Lowering herself back to her chair, she crossed her arms over her chest, the movement stiff. "Tell them I'll be down in ten minutes. I just have a few more lines to finish."

"Forget the lines, babe." Theo's smile was charming, deadly when he aimed it at you, but Jo had known him long enough that she could steel herself against it—well, sometimes. "It's your birthday. Finish them another time."

"I can't." Her eyes narrowed—why was he pushing? "My deadline is tonight. I should have handed the piece in already."

"Does it really matter?" Clearly confused, Theo waved a sure hand through the air—the lord in his manor. "Blow off the deadline. I don't see what the big deal is."

"The big deal is that they're counting on me to hand the piece in. If I don't, they have to scramble to find something else for that spot." Jo's voice was incredulous—why was this so hard for Theo to understand? "And also, if I don't hand the article in, I don't get paid."

"They pay you peanuts. What's the point?" Theo reached for her hands again, and this time instead of just avoiding him, she swatted them away. Rising from her chair, she stood to face him, clenched fists growing sweaty at her sides.

"A hundred dollars is not peanuts." Her voice was shaking. Damn it, Theo knew—he *knew*—that this job was important to her. "I'm saving it for school, and you know it."

"Well, a hundred dollars isn't anything to me." He shrugged dismissively, and Jo felt the bottom drop out of her stomach. "Just...please. Just forget about the article. I'll give you thc hundred dollars, okay? Just please come back downstairs so that I can give you your birthday present."

For a long moment she was speechless. She actually kind of felt like throwing up.

She and Theo had their differences, but she *loved* him. She'd given him her body. Her heart.

And here he was pushing her to forget something that meant the world to her, just so he could get his way right now.

"You think I'm going to take money from you?" Horrified, Jo rubbed her hands over the hips of her jeans, trying to ease the clamminess. "After what we just did last night, how do you think that makes me feel?"

Understanding dawned on his face—at least, the tiniest inkling of it. "No, no. Jo, Jojo, that's not what the money is for. Please—"

"No, of course it's not." Damn it, she was shouting. This was nothing new for her, not with her temper, but she couldn't ever remember feeling exactly like this, sickness mixed in with the growing rage. "The money is so that I will ignore what I have repeatedly told you that I want right now, on my own damn birthday, and so that I will go do what you want. Lord Lawrence gets his way yet again."

"Don't call me that." A dangerous spark flickered through Theo's eyes. Lord Lawrence was what they'd all called him when he'd been younger and acting like a bit of a brat. "You know I fucking hate that."

"Sucks, doesn't it," Jo taunted, finding a sick pleasure in getting some kind of reaction out of him. "When someone ignores what you've repeatedly said you want so that they can do what they want instead."

"Wait a minute." Theo suddenly stood up ramrod straight. He scrubbed his hands over his face before looking back at Jo. "You're not talking about last night. Please tell me you're not talking about last night."

"Jesus Christ, Theo." An inarticulate scream burst from her throat. "No, I'm not fucking talking about last night. If I hadn't wanted your hands on me, you would have bloody well known it."

"Right. I know," he replied hastily, his restless hands now moving to rake through his hair. "You're just so mad. And if we're just talking about the article..."

If we're just talking about the article, then I don't know what the hell you're so worked up about.

Her mouth, the mouth she'd used all over his body not twenty-four hours earlier, fell open with disbelief. Theo's indifference to the gifts he'd been given had been a bone of contention between them before, but it had been...a small bone. A fish bone. Something that a sweet smile from him could help send into the garbage disposal.

This? This was a dinosaur drumstick, too big to be ground down in the kitchen sink.

"Look, I shouldn't have done that." Theo spoke

hastily, trying to smooth over what he'd said. "That was wrong. Let's not fight on your birthday."

"Are you saying that because you're actually sorry?" Resentment was bitter on her tongue. "Or are you saying it so that you get your way?"

She watched, almost as if she'd stepped outside herself, as temper flared in those caramel-colored eyes. Copper fire—that was what it looked like.

"Why are you acting this way?" He bit his words out the way he always did when he was angry, as though it took more effort to form them. "I just wanted to spend your birthday with you."

"That's not an answer." He growled in response, actually fucking growled, and took a step toward her. She held up both hands and thought she might even have hissed. They'd been reduced to animals in their fury, and she was really fucking tempted to bite him.

And not in a fun way.

"Get out of my room." Her voice was shaking. As she pointed at the door, she noticed that her hand was, too.

"What?" Incredulity lent an almost comical cast to his face. "Are you fucking serious right now?"

"I said get *out*!" she screamed, her voice echoing off the small confines of her room. Theo reeled back as if she'd slapped him, and her palm itched to do just that. He must have read the desire in her eyes, on her face, because his face reddened, the effect of his own temper, but he took a step back. With one last look, he spun on the heel of his ridiculously expensive shoes and stormed out of her room, slamming the door behind him. Minutes later, Jo felt the frame of the house shake as he slammed the front door as well. Crossing to her window, she hugged her arms to her chest and watched as Theo's tall, lanky figure strode across the lawn, climbing over the short fence that separated their properties, his movements jerky.

He would drink now, she knew that absolutely. He'd pull one of his dad's priceless bottles of scotch from the ornate liquor cabinet and numb everything he felt with the gilded liquid. He would retreat into a sullen cocoon, erecting the barriers that were his first line of defense.

He'd never erected those same barriers against her, but she knew him inside and out. And knowing him as she did, she saw with sudden, startling clarity that he truly wouldn't understand why she'd responded the way she had. Why she hadn't been able to just jump onboard Theo's Fun Train… because to him, responsibility didn't exist.

Knowing him the way she did, she wondered why she only now understood that this particular quirk of his meant that they were never, ever going to be able to work.

Acid churned in her belly as she sank down to the floor. It rose to her throat when Beth, the sister she was closest to, cracked open the door and stuck her head in, and she couldn't reply.

"We heard you guys yelling." Her sister's bright blue eyes were wide, meaning that she was as shocked by the argument as Jo was. "Are you okay?"

Jo looked up at her younger sister, the one she most often confided in, and felt the first small crack reverberate through her heart. Wordlessly, she held Beth's gaze and shook her head, just the smallest bit.

And when Beth crossed the room, sank to the floor beside her and wrapped Jo in her skinny tween arms, Jo burst into tears.

And that pissed her off, too.

CHAPTER FOUR

Then

THEO LAY SPRAWLED in the massive leather chaise that occupied the corner of his bedroom at one… or was it two in the morning? He lifted the bottle of scotch that he'd brazenly lifted from his dad's supply, squinting as he tried to discern just how much he'd had to drink.

He was pretty sure that the bottle had been full—a brand-new one, in fact. After the first couple of shots from a heavy crystal tumbler, though, he'd decided to forgo the glass and swig straight from the bottle. And then he'd spilled some on the floor in the hallway, leaving a sticky lake of amber liquid for the cleaners to find in the morning.

So basically…he had no idea. He knew he'd drunk a lot, but it wasn't having the effect he'd hoped for. The buzz he was chasing kept dancing just out of reach, and instead the alcohol was filling him with lead, weighing him down until he thought he might never move again.

"Why do you do this to yourself?"

He didn't have to move to know that Jo was standing in the doorway of his room. He caught a whiff of spicy cinnamon, heard her quiet sigh as she entered, closing the door behind her.

He remained motionless, listening as she moved around his room. She straightened his sheets, probably pulling down his covers for him. He tracked her footsteps to his bathroom, heard the tap and knew that she was getting him water and aspirin. Finally she closed the space between them, reaching out for the bottle he still held.

Because he was in the mood to be a dick, he held tight. He heard a grim hum from her lips, and then she smacked the bottom of the bottle, twisting it over in his grip and upending the contents onto his lap.

"Fucking hell, Jo!" Shocked into motion, he scrambled upright. A tight smirk of satisfaction was on that fascinating face of hers, and she simply stood back, arms crossed over her chest as he reached for the closest thing he could find, a sweatshirt, to mop up the liquid on his lap.

"I'm going to bed," he informed her. She didn't

move. He wasn't surprised. Damn it, what the hell was going on with her? All he'd wanted to do was make sure that she enjoyed her birthday. She didn't have to write those freaking articles. She'd just turned eighteen today—no one expected her to contribute. And if she was worried about money, he had plenty, and he was happy to share. So what the fuck was the problem?

"Theo." Her voice was a sigh again. He glared up at her as she pulled his footstool closer to his chair, lowering her small frame to a perch. "We need to talk."

He was just drunk enough that talking seemed like a horrible idea. As he looked at her sitting there, her pert, perfect breasts clearly outlined in the flimsy blouse that he knew Meg had made her wear for her party, he thought of something that sounded like a lot more fun than talking.

"C'mere." He gestured, overshooting and making his arm swing wildly. "I still need to give you your birthday kiss."

She closed her eyes, muttered something beneath her breath and then pinned him with thunder in those storm-gray eyes. "It's not sexy time, Theo. Sexy time is not on the menu anytime in the near future. Just sit up and answer something for me."

Theo rather thought that he could convince her on the sexy-time front if she gave it a fair shot, but the clipped quality of her voice finally sank through the scotch-soaked folds of his brain. Warily, he scooted to the edge of his seat, bracing his elbows on his knees and trying to look like he was sober.

From the grimace she made when she caught a whiff of his breath, he knew he wasn't fooling her. Sighing, he scrubbed a hand over his face, then gave her his full attention. "What do you need to say, Jojo?"

Her question was like a punch in the kidneys. "What are your plans, Theo?" He waited for her to elaborate, but she just waited for his response, her entire frame unnaturally still.

"You mean like…my plans for you?" Anxiety pitched his words higher than usual. He loved her, but wasn't it a little…soon…to have that talk?

"You are such a jackass," she muttered. He scowled, opening his mouth to reply, but she forged on. "No. Not your plans for us. Which, incidentally, would be *our* plans, but whatever."

His brain wasn't moving quite fast enough to keep up with that train, but he put all his energy into focusing so that he could catch her next sentence.

"I'm talking about you. Your plans for your own life. What are you doing with it? What do you even *want*?"

"I—" He paused, unable to verbalize the tangle in his head. "I don't—what do you mean?"

She studied him, the sharpening of her features making her appear faintly birdlike. Not like a sweet bird, though, he thought grumpily, like a canary or something. No, she was putting him more in mind of a raven, or a crow, maybe a hawk—something gorgeous and wild and more than a little bit dangerous.

"What I mean, Theo, is that you have so many opportunities. *So many.* More than anyone I know." When he didn't respond, she threw up her hands. "What I *mean* is…do you see yourself going into business with your father? You could, you know. He'd love that."

"Not bloody likely," Theo muttered, thinking of the nasty little altercation he'd had with Theodore Sr. last night.

Jo ignored him, plowing on. "What about school, then? You can afford to go anywhere. *Anywhere.* Doesn't that excite you, even a little bit?"

"Don't be stupid. There isn't a school in the world that would take me with my SAT scores." Theo snorted with disgust, making sure Jo didn't know that disgust was actually with himself. "College isn't an option."

"That's ridiculous." The glare she shot him was

like a laser beam, slicing right through to his core. "You can retake those any time you want."

"I can retake them, but I won't be any smarter." Shrugging as if he didn't care, he took another large swig from the scotch bottle. When he swallowed, the alcohol felt like acid in his gut, eating away at him from the inside out.

Jo threw her hands up in frustration. "You won't get any smarter if you won't freaking *try*, Theo. It's called studying. The people who get good SAT scores do it."

"Why are you on my case like this?" He couldn't handle even one more of her biting observations, because each one was like the lash of a whip, slicing away another sliver of his defenses. Soon he'd be left open, raw and bleeding, all of his insecurities out for her to see.

No one was allowed that close. Not even Jo.

"I'm on your case because I don't understand what's going through your thick skull." Her temper was up now, and so was her voice. "You have opportunities that some people only dream of, and you're throwing them all away because…what? You're just going to lounge around and drive your dad crazy forever?"

Theo stilled. "My dad treats me like shit. Since my mom died, he can't even look at me. You know that."

"You don't treat him any better!" Jo's harsh words reverberated off the walls of the room. "You might not get along, but he's still trying to help you make something of your life, and you thwart him at every turn!"

Theo had known that Jo had a temper since the second day of their acquaintance, when they'd gotten into a fight during an impromptu softball game and she'd accidentally beaned him with the bat when she'd thrown it in a rage. His anger management wasn't much better, though, and she'd just stuck a crowbar into his most tender parts and cranked it.

He fisted his hands at his sides, blood rushing to his head so fast that he felt dizzy.

"Thwart? Who actually says that in conversation?" he sneered, his words aimed to pierce her delicate skin. "I get it now. It's not that you *care*, that you're *worried* about me. It's that I have chances you don't, and it's driving you crazy!"

Jo's mouth fell open in disbelief, and her eyes were wild. "I've known you were a lazy prick with entitlement issues since the day we met, but stupid me, I thought you'd grown up a bit. But you never will, will you? You'll never figure out what you're going to do with your life, because you don't want to do anything!"

She sucked in a big breath before continuing.

"Your mom is the one who died, Theo! Not you! So why the fuck do you keep acting like you went with her?"

Theo couldn't think past the roaring in his ears. Grabbing her by the shoulders, he fought the urge to give her a shake. He'd never hit a woman in his life, and he didn't intend to start, but Josephine Marchande sorely tempted him to.

He growled, an unintelligible sound low in his throat. He had so much to say, to try to make her understand, but the words were stuck in his suddenly dry throat, choking him. He needed an outlet for the rage, the confusion, even the hurt that was storming through him, and Jo was safe. She'd always been safe.

Instead of shaking her stupid, he tugged her against him, crushing her lips against his. She shoved at his shoulder seconds before he felt a hint of the tension leave her body, her lips softening beneath his.

And then a stabbing pain as she sank those razor-sharp little teeth of hers into his lower lip.

"Motherfuck—" He reared back, clapping a hand to his injured lip. It came away bloody, but before he could utter another word, Jo followed the bite with a straight shot to his solar plexus.

His breath escaped his body in one giant cloud. Wheezing, he doubled over, sinking back into his chair, one arm around his stomach, the other pressed to his lip.

"What the actual fuck, Jo?" If she'd wanted to stop him in his tracks, she'd done it—he couldn't believe she'd hit him. He'd have been proud of her right hook if he didn't think there was a distinct possibility that he was going to vomit all over her bare feet. "What was that for?"

"Are you serious right now?" She laughed, but the sound was dry and harsh. "I can barely look at you right now, so you sure as fuck don't get to touch me."

"What?" He tried to focus on her face, but his head was spinning. "Jo. What?"

She sucked a breath in through her nose before jamming a finger right in front of his face. "You don't touch me unless I want to be touched. And you sure as hell don't try to kiss me when you're breaking my heart."

He watched, at a complete loss for words as she stepped back, putting some much-needed space between them. Crossing her arms over her chest, she started to shake, and when she looked back at him, her eyes were shiny and red, though not a single tear actually spilled.

Without another word, she turned and made her way to the door. She didn't slam it, didn't even close it—just left it hanging partway open like a wound that needed stitches but couldn't be closed.

He should call out. Go after her.

He couldn't. Wouldn't.

She'd cut him open, flayed his flesh, and he didn't know how to fix it. Didn't know if he could.

Instead, he sat motionless in his chair until the sun came up, warring with himself. He was furious with Jo, with his dad, with his dead mom, with himself. He was absolutely, utterly incapable of dealing with any of it.

When pale golden light began to filter through the paned glass of his window, he stood. Strode to his closet. Opened the small safe inside it, retrieving his passport, birth certificate and the stacks of cash that he kept just for the hell of it. Pulling a supple, chocolate-brown leather trench coat from his closet, he stuffed the retrieved items into the pockets and threw the coat over his shoulders.

By the time the sun was fully up, shining fat and high in the sky, Theo was gone.

CHAPTER FIVE

Now

THE NUMBER ONE question in my in-box? The biggest thing that readers want to know? It's how much of what I report on is something that I actually do. Yes, you filthy-minded little freaks want to know all the dirty details, and I know why...because if I've tried it, then you're not so weird if you do, too.

If you're waiting with bated breath for me to answer, you're going to have to keep on waiting. Why? Because I think that if you want to let your freak flag fly, you should find the guts to hoist it yourself. Color it with your own kinks, and don't be afraid to invite a partner...or three.

Now keep reading as I chat with Emma Muse, a cam girl with over six hundred thousand Instagram followers, about why so many women are choosing to pleasure themselves on camera for money, and why she thinks it's a viable career—not to mention fun!

Sluttily yours,

Jojo Kink

Exhaling hugely, Jo sat back in her rickety desk chair. Lacing her fingers together, she twisted them outward, extending her arms and arching her back in a giant stretch. She'd only been working on this post for a couple of hours, but she'd been so into it that she hadn't been paying attention to her posture, and as the minutes had ticked by, she hunched up tighter with every word that she typed.

Scrolling back up, she reread the introduction and couldn't quite hold back her grin. The post was good, and she wasn't one for false modesty, especially when she was alone in her bedroom with no one to see her crow over it.

She knew that she could write. She'd been doing it steadily for pay for years, which was a pretty good sign that she wasn't a complete hack. But after a seemingly endless period of churning out things that other people wanted, writing about something that interested *her* felt like she'd grown a pair of giant, feathery wings.

Reading the post through one more time, she

made a few small edits before copying the text to her blog site, Jojo Kink. As it uploaded, she opened her blog's email in-box, scanning through the messages and the alerts of comments on her blog, which ranged from rapturous praise to things like *Die in hell, skank.*

Skank. Ha. If only they knew.

Checking the box that would allow her to delete everything with one click, she emptied her in-box, then blinked at the single message that slid in right after. Marked urgent, it carried the subject Job Opportunity.

"Oh, I just bet." She rolled her eyes and almost deleted this one, too. She received "job offers" every week, and most of them were invitations to meet up with very gracious gentlemen who were interested in letting her blow them. She mostly ignored them, but once in a while she skimmed over one of these fascinating missives and her temper—her Achilles' heel—would get the better of her. It never failed to amaze her how many men couldn't understand that no woman on this earth wanted an unsolicited dick pic. Actually, most didn't want a dick pic, period, but pointing that out usually just resulted in a flurry of them.

She was in the mood to argue, though, so she opened the email, bracing herself for a veiny close-up. She was surprised that, instead of an image of throbbing male genitalia, the email contained an actual message, complete with a website link.

To Ms. Kink,
My name is John Brooke; I'm a freelance business mentor currently working with the dating app Crossing Lines. We at Crossing Lines would like to meet with you to discuss the possibility of writing some blog posts for our site. We love your voice and think that you are just what we need to appeal to the female demographic.

We would love to hear back from you, at your earliest convenience.
Sincerely,
John Brooke and the Crossing Lines team

"Say what?" Jo sat up straight as hummingbirds of excitement flocked through her veins. Clicking on the site link, she found herself staring at a logo that she actually knew. Crossing Lines had been everywhere lately—she was pretty sure her youngest sister, Amy, actually had a profile on it. Their advertising was slick—they clearly had a lot of money behind them.

And they wanted *her*? How the hell had they found her blog, anyway? Her blog had decent traffic, but she was a medium-size fish in a gigantic pond.

"Who the hell cares?" She wasn't an idiot. This was huge. Palms suddenly slick with sweat, she scrambled to reply. John Brooke, whoever he was, must have still been in his email, because he came back again almost instantly, asking her if she had time to meet the next morning. When she agreed, he gave her an address close to the financial district in downtown Boston and told her they looked forward to meeting with her. She didn't have a clue who else was included in the *they*, but the thrill fizzing through her wouldn't let her care.

Shoving back from her desk, she closed her eyes and savored the moment. She could hear music coming from Beth's room, some kind of weird electro-pop that she normally couldn't stand, but right now it was perfect, and she did a little walk-dance of joy around her cramped room to the beat.

She'd been writing for years. *Years.* She'd started with the local paper, and her secret dream had been to go to journalism school. When her sister Beth had gotten sick, though, and the family had started to drown in debt, she switched tracks. Words were her skill set, so she searched out the best way to make quick cash from them. Her ghostwriting gigs—writing stories to spec for other people—had been what allowed them to stay in their grand old historic home, but she'd always felt like she lost a bit of herself when she signed away the rights to something that had come from within her.

Now Beth had hooked up with Ford, and while at first Jo had been certain he'd been using her little sister as a stroll through a kinky park, she now had to admit that he'd saved their asses, for no reason other than his love for Beth. His idea to build a small boutique hotel on part of their massive property had led to a source of viable income for their family, which meant that Jo could finally, finally, write whatever the hell she wanted.

She'd been surprised at how much she'd enjoyed ghostwriting erotic stories, and that was what had led to the idea for Jojo Kink. Researching and interviewing people about freaky sexual topics threw in that love of journalism and, it turned out, was just *fun*.

But writing for a big company didn't mean that she couldn't still blog—at least she hoped it didn't. And writing for a big company meant money. She brought in a bit through ads on her site, but a regular paycheck…

She couldn't even imagine what she'd do with that. She'd never had one.

Thinking of the hotel reminded her that Ford had organized a sneak-peek open house for

Marchande Boutique for that evening…and it was in just over an hour.

"Shit." Breathing a bit heavily from her dancing, she looked around the room, a bit lost.

Dressing up? She hated it.

Socializing with human beings who weren't part of her social circle? She hated it even more. There was a reason that she chose to make a living from behind a computer screen.

If she tried to stay home, though, her sisters would drag her bodily from her room, and experience had taught her that Amy went for the hair, the bitch. Sighing as though the world was ending, which the stone in her gut told her it was, she shuffled across her room to her tiny closet.

She hoped that Ford would be okay with ripped jeans and a T-shirt, because that was all that she owned.

"Aah!" Opening her closet, she ducked when something flew through the air. Batting at her head as though something might be nestled in her hair, she exhaled on a laugh when she realized that the flying object had been something swooshing on a hanger—a dress. No wonder she hadn't expected it.

A dress. *What the hell?*

Scowling, she unhooked the hanger from her closet door. A note fluttered to the floor as she did.

Jo,
No, you can't wear jeans to the open house. Wear this instead.
Meg
(PS: Matching shoes are under your bed.)

"Shit." Jo groaned out loud. She did not wear dresses. In fact, she mostly wore men's clothing. She was used to people wondering if she was a lesbian—the way she dressed, the way she carried herself, the lack of any long-term relationship seemed to invite the question. She'd even wondered herself for a while if the lack of sexual interest she'd had in men since Theo was because she wasn't attracted to them as a species.

One female fling later and she'd discovered that that wasn't right, either. She was who she was—not a lesbian, not a boy trapped in a girl body. She was just Jo, and she was far happier when she dressed how she wanted, behaved how she wanted, dated—or didn't—who she wanted.

She thought her sisters understood that, and she felt her infamous temper rise as she examined the offensive garment.

The fabric was actually quite nice—some kind of heavy, silky stuff, none of that wispy, flirty fabric that always made her feel like she was half naked. The top part had a halter neck, which she liked, and though the back dipped lower than she was comfortable with, she actually quite liked the fact that the tattoo on her back—a stunning phoenix inked by her sister Amy—would be shown off.

That left the skirt part, which she didn't think she could get past—except that when she examined it, it wasn't a skirt at all, but rather shorts. Meg had gotten her what she supposed would be called a romper, and the relief was like chugging icy lemonade on a scorching-hot day.

A quick glance under the bed showed that her older sister had had enough sense not to get her high heels, either—the shoes Meg had chosen were flat, gladiator-type sandals, with straps that wound up her calves. She could deal with that.

After slithering into the simple garment and struggling with but ultimately conquering the shoes, she looked in the mirror and thought that maybe, this time, Meg had known what she was talking about. Jo didn't feel like she was playing dress-up, she was fairly comfortable and she wasn't wearing jeans—everybody won.

Flicking a glance at the time on her phone, she saw that she only had five minutes to get across the grounds to the hotel. With any luck, her sisters had already left, and no one would try to attack her with lipstick or a hair straightener.

"Slayyyyy." Giving one last look in the mirror,

she tried out the word that Amy used whenever she was trying to tell someone that they were looking hot. She placed a hand on her hip and tried out a seductive, come-hither expression before bursting out laughing.

Ironic for someone with a blog called Jojo Kink, she thought as she clattered down the stairs and out the front door, that its owner wasn't the least bit, and had never been, sexy.

CHAPTER SIX

"IT'S JUST LIP GLOSS," Meg insisted as she aimed the wand from a glossy tube of red goop at Jo's face.

"I don't want it!" Ducking, Jo tried to avoid the lip gloss, and Meg missed, swabbing Jo's cheek instead.

"Now look what you did," Meg sighed as Jo scowled. Leaning in, she rubbed at the red stuff on Jo's cheek and then, lightning quick, swabbed a matching stripe on the other cheek. "There. It'll work as blush. Now you at least look like you've seen the sun sometime in the last decade."

"For fuck's sake, Meg." Holding up her hands to fend off another attack, Jo took a giant step back, putting space between herself and her fashion-loving older sister. "I'm wearing the outfit. Isn't that enough?"

"The blush looks good," Meg continued as if

she hadn't heard Jo speak, "but you'd look even better if you'd just let me comb your hair."

"Don't touch it," Jo warned, backing up yet again. She'd kept her formerly long, chestnut waves in a sleek bob since she'd hit her twenties, the only reason being that, in her opinion, she never needed to do anything to it—it always looked the same. "Seriously, Meg. The energy it takes me to fend you off is the energy I should be using to smile at strangers without baring my teeth."

"Fine," her sister huffed, turning her attention to her own reflection. As usual, she looked like an Instagram post—something Jo knew she could never achieve, even if the thought of spending several hours on her hair and makeup didn't make her want to stab herself in the eye.

"You look good enough for both of us," Jo insisted, herding her sister to the door of the funky little bathroom in the lobby of the hotel. There was a fireplace and a lounge chair inside the room, which puzzled her—why would anyone want to hang out in the bathroom?—but she supposed that Ford knew what he was doing. Actually, maybe she'd sit in that chair and hide here for the rest of the evening…

Before the door closed behind Meg, though, she turned and grabbed Jo's hand, tugging her back into the lobby. Snagging a fresh glass of sparkling wine from a passing waiter in what looked like a vintage tux, she pressed it into Jo's hand, then gestured around the room.

"Chug that, then go mingle," she ordered, straightening her sequined, spaghetti-strapped sheath. "Ford said we had to. You don't want to disappoint Beth."

Damn it. Meg knew that Beth was Jo's kryptonite—the sister she'd always been closest to, the sister she still was terrified of losing if her illness came back.

Yeah, she'd do anything for Beth—even mingle.

Pasting what she suspected was a terrifying smile on her face, she shuffled a few awkward steps farther into the room. Chugging down her sparkling wine so fast that it burned, she grabbed a second glass as a prop while she stood awkwardly, shifting her weight from foot to foot.

"You look like you could use some company." Jo looked up as a man sidled up next to her. He smiled, revealing toothpaste-commercial teeth, and she cocked her head, taking him in.

He was good-looking, she supposed. Objectively, he was tall and well built, with the kind of body that wore a suit well. His features were distinct, with high cheekbones and a strong jaw. He even had a dimple in his chin.

"Are you all right?" His blinding smile faltered,

and she realized that she'd left the silence run on too long as she studied him. She had a bad habit of doing this, losing track of the conversation as she scrutinized a potential partner, wondering what the hell was wrong with her when she inevitably wasn't interested.

Again.

"I'm fine, thank you." She smiled politely, sipping at her wine. "Why are you here?"

Her potential suitor blinked, and Jo winced. Man, she sucked at small talk. "What I mean is, what brings you to this event?" There. That sounded fancy enough.

"I'm one of Ford's friends from back home." He sipped his own wine, looking at her over the edge. "I'm barking up the wrong tree here, aren't I?"

"Pardon?" Jo blinked, even as his meaning flooded through her. She could have recited his next words along with him.

"You're not interested." He smiled at her, though he seemed slightly puzzled by her reaction. At least he hadn't said *You're not interested in men*, which was what she'd been expecting.

"Sorry." She shook her head and offered what she hoped was a winsome smile. "Better luck elsewhere."

He was clearly startled by her response, but then she was gone, scurrying across the lobby floor as fast as she could in her slightly slippery shoes. She gulped at her wine, leaving the empty glass on a table as she headed unerringly for the wide, stone-tiled stairs, desperate to get away.

She wasn't good with words in person. She was socially awkward to the extreme. And Dimples had picked up on her one insecurity, the one thing that she just couldn't figure out about herself—no, she wasn't interested. Not in him, not in any man. Hell, not in any woman, either.

She hadn't been since Theo. She'd tried, and sometimes she managed a mild affection, but attraction? Sexual arousal?

Forget it. That was why she'd fallen in love with her blog—it was an outlet, a place for her to explore her sexuality in a place where her own biology had failed her.

She could rage against it, she supposed, as she reached the upper floor and sighed with relief at the sudden muting of the party noise, the voices. But what was the point?

Footsteps sounded on the staircase behind her, along with the hushed murmur of voices. Shit. Her encounter with Dimples had drained her—she just couldn't handle interacting with even one more person.

Desperate, she tried the handle of the closest

door. It opened, and she wasn't going to question it. She hurriedly ducked inside.

The heavy door swung shut behind her, enclosing her in a dim, quiet space. She ran a hand over the wall, searching for the light switch, then decided to leave the room in the dark. The lack of stimulus after the sensory assault of the party was soothing.

She'd recharge here then go downstairs and force herself to mingle for twenty more minutes—long enough to say that she'd given it a go.

Then she'd go home, put on her jeans and tank top and return to the cocoon of blissful aloneness.

The doorknob turned. A feminine giggle shattered the womblike tranquility, followed by a deeper voice that was undeniably male.

She had no idea why she ducked into the closet—maybe just the urge to not have to interact with even one more person. She stood in the small space, behind the half-opened door, fisting sweaty palms as the people entered the room, letting the heavy door fall closed behind them with what sounded like an ominous click.

"How much have you had to drink?" The man's voice made her straighten, like she was in school and her knuckles had been slapped with a ruler.

"Not so much that I don't know what I'm doing." The woman giggled, a bubbly, breathless sound.

Jo squinted across the room. It was dark in the room, more shadows than light, but she could see shapes, outlines.

She could certainly hear, and knew that the metallic rasp couldn't be anything but the lowering of a zipper.

"This wasn't what I had in mind when I invited you to this party as my date," the man said, his voice wry. The woman shushed him. Jo's eyes were gradually adjusting to the dark, and she watched the woman drop to her knees in front of the door the man was leaning against.

The woman inhaled sharply, and the man exhaled slowly, a circular dance. Jo fought to hold her own breath, lest she give herself away.

Why, oh why, had she ducked into the closet? It was past the point where she could announce her presence. *Oh, pardon me, I'll just look the other way if you don't mind letting me through.*

"Chill out," the woman said, voice exasperated. "This doesn't mean anything, okay? I'm your assistant, and I'm supposed to make your life easier. I don't know why you're all keyed up tonight, but let me take the edge off. It's nothing we haven't done before."

The man said nothing, did nothing for a long moment. Then a low rumble of pleasure escaped his throat, followed by the wet sound of mouth on skin, sounds that screamed sex.

Close your eyes, Jo. Close them now.

A rustle of movement, then a groan as the man tangled his hands in the woman's hair. That groan should have been a sound of surrender, the man acquiescing to the woman's desire to please him, but somehow he still sounded like he was the one in control.

Jo shifted in her hiding place as something dark and wild tangled in her belly. She found herself rubbing her thighs together against the sudden ache. It took her brain a few moments to catch up.

Was she actually *aroused* by this? By hiding in the closet, watching a woman she didn't know suck on a strange man's cock? How could that be, when nothing had turned her crank in the years since Theo had left—absolutely nothing?

She swallowed, hard, pressing her forehead to the cool plaster of the wall. Watching this when they didn't know she was here was so, so wrong. But this was the first hint of arousal she'd felt in so long—she knew she wasn't going anywhere.

Taking another quiet breath, she focused in. The woman's mouth made obscene sucking noises as she worked on the man, but she wasn't what held Jo's attention, though she supposed that the woman's inherent enjoyment in the action of pleasuring the stranger was erotic. No, it was him, something about the man. About the way he looked downward, attention focused on the point of contact. And something else about him—the outline of an imposing body, the unapologetic way he held himself, as if he deserved to be serviced.

Like he was doing the woman a favor by letting her place her mouth on his cock. He almost seemed impatient.

How strange.

Jo watched, now entranced, as the woman seemed to redouble her efforts. The sounds she was making said that servicing the man was pleasurable for her as well. How could that be?

Her attention was caught on him as he sucked in a breath that sounded pained, his focus sharpening. Sliding his hands through her hair, he caught the woman's face in his palms. The thin, inky darkness seemed to thicken, to throb along with the pulse between Jo's legs.

"Pull off," he growled, and the woman did with a sound so wet it was obscene. She hummed, low and satisfied, like she'd just indulged in some delicious treat, and a jolt of hunger struck Jo.

She sighed, just the quietest of sounds, but it was enough to be heard. The man's head snapped up, his head orienting right in Jo's direction, even as he exhaled harshly, thrusting into the woman's cupped hands.

Oh shit. Had he heard her? Could he see her? Did he know she was there? Spell broken, Jo pulled back farther into the closet. A single bead of icy sweat rolled down her spine.

"See? I told you you'd feel better," the woman purred, satisfaction thick in her voice. This puzzled Jo as well.

The man had come. The woman had not. Why, then, did the woman seem so pleased?

The man simply grunted. The unfamiliar slickness between Jo's thighs and the buzzing in her head, the flush of her skin begged her to step from the closet, to get one more look at the shadowy figure who'd brought her senses to life. That, though, would be pure insanity, so she forced herself to stay crouched in her hiding place, her pulse thrumming through her veins.

She listened, trying to slow her breath, as the man zipped himself up. Listened as the pair exited the room, the door closing heavily behind them, and then listened to the silence left in the room as she absorbed the fact that she was alone.

"Jesus." Cautiously, Jo pushed off the wall, stepping softly onto the thick, luxe carpeting of the hotel room. Part of her thought—hoped?—wildly that the man might still be here. He was gone, though—of course he was gone. She was left alone with the vague sense that it had all been a very dirty dream.

And, of course, that suddenly pressing need to fill the aching space between her legs. That was new. Actually, it was old—so old it was new again.

Throwing her head back, she huffed out a laugh at her own expense. She was a disaster.

Against her hip, her phone buzzed. Since the romper had no pockets and no back, the only place she'd been able to tuck her phone was under the elastic waist of her panties. She pulled it out, frowning when she saw a message from Beth.

Ford says he's sorry. He didn't know.

Well, that was clear as mud. Shrugging it off, Jo replaced her phone, took a cleansing breath and left the room. She held her breath as she walked down the empty, elegant hall, still half expecting to see the couple who had just awakened her slumbering carnal appetite.

She didn't see them. Of course she didn't, and even if she had, how would she have known?

What is wrong with me?

Descending the ornate staircase, Jo made a beeline for the bar. She both needed and, she thought, deserved a drink—something a little stronger than the cheerful glasses of sparkling wine that were still being circled.

Standing on her toes, she leaned against the polished dark wood of the lobby bar, trying to catch the bartender's attention. The gray-haired, heavily mustached server didn't even spare her a glance.

Meg was way better at this. Then again, Jo thought as she looked down at her rather flat chest, Meg had a little more to work with.

"Scotch on the rocks with a twist." The voice came from behind her. Jo turned as irritation snaked over her skin—she was here first, and also, that was her drink.

Slapping a palm down on the counter, she angled her chin up as she pivoted on her fancy sandals. "Back of the line, buddy."

"I've been lots of things to you, Jo, but *buddy* was never one of them."

Jo whipped her head the rest of the way around so quickly that she felt a pinch in her neck. A roaring sound filled her ears as she found herself staring at a wide, hard chest, then up to broad shoulders. Tequila-gold skin started at the neck, covering chiseled features that were set off with night-black hair and eyes just as dark.

"Hi, Jo."

Her mouth fell open. She must have looked like she'd gone simple, staring up at him like she'd never seen a man before. Though it was true enough that she hadn't seen this particular man for quite some time—years, in fact.

"Theo," she managed, her tongue thick and cottony in her mouth. She'd always known he would come back, had known it right down to the marrow of her bones. And yet of all the ways she'd imagined that the reentry of Theo Lawrence into her life would go—and she'd dreamed up plenty—she'd never expected that she'd actually manage to smile and be charming. To hide her innate social awkwardness and show only what she wanted of herself, the way so many women seemed able to do.

After all, this was the man who'd been like a part of her family. Who'd spent holidays with her family, who'd been her first kiss, her first love.

Her first experience with the kind of pain that could tear a person in two.

Drawing on every ounce of strength she had inside her, she turned back to the bar. She couldn't deal with this without some liquid courage.

When Theo snagged the drink from the bartender's hand, she felt anger whip through her. When he handed her the heavy tumbler, ice clinking merrily against the glass walls, the anger evaporated into a dense cloud of confusion.

"Scotch on the rocks with a twist, right?" He studied her with those coal-dark eyes, the ones that still haunted her dreams. "You never could stomach the hard stuff without a little ice."

The rage winked back to life. "Do you really think that remembering what I drink will make up for ditching out on life?"

His smile dimmed, and Jo cursed internally. Damn it. *Damn it.* After that, how could she smile and pretend that she was doing just fine?

"So that's how it's going to be." He smiled at her, but the press of his lips was tight. Still, she was distracted by it—the way that full, beautiful mouth moved. She'd always thought of his mouth as his Latin-lover lips, inherited as they'd been from his gorgeous Latina mother.

Well, she could look, but she was no longer interested in his lips, gorgeous or otherwise. Since she'd already blown the cool card, this was where she should scream. She should rage, pummel his chest with her fists. Flood the lobby of the hotel with angry tears.

At eighteen, she would have. She still had a temper, but she was also no longer that young—or that innocent. It took enormous effort to reseal the bottle that contained everything she felt and had felt for Theo Lawrence, but she did it, shoving the cork back in until she could get somewhere alone, a safe place for that bottle to explode.

Instead, she took a deep swallow of the drink

he'd pressed into her hand, even though she resented that he'd been the one to procure it. Then she finally managed that civil smile, though it felt like pushing through a thick wall of cement.

"You look well, Theo." There, that was normal. No hint of weirdness there. "What brings you back to Boston?"

For just the merest blink of an eye, she thought she saw something like confusion flicker through his stare. Then it was gone, and she was sure that she'd imagined it, because he turned the charm back on—and he still had plenty—showing her a flash of teeth against that delicious skin.

"Business." He didn't elaborate; she didn't ask. "And you're still writing."

It wasn't a question, and she resented the hell out of what he hadn't said with that, with the drink. "You don't know me anymore, Theo. Don't presume that you do."

"I suppose that's true." She didn't miss the hint of danger that snaked its way into his voice—he never had enjoyed being told that he was wrong. "For instance, I never would have pictured you as a voyeur."

Time crashed to a standstill. Jo's fingers, suddenly sweaty, slipped on her drink, which would have crashed to the ground if Theo hadn't caught it, setting it back down on the bar.

"What did you say?" she finally gasped, her pulse stuttering before starting to throb double time. Her mouth was dry—she wanted her drink but didn't trust herself to pick it up.

"I think you heard me," he replied mildly, gesturing to the bartender, who brought him a glass of something that looked like club soda. In some dim recesses of her brain, Jo noted that it was odd to see him drink something nonalcoholic in a party setting, but she couldn't give the matter more than a passing thought.

"I heard you," she managed, narrowing her eyes. She tucked a strand of her loose hair behind her ear for something to do with her hands, and when his stare tracked her movement, it caused conflicting sensations to reverberate off one another inside her. "Explain."

"I know you were just in that room upstairs." The way he was looking at her was like a dare. He knew—there was no sense in denying it. He knew she'd just watched him get sucked off.

Of course, she hadn't known it was him. Though really, it seemed like some part of her had. Hadn't he always been the only person in existence able to arouse her? Just her fucking luck.

"I was already in the room when you and your little friend decided to have a private party," she replied tartly. Damn it, now she sounded like a jealous shrew when in fact she felt nothing of the sort. No, when she thought of what she'd seen, she got that sticky, sweet sensation between her thighs again—and knowing it was Theo was a new but not entirely unwelcome element. "I couldn't exactly go anywhere while your dick was in her mouth."

"I suppose not," he replied thoughtfully, looking at her over the rim of his glass. To avoid that stare, Jo looked up, down and around, but all she managed to do was note that he still wore a suit better than any man she'd ever met—and that even to her unskilled eye, the suit looked like it cost more than she made in a month. "But you didn't have to watch, either."

Jo cleared her throat. What the hell was she supposed to say to that? It was one hundred percent the truth. She'd gouge her eyeballs out with one of those little plastic cocktail swords, though, before she admitted to him what watching had done to her—for her.

"How did you know it was me?" This seemed safe enough.

His grin was both wry and the tiniest bit wolfish. Her pulse responded, even as her brain scolded it. "You still smell like cinnamon."

She'd never cared about makeup, but she'd always like to smell good, and she always had a little bottle of cinnamon essential oil on the go, ever since she was thirteen. That he remembered should maybe have been touching, but instead it brought out her caged fury yet again.

"I'm surprised you noticed it. You were a little busy." Her words were too loud, too sharp—social awkwardness was back in the room. But where lots of people would have recoiled, starting to look at her like she was a bit odd, Theo didn't even seem to notice.

Nor did he apologize, though Jo certainly didn't expect him to—not for this. But neither did she expect what he said next.

"Then I suppose my next question should be, did you like it?"

Jo barely held back a strangled sigh. He was deliberately pushing her buttons, but for the life of her, she couldn't understand why. Surely he didn't think they were just going to pick up where they'd left off? Theo was a lot of things, but he'd never been crazy.

She didn't answer. He let the silence between them stretch and thicken.

"Everything all right here?" Like a wave of fresh spring air, Beth appeared at Jo's elbow. Gratefully, Jo tore her focus away from her ex to pay attention to her sister.

Clad in a slinky little red dress, Beth looked

like she'd never been sick a day in her life. The spaghetti straps and short hemline left her many tattoos on full display. The purple streaks in her dark hair should have clashed with the deep crimson of her dress, but instead they made her look effortlessly cool.

On her other side, her fiancé, Ford Lassiter, was dressed in a suit that was probably even more expensive than Theo's. He looked like he'd stepped out of an issue of some men's business magazine. He definitely didn't look like the kind of man who would be enamored of a woman who was a walking advertisement for a tattoo parlor—namely, her sister's tattoo parlor—and yet somehow they worked.

"Theo!" Placing her hand on Jo's elbow, Beth offered up a polite smile. "It's been forever. What brings you back to Boston?"

"Business." Theo offered the same one-word explanation he'd given Jo. The smile he offered Beth was genuine, however, with none of the layers of undertones that his voice had when he spoke to Jo.

"I haven't seen you since that tournament...was it at Palm Springs? Two years ago. What are you into now?" Ford, too, seemed friendly as he offered Theo his hand, but the other man had been hanging around the Marchandes for long enough now that Jo caught the hint of stiffness in his voice.

"It's funny that you didn't mention you knew my girl's family when you accepted this invite."

"I didn't put two and two together." Theo smiled smoothly, but Jo's bullshit alarm screamed. He was lying through his teeth—but why? "I never would have imagined the girls opening a hotel on their property."

"The girls, huh?" Ford rocked back on his heels. "You must go way back."

Jo exchanged a glance with Beth as the two men puffed up like peacocks, each trying to posture their way to dominance.

"I've known the Marchandes for a long time," Theo started, and Jo had suddenly had enough of the bullshit. Holding up her hands, she waved them in the air to stop the argument in its tracks.

"Let's just cool it before we get to the point where you guys hose each other down with testosterone, okay?" Both men grunted, and Jo turned her attention to Ford. "Thanks for defending our honor and all that, big bro, but if you don't like the dude, don't invite him."

"I liked him just fine before I knew what he'd done to you," Ford muttered, "but I'd like him better back on one of the golf courses in LA, where I could go after him with a nine iron."

Beth turned away, her shoulders shaking as she tried to hold in her laugh. Her laugh died as Ford dipped his head to whisper in her ear. Jo watched as her younger sister flushed from head to toe, her posture changing just slightly as she took in whatever dirty thing Ford had just said to her.

"I might be wrong, but I think they've forgotten about us," Jo said wryly as Ford caught her sister's elbow and led her from the lobby. She felt the pang of envy reverberate around her rib cage.

She was happy for Beth. She was. But was it too much to ask that she have someone who made her feel like that, too?

"Never would have thought that sweet little Beth would hook up with Ford Lassiter." Theo took another sip of his club soda, calling Jo's attention back to him. She watched as he swallowed, cursing inwardly when she caught herself watching the lines of his throat.

Couldn't he have gone soft under that suit? Did he still have to look so damn *physical*?

"What's that supposed to mean?" Jo felt the flare of temper as a knee-jerk reaction. "You don't think one of the Marchande girls is good enough for a hotel tycoon?"

"Jo." The exasperation he managed to inflect that single syllable with was a talent of his. "I was actually referring to the fact that, according to rumor, he's a kinky fucking bastard."

"What rumors? He said you were golf buddies."

Jo glowered up at Theo. Man, he'd been gone for so long, and yet within seconds he'd managed to tap right back into that special talent he had for getting under her skin.

It was during those times, when he would put his mouth all over her body except the place she most wanted it, that made her hate the fact that he made her wait.

"Golf buddies," Theo agreed, a slight smirk curling the corners of his lips as he watched her. Heat rose into her cheeks—he knew. Damn it, he knew where her mind had gone. "And we also had some mutual friends. Friends who were into things that would shock you."

Jo's mouth went dry as Theo looked her over, top to bottom and up again. His eyes glinted with mischief, and also something darker.

"Shock me more than being trapped in a room watching you get blown by some other woman?" She found her voice and used it as a weapon. She no longer cared if she sounded jealous—she wanted an excuse to leave, leave this conversation and leave Theo, because the longer she stood here with him, the more she started to want things that she could no longer have—at least not if she was smart.

Theo. The dark. The rasp of a zipper, the wet sound of lips on skin. Without warning, Jo felt moisture surge between her legs, just from the memory.

She wasn't jealous at all. Rather, being a voyeur on that little scene had awoken something she'd thought she'd never feel again.

Theo didn't reply—he just kept on watching her with those dark eyes. And she absolutely did not have to fight back the urge to rise to her toes and trace her tongue over the golden line of his jaw.

"Fun as this has been, I'm going home." Setting her now empty glass down on the bar, she wiped her palms over her thighs to hide the fact that they were trembling. "Good night."

The way that Theo had been acting, the way he'd been flirting—for that was what it had been—Jo was surprised that he remained silent as she walked away, though she knew, just knew, that he watched her until she was out of sight. It wasn't until she was back in her own room, her back pressed flat against the door she'd just closed, that she acknowledged that she was disappointed that he'd let her just go.

"No way, Jo. Not happening." She shed her romper and the sandals as quickly as if they'd burst into flame. Pulling on white cotton panties and a worn Marilyn Manson concert tee, she exhaled with relief, as though in taking off the party clothes, she'd shed the Jo who was tempted by Theo Lawrence.

It was still there—that thing between them, that indescribable connection. Even in the dark, even not knowing who he was, he'd managed to turn her on.

"Don't be stupid," she muttered to herself as she climbed into her bed, crawling beneath the covers.

The only man who made her crave was also the man who had broken her heart. What kind of person would she be if she took him back? Not that he'd asked. Not that she would.

But as she lay there in the shadows of nighttime, listening to her sisters return from the open house, she couldn't stop shifting back and forth in her bed. If she got up and looked out the window, she could see the Lawrence house. Was he staying there? Probably not, but the thought of him being so close after so many years made her pulse race.

So she stayed in bed, but when she finally fell into a fitful sleep, she was chased by images of dark eyes, golden skin and wicked hands that woke her up from the sleep she'd been in since he'd left.

CHAPTER SEVEN

LET'S TALK ABOUT VOYEURISM. If you're reading this blog, chances are you're a dirty birdie and you already know what it is, but for those of you who don't, it's getting hot and bothered watching someone else involved in illicit activities. Now, while this sounds like it could be a sexy good time, if you take it too far, it ventures into crime territory, so don't expect to peep into your sexy neighbor's bedroom window without consequences. But say you're at a party and you're grabbing some alone time. A couple with oral sex on their mind stumbles upon your hidey-hole, and before you can make your presence known, she's giving him a happy ending and you've been whisked along for the ride. Is this awkward, or is it hot? Is it hotter if they discover you're there?

Food for slutty thought,

Jojo Kink

* * *

The offices for Crossing Lines took up the entire third floor of a tall office building just outside the financial district in downtown Boston. The building was sleek, the smell of latex paint still evident as Jo closed herself in the shiny silver elevator that was so eerily silent she double-checked to make sure she was actually moving.

The woman at the front desk was the type who intimidated lesser specimens without having to lift a finger. She barely even looked up as Jo crossed the plush carpeting to the massive chrome desk, clearing her throat when she arrived.

"Can I help you?" When the woman finally did look up, she flicked a glance over Jo, and though there was no visible change in her expression, Jo felt her distaste flavoring the air. Jo knew what she saw and couldn't help but squirm a bit under the assessing stare.

She'd never gone on a job interview. The position at the paper so very many years ago had been offered to her over the phone based on her work on her high school paper. When she ghosted stories for other writers, they didn't care what she looked like or how she dressed. She deliberately left images of herself off her blog.

That left today. She hadn't had time to go shopping for something more appropriate and didn't know what that was at any rate, so she'd settled on a pair of black jeans that were free of rips and tears, a black sweater from the men's department, and a clean pair of sneakers. Face-to-face with this woman, whose hair was glossy and highlighted, and who wore a white blouse without a single wrinkle, Jo knew that she'd missed the mark, but there was nothing she could do about it now.

"I have a meeting with John Brooke," she stated, drawing herself to her full, if insignificant, height, trying to look like what she was wearing was just fine. "At ten o'clock."

"I'll take you to his office." When the woman stood up, Jo noted that she was also wearing heels that added at least three inches to her height, and that her skirt came to midcalf, hugging her legs like a second skin. How did she walk?

The woman, who hadn't introduced herself, seemed equally interested in Jo, taking a long moment to look her over, her expression faintly puzzled. Maybe, Jo thought, she was wondering how security downstairs had let someone with such little fashion sense into the building.

Finally, the other woman turned and walked down the hall, gesturing for Jo to follow. Jo watched the sleek length of the woman's ponytail, thinking of the woman last night, savoring the resultant heat.

Not now, Jo!

The woman paused outside a glass door. It was cracked open, but she knocked on it smartly. A voice called out for them to enter. The woman didn't follow Jo in, just studied her intently again as she gestured her in, and Jo felt her stomach slowly roll with nerves.

"Miss Marchande?" The man who stood up from behind the desk was tall, well over six feet, and absolutely gorgeous. Light brown skin set off pale green eyes, and the short buzz of his black hair showed off the strong lines of his face. Dressed in a well-cut suit, he was, quite simply, hot. "I'm John Brooke."

His smile was friendly enough that some of Jo's nerves eased. He didn't make her feel out of place like Miss Tight Skirt had, and when he offered a large palm for her to shake, she felt some of her confidence return.

"Nice to meet you." She winced a bit as the words came out just a bit too loud, but he didn't seem to notice. Gesturing for her to sit, he checked the expensive-looking watch on his wrist. "The owner will be here momentarily. While we wait, would you like coffee? Water, tea? I can have Ava get you whatever you'd like."

Assuming that Ava was the girl at the front desk, Jo was tempted to ask for something as a petty revenge for the scrutiny. She knew she wouldn't be able to swallow a thing, though, since the news that another person would be joining them had ratcheted her anxiety back up again.

"I'm fine." Doing her best to smile like a normal human, Jo took a second look at John Brooke. He'd said in his email that he was some kind of adviser to the company, which made her think of endless travel, city to city, clandestine encounters in airport bathrooms. He looked the part—sleek and sexy.

He did nothing for her, roused nothing more than a mild appreciation for a fine-looking man.

"Sorry I'm late."

No. Oh, hell no.

Jo hadn't recognized Theo's voice last night because she hadn't heard it in so very long. Now, with it fresh in her mind, she was on her feet before he'd even cleared the doorway, his voice triggering an instant surge of adrenaline.

"Miss Marchande." He cast her a polite smile, almost as if they were truly meeting for the first time—almost. There was a glint in his eye that told her he was looking forward to seeing how this played out.

It pissed her off.

"What the hell, Theo?" Still standing, she planted her hands on her hips and stood up straight. "What are you doing?"

"Do you know each other?" John stood as well, furrowing his brow in Theo's direction. "I thought Miss Marchande was the writer of that blog you showed me."

"She is the writer of that blog," Theo replied, fully entering the room. Crossing the room, he propped a hip on the massive desk, looking like he truly didn't give a fuck about the tension brewing.

He'd never given much of a fuck about anything…anything except her. She couldn't make out what his game was here, though, and she didn't like being a pawn in it.

"Explain yourself," she demanded crisply. He gestured for her to sit, but she remained standing, refusing to do anything he told her to.

"I'm going to go," John announced, clapping his hands together as he cast Theo a stern look. "Please stop by my office after…whatever this is."

Theo acknowledged the other man with a jerk of his chin, and then John was gone. He closed the door behind him, leaving Jo alone with Theo.

Her pulse tripped, then started to beat double time.

"What are you doing, Theo?" Her voice trembled, and she told herself that it was with anger. "You had a chance to talk to me last night. You didn't have to drag me all the way here with a made-up story."

"Let me be quite clear." Theo's voice was suddenly sharp, commanding in a way that she'd never heard before. It caught her attention, and she eyed him sharply. He still lounged against the desk, but he'd straightened.

Rather than the lazy, hedonistic Theo she was acquainted with, this man looked in control. She had no idea what to make of it.

"There was no false story. I own Crossing Lines. I am looking for a unique voice to draw in new users. The offer of a job is real." His expression darkened, and he didn't hide the way his gaze swept over her small frame. "But at the same time that John and I came up with that idea, I was looking into what my ex-girlfriend was up to, since I was coming back to Boston. Imagine my surprise when I discovered that the sweet girl I'd left was the writer of a blog exploring all things kinky."

"I've never been a sweet girl." Jo made air quotes around the last two words with her fingers. "And you didn't discover that I was the writer of my blog with a simple internet search. I've made sure of that."

The corners of his lips twisted in a smile. "Touché. I may have had one of my programmers dig a little. But your secret is safe with me."

"Why offer me the job, Theo?" Jo's voice was quiet. "There are a million writers out there who could write what you want. This has messy written all over it."

He paused.

"I owe you," he finally said, tapping a finger on the desk. "Though of course, if you weren't qualified, this wouldn't even be an issue."

"You *owe* me?" Jo heard her voice echo off the high ceiling and realized she was shouting but didn't care. "Fuck that noise, Theo. You thought you'd come throw a job at your fancy new company at your hard-up ex and all would be forgiven? I don't need your charity. I don't need *you.*"

That was it—she was done. Her fury at his actions overrode the very real disappointment that the job wouldn't work as she stormed toward the door.

When Theo grabbed her arm, she slapped at it with angry hands. "Stop manhandling me!"

"Then stop acting like an ass and listen." Hauling her around so that her ass was pressed against the desk, he leaned in, a hand on either side of her hips, forcing her to rear back.

She could smell him, some kind of pricey cologne that made her throat go dry. She could feel the heat of his body all along the line of her own, and damn it, that ache between her thighs decided that it would be a fine time to wake up.

It was Theo. It had always been him.

"The reason I offered you the damn job, and the reason that you're going to take it, is because we have unfinished business." He leaned in, and she felt his warm breath mist over her lips. "I didn't leave because of you, or us, and you damn well know that. And there's still something here. You can't deny that."

Opening eyes that she didn't realize she'd squeezed closed, Jo looked up at Theo, saw the glint of truth in his eyes.

Her heart felt as though he'd placed it in his fist and squeezed.

"You may not have left because of us, but you still left." She did her best to keep her voice level. "You really expect us to just pick up where we left off? Unbelievable."

She placed her hands on his chest, intending to push him away, but the feel of his body beneath her palms made her hesitate. Like a shark sensing her weakness, he closed the ribbon of space between their bodies, pressing himself against her.

"Tell me you don't want me to touch you." He touched his lips to the thin skin behind her ear, and she couldn't hold back the shudder. When her fingers dug into his chest, he slid those lips down her neck and over, measuring the beats of her heart in the hollow of her throat.

Damn it. Damn herself. She'd gone for so, so

long without feeling this heat, and now that she'd had a taste, she wanted another hit, and another after that. Would it really be so bad to just let herself go, one more time?

Slowly, giving her time to say no, he moved his hands from the desk to her hips and up, until his long fingers framed her waist. He squeezed gently, and she remembered what it was like to have him grip her like that when he was inside her.

She also remembered what it had felt like after he'd left, in the days and weeks and months when she'd missed him so much it felt as though she'd been stabbed with a ragged shard of glass. It had taken everything she had to move past that—was it worth feeling that again, in exchange for just a few moments of pleasure?

No. No, it was not.

Pulling back abruptly, she pushed him away and broke the embrace. Her breath came fast and hard as she made space between them, wiping sweaty palms on the thighs of her jeans.

"We're not doing this." If only she felt as sure as she sounded. If he so much as crooked a finger at her, she'd strip off all her clothes and lie down on the desk for him to play with. "It's not fair to ask that of me."

Theo looked as though she'd clocked him in the head. He, too, was breathing hard, and when she saw the outline of his erection pressing against those fancy suit pants, she almost gave in again.

"I have to go." Shaking her head, she blindly pushed her way out of the office, heading straight for the elevator doors. Once inside, she turned and saw the satisfied smirk on Ava's face, realizing that she must have been the woman she'd caught with Theo. She should have felt jealousy, but instead the memory sent another bolt of heat through her. So long feeling nothing, and the sudden onslaught meant she was about to self-combust. But she held firm, and as the elevator doors closed, she pressed her damp forehead to the chilly steel of the elevator wall.

What the hell was she going to do?

"Want to explain to me what that was about?"

Theo was slouched in the chair at his desk, a can of icy club soda open in front of him. He desperately wished that it was three fingers of hideously expensive scotch.

"Is this where you spank me for not telling you that I knew Jo?" he asked wryly as John came in, closing the door briskly behind him.

The other man rolled his eyes. "Don't be such a drama queen. But yes, I'd like an explanation. You're paying me a lot of money to help get this company off the ground, Theo, and I'm not interested in being blindsided with whatever shit that was that you just pulled."

Theo took a large swallow of his club soda. It was flat and tasteless—why did he drink this shit, anyway?

John remained silent. Theo knew the tactic well—he often used it himself to make the other person talk first, to establish power.

He didn't have enough energy to fight it.

"Jo was my girlfriend when I was nineteen, but I've known her family since I was a kid. We lived next door to each other."

"And what did you do to piss her off like that?"

"What makes you think I did something?"

John snorted inelegantly. Reaching across to the sleek minifridge, he pulled out a club soda for himself. He grimaced after he took a sip. "This stuff is nasty."

Theo shrugged. "I realized that I wasn't good for her, and I left."

John cocked his head, as if waiting for the rest of the story. When he realized that there wasn't any, he slammed his can down on the desk.

"Let me guess—you haven't talked to her in all this time, am I right?" Theo didn't answer, but John was already building up a head of steam. "And you lured her here with a job offer in the hopes that—what? She'd be so thrilled at your return that she'd jump right back into your arms?"

Well…yeah, that had essentially been his plan. Hearing it come from someone else, though, made Theo wince.

He hadn't thought that out very well. With Jo's legendary temper, he was lucky she hadn't pushed him through the window.

"You." John pointed a finger at him before rising to pour the rest of his club soda into a plant. "You don't approach her about the job again. I'll handle that end so that we have a hope in hell that she takes the job, assuming you haven't fucked that up beyond repair. That blog of hers is the ticket to a successful launch, Theo, and that is my very expensive, professional opinion."

Theo cast his colleague as a sidelong stare. "You done yet?"

"Not even a little," John replied cheerfully, sitting down again and bracing his elbows on his knees. "Now, as someone who is an absolute magnet for the ladies—"

Theo interrupted him with a snort before waving his hand through the air. "Sorry. Carry on, Casanova."

"As I was saying before I was so rudely interrupted, you can't just come back after something like that and expect a woman to jump for joy at your mere presence."

"Then what the hell am I supposed to do?" Theo burst out, frustrated. "She's the most difficult woman in existence, ever."

"Ah, but the greater the challenge, the sweeter the reward." John grunted when Theo furrowed his brow. "You know, for the brilliant, maverick owner of a start-up valued at over ten million dollars, you can be an idiot." Standing, he tossed the empty can into the recycling bin, then leaned over the desk to pat Theo on the shoulder.

"Woo her, my man. Woo her like you've never wooed before."

CHAPTER EIGHT

When Jo got home, she headed straight for the garage. The small space housed her sister Beth's mechanic shop, and the sister she was closest to could almost always be found there during work hours.

She didn't want to be alone, but she wanted someone she could be silent with.

"Beth?" She strode into the garage, throwing her arms up at the last second when she saw her sister, who was very much not alone. "Oh shit! Sorry! I'll go!"

"No, no. Stay." Beth pushed Ford away with a mock-stern stare and pulled her coveralls back up to her waist, where she tied the arms in a knot, then straightened her tank. "Mr. Handsy here was just trying to convince me to take a break, but I have too much to do."

Beth stopped when she caught sight of Jo's face.

Jo thought she'd done a pretty good job at masking what she felt, but her sister knew her well enough to know that she wasn't all right. "For you, I'll take a break. Sit."

Beth gestured to her workbench, then shot Ford a look with eyebrows raised. He took the hint, buckling up his pants as he entered the house through the door that joined the two.

"I'm not going to bug you if you're busy," Jo started, but Beth waved her off.

"You can talk while I work," she said, ducking under the hood of the car she was working on. Jo saw something spark and took a cautious step back, out of range.

"It's nothing. Really," Jo insisted, but she didn't leave, instead opening up the mini fridge that Beth kept in the corner. The door was lined with shiny glass bottles of kombucha. So gross. Jo wrinkled her nose and shifted things around, finally locating a can of Diet Coke in the back corner. She didn't love soda, but she did like having something to do with her hands.

When she closed the fridge, Beth was watching her. Her sister's skin was still flushed from what she and Ford had been doing when Jo entered the garage, and Jo felt a pang of what was undeniably loneliness.

She wanted what Beth and Ford had. Not just

the companionship, either, damn it. She wanted the lust, the can't-keep-your-hands-off-each-other headiness.

And the only person who had ever done it for her was Theo.

Fuck her life.

"I'm going to take a wild guess and assume that it's Theo who's gotten that crazy look in your eyes." Beth eyed Jo's drink, then crossed to the fridge and retrieved a kombucha for herself. Jo couldn't hold back a grimace when her sister downed half the bottle. Sure, it was supposed to be good for you, but it had little floaty things in it. Yuck.

"So, tell me." Beth gestured with her bottle. Jo squirmed. She'd come here because she'd wanted to rant to her sister, absolutely. But after seeing Beth and Ford together, she felt more like curling up into a ball in her room. Alone.

"How can you drink that?" Both Jo and Beth jumped when the door Ford had just disappeared through banged open, smacking into the unfinished drywall of the shop. "It has chunks in it."

Beth arched an eyebrow at the bottle of beer Meg carried. "But beer before noon is okay?"

"It's craft beer." Meg smiled sweetly. "Doesn't count."

Looking to Jo for support, she stopped short. "What's going on?"

"Theo," Beth supplied before Jo could answer.

"Damn it." Meg handed Jo the beer. "Want to talk about it?"

"No." Jo scowled. She'd come here wanting to talk to Beth, but now she didn't know what the hell she wanted.

"Hello?" All three sisters turned at the sound of the male voice. Jo felt awkwardness weigh down on her like wet wool as she saw John Brooke standing in the open door of the garage. His pristine suit looked completely out of place against the oil-stained walls.

"Mr. Brooke." *Shit.* Jo had no idea what the social nuances of a situation like this were. She also had no idea what the hell he was doing here.

"Miss Marchande." Sidestepping a slick of oil on the floor, John closed the distance between them, offering her a hand. "I don't feel that we had an adequate discussion of the position at Crossing Lines. I'd like to remedy that. Perhaps we can try again, tomorrow morning?"

"What?" Jo blurted, ignoring the hand that he still held out. "But didn't Theo tell you about us?"

"I don't know what you're talking about." John arched his eyebrows in a way that he suggested he didn't *want* to know, either. "If you need time to think about the offer, I can give you twenty-four hours. But I don't think you were informed of the compensation for the job, which might influence your decision."

He named a sum that made her two sisters gasp and left Jo gaping. It wasn't astronomical, but it was far more than most writers made…ever.

"Apologies—I didn't think that it might be crass to drop numbers in front of others." He looked over at her sisters as he spoke, then did a double take at Meg. She looked right back, and the smirk that curved her lips said she liked what she saw.

"Thank you," Jo said, a little too loudly, but this time her volume was on purpose. John cleared his throat and forced his attention back to her. Working on anything connected with Theo was a bad, bad idea, but she was human, and she had no money. The sum he'd named had her mind spinning wildly with possibilities.

Shc could maybe, possibly awaken that dream of going back to school. At the end of the day, she supposed that she was like most peoplc—money was a powerful motivator.

"If I come in tomorrow to discuss this, will I be speaking with you?" She chose her words carefully. The last thing on earth that she wanted to do was discuss her complicated history with Theo with his business partner, so she was relieved when he simply nodded.

"Yes. I'll go over the job with you, what we hope it will bring in terms of visibility to the company." Tucking his hands into the pockets of his well-tailored trousers, he looked her in the eye. "But there will also be some input from the owner on the creative side."

"I see," she replied slowly, swallowing past a dry throat. Could she really do this? Could she work at a job where she knew she'd have to see Theo every day?

For that kind of money—life-changing money—could she not?

She could feel her sisters watching her—well, Beth was watching her. Meg was staring at John while licking her lips. She sucked in a deep breath, then nodded decisively.

"I'll see you then."

Beth jumped in place as John turned and exited the garage. Meg stared blatantly at his ass. And Jo felt as though all of the air had been sucked from her lungs.

What had she done?

Theo heard them as soon as he turned his ignition off. Taking advantage of the warmth of the early spring day, he'd taken his convertible, leaving the top down. He'd meant to pull his car into the yawning garage of the estate, which he had to do manually since he had no idea where the fob was—his dad had left an insane amount of personal things to sort through. But when he heard the feminine laughter, he was reminded of all the times he'd hung out with the Marchande girls on the very same lawn that they were on now.

Woo her like you've never wooed before.

His partner's words reverberated in his head. He wanted to balk—he was Theo Lawrence. He'd made something of himself, even though no one had ever thought he could. He could have any woman he wanted, and he frequently did. He didn't have to *woo.*

Those women weren't Jo.

"How the hell am I supposed to *woo* her?" He waited for inspiration to strike, and when it didn't, he reached for his phone. A few taps later, and his screen was filled with images of flowers, chocolates and people eating dinner with napkins in their laps.

A date. He should ask her on a date—a real one.

An unexpected pang of nerves shot through him, and he mercilessly squashed it down.

He needed to approach this like he would approach a business meeting, confident in his success.

As he strode back down the driveway, the rosebushes that had grown wild since his father's death caught his eye. Among the tangle of branches were a handful of early blooms.

He'd never given Jo flowers. What an ass he'd been.

"Ow!" The branches were thorny, but he managed to gather enough stems to make a small bouquet. Arranging them clumsily in one hand, he took a deep breath and headed for the house next door.

"It went through!" Triumphant, Meg brandished a…was that a croquet mallet? Yes, they each had one, and there were thin wire hoops set up all over the lawn.

"No good! You weren't holding your drink!" Amy pulled a fresh can of beer from a small cooler and tossed it to her eldest sister before taking a long drink from her own. "This is how you do it!"

Holding her can in one hand, Amy waved her mallet in an inelegant arc that somehow managed to connect solidly with a black ball. It flew through a wire hoop and smacked against the orange ball that Meg had just hit. "Yes! Two extra strokes for me!"

"From what I've heard, you don't need any extra strokes to get the job done." Beth grinned wickedly at her youngest sister, waving her mallet in the air like a pointer finger. "Who is it this week? Mason? Caroline?"

"A lady never kisses and tells," Amy sniffed before sending a ball through the next hoop. Jo snorted in response.

"Since when are you a lady?" She'd been lying out flat on the grass, but now she propped herself up on her elbows, shielding her eyes from the sun. He could tell the moment she spotted him, because her spine straightened, her body tense. "Oh."

"What?" Beth turned to look in the same direction. "Oh. Theo."

"Hi, Beth. Meg. Amy." He nodded at each of them in turn, suddenly feeling as though he was facing a firing squad. He'd never met an opponent he couldn't best in the boardroom, but facing these four women that he'd known a lifetime ago made him wish for a drink. "May I ask what on earth you're doing?"

"Playing beer croquet. Obviously." Amy looked him up and down. At least he was assuming it was Amy—he could see whispers of the girl she'd been in the lines of her face, but this woman had blond dreadlocks and so many tattoos that he could barely see the ivory of her skin. "Wanna join?"

"Amy!" Meg glared at her sister, gesturing toward Jo with her head in a not-at-all-subtle manner.

"What?" Amy tossed her mallet to the ground with exasperation. "We've known him forever. You can't just erase that because he went on some rich-boy rumspringa and grew up."

"That's right." The sound of his own voice surprised him—he hadn't intended to say anything. But as all four of the women looked at him curiously, he cleared his throat and continued, flying by the seat of his pants. "You can't erase it."

He focused in on Jo, offering her the bouquet he'd plucked. "Here."

The expression on her face wasn't one he'd seen before, a cross between confusion and terror. "Did you pick these?"

"I—yes." Damn it. He should have thought this through better. Gotten something made up at a fancy florist. Something spiky and tropical, with lots of wild greenery—something that suited her better than a bunch of garden roses. "I'm here to woo you."

"What?" Jo threw her hands in the air. Behind her, Meg choked on her swallow of beer, and Amy cocked her head, watching him intently. "*Woo?* What the hell does that mean? Who says that anymore?"

"Shush, Jo." Meg wiped the back of her hand over her mouth. "Or you won't be able to hear the wooing."

Jo growled at her sister, who smiled beatifically back at her. The fact that Jo's sisters hadn't run him off the property with their mallets restored the smidgen of confidence that had been misplaced by doubt.

Jo hadn't told him to leave yet, and the heat of her skin was still on his lips. She wasn't immune to him, and her sisters hadn't chased him away. He was going to take that and run with it.

Shutting out the other women, he crossed the lawn to Jo. Her expression was stony, but he saw her swallow thickly when he got close.

He held out the roses. She looked like she'd as soon eat them as accept them, but she reached out a wary hand.

"I want to take you on a date." She sucked in a sharp breath, and he felt a stab of vindication. No, she wasn't immune. "Tomorrow night. Dinner. You and me."

Jo opened her mouth but never got a chance to speak.

"She'll go!" Meg and Amy shouted at the same time. Jo turned to glare at them, but her gaze stopped at his hand.

"You're bleeding."

He looked down at his hand. Multiple scratches from the rosebush striped his skin, and a drop of blood welled up from one. "I didn't notice."

He wiped it on the thigh of his suit pants, and Meg winced. Amy watched him thoughtfully, and Beth pretended to be busy moving clips on the hoops, though he knew that she was paying attention, too.

Jo, though, squinted at him as though trying to peer into the dark recesses of his brain to find what his motivation was. He really thought she should have known.

Her. His mind was full of her. She'd never been far from his thoughts, even when he'd tried to tell himself that choosing to locate the offices of Crossing Lines in Boston was because of the location, or when he'd dated other women—fucked other women—in a desperate attempt to wipe her out of his mind.

He'd gone to that party knowing damn well that he'd see her, but he hadn't been able to stop himself. He'd let Ava give him what she wanted—his cock in her mouth—to try to tell himself that the only reason he wanted to see Jo was to check in, to make sure with his own eyes that she was doing all right. That the job offer was really just a job offer.

And then there she'd been in the dark, watching him. Watching him and liking it. And just like that, it all came roaring back.

She looked up at him with an indecipherable glint in her eyes.

And then she nodded. “Okay.”

CHAPTER NINE

"WHAT DO YOU know about Crossing Lines?"

Jo rocked back and forth a bit in her chair. Unlike the hardware store special that was at her desk at home, this one was sleek leather, softly cushioned, and had wonderful support for the achy back that Jo figured most writers probably had.

She was enjoying the chair so much that it took her a moment longer than usual to answer John's question. When he cleared his throat, she looked up, realizing that she'd taken too long.

"I looked it up," she admitted, "after you emailed me. I read the Wikipedia entry on it and took a look at the site. But I'm afraid I didn't really understand the specifics of it."

"Did you download the app?" John asked. Jo shook her head, trying to hold back her grin.

"I'm sorry. I know most people would have, but

I don't have many apps on my phone at all. I use it for email and jotting down story ideas when pen and paper isn't around. That's it."

"You don't use it as a phone?" John's expression registered horror at this, prompting Jo to laugh. He'd had to pause their meeting several times already because he'd gotten calls that he couldn't ignore.

Jo was the opposite. "Hell, no. I hate talking on the phone." She shuddered.

John stared at her, perplexed. "You're a unique woman, Jo."

"Is that bad?" She might have felt nervous, but she had a sneaking suspicion that John was one of the few people in the world who both wasn't related to her and genuinely liked her.

"Not at all. It's very refreshing." His smile was very nearly dazzling, and Jo might have thought that he was flirting—except that she knew she very much wasn't his type. Never mind that he hadn't been too subtle in checking Meg out yesterday, but she wasn't most people's type. Antisocial tomboys with tempers weren't in high demand.

"Okay. Where to start, then..." John stopped his pacing—he was constantly in motion, full of energy—and pulled a second chair up to the massive desk. "What dating sites are you on?"

Jo couldn't hold back the laugh this time. John looked at her, perplexed.

"I'm not on any dating sites." She wasn't sure how she was supposed to interpret the look that John cast her then—not quite pity, but like he couldn't figure her out.

She didn't really like it. Romance was for other people. She'd mostly accepted it, until Theo had crashed back into her life. She was the one who was friend-zoned, considered one of the guys. On the rare occasions that another person seemed interested in her, she was too awkward to figure out the interaction—and she rarely found it worth it at any rate, since none of them ever made her hot and bothered.

She wasn't about to express this to some slickly suited guy that she'd met yesterday, though, so she searched his face for a cue and decided to deflect. "I think my sister Amy is on this one, though. She's on a few."

"Amy." He rolled the name over his tongue. "Is she one of the sisters I met yesterday?"

Jo refrained—barely—from rolling her eyes. "The sister you're ever-so-delicately inquiring about is Meg. She's a caterer with small-business dreams. She tells very dirty jokes, treats thrift-store shopping like an Olympic sport, and she's single."

John blinked, then ran a hand over the buzzed ebony hair on his head. "I guess I wasn't that subtle, huh?"

"Not even a little bit." *Damn.* Should she be more formal with someone who was now her boss? She wasn't the formal type. And hadn't he said that he liked the fact that she was unique?

Theo always had.

Do not go there, Jo.

"Okay. The Wikipedia article said that Crossing Lines is revolutionary. Can you explain that to me?" She tugged on the hem of the black tunic thing that Meg had shoved at her that morning. She was wearing it with some stretchy leggings that her sister had also strongly—forcefully—recommended, but she'd ignored the ballet flats in favor of her Converse sneakers.

"Okay. I'm going to explain as though you don't know anything about dating sites, so apologies if any of this is redundant."

Jo nodded. *It won't be. I know nothing.*

"So on most dating sites—Cupid.com, PlentyOfFish, even older ones like Match.com and Lavalife—people set up a profile. They talk a little bit about themselves, about what they're looking for, and then they conduct searches for matches with their criteria. Often the sites will have algorithms that suggest profiles that members might want to check out. Following?"

"Yes." It sounded a little bit tedious to Jo. She spent enough time at her computer, and the thought of scrolling endlessly, looking for a partner, didn't appeal to her.

"What makes Crossing Lines different is that it adds back a bit of the meeting-in-person element. You know, how everyone up to our generation was stuck meeting." He grinned, tapped on the keyboard, then turned the monitor to show her the screen. "What our site does is connect you with people that you come across in real life."

"I'm not following." Wasn't that just…meeting in person?

"Bear with me." John tapped on the keyboard again, and she was surprised to see him bring up what appeared to be his own profile. "Okay. So let's say that your hot sister and I were both members of Crossing Lines."

Jo couldn't hold back the smirk.

"Then let's say we both happened to go to the same Starbucks at the same time—crossing lines, so to speak. We would each receive an alert that someone else from the app was in the vicinity. You could then check out their profile and indicate whether or not you're interested."

"Oh…" Jo cocked her head to the side. "Oh, so

that saves the nerves of approaching someone you find attractive for a date, too."

"Exactly!" John beamed at her like she'd performed a trick and earned a treat. "So then let's say your hot sister and I checked out each other's profiles and indicated that we were interested. Then I could approach her, or she could approach me, and we could set up a date."

"What if one of you didn't hear the alert?" Jo didn't hear her phone most of the time, though in her case she kept her notifications on silent deliberately, so they didn't annoy her. "Doesn't that kind of screw things up in this magical meet cute?"

"No matter when you catch the alert, you're still able to see the profile," he assured her, pointing at the screen. "So even if you check an hour, two hours later. The next day. You still might think, oh, that's the cute girl from the coffee shop. Or, oh, that guy was with his kids, but now I see that he's a single dad, so I'm going to hit him up to *install my kid's car seats*."

Jo snorted at the innuendo that John infused his last words with. Pushing back in her chair, she took a moment to let it all absorb.

"This is actually kind of brilliant." She drummed her fingers on the arm of the chair. "Who thought this up?"

"Theo did." John suddenly, deliberately, busied

himself with closing out his profile and readjusting the screen.

Yeah, Jo was pretty sure that Theo had filled him in on their history. She wondered if he also knew about the upcoming date, and what he thought about it.

She still wasn't sure what *she* thought about it. She didn't—couldn't—dwell on it right now, or she'd think herself into a spiral of doom, so she changed the subject again. She was becoming an expert at it.

"So where do I come in?" She couldn't really think what place a creative writer would have on the staff of a cutting-edge dating app. She especially couldn't imagine what her kinky sex blog could contribute to anything.

"We're still what's considered a start-up company," John explained, pushing out of his chair and starting to pace again. "We're the new kid on the block—the *weird* new kid on the block. Our business model tells us that we can be incredibly successful, but we need to find new and creative ways to bring in users. Millennials and Gen Z are statistically the most likely to give something a bit different a try, and they are also the generations that are more open to new things when it comes to sex and relationships. They're intrigued by kink, and that's where you come in."

"You don't expect me to put up a profile, do you?" Panic was a flock of tiny birds in her belly. She couldn't imagine something less appealing. "I just write about it. I don't want to get kinky with strangers."

John looked at her as though she'd grown a second head. "Of course not."

She exhaled, trying to expel those tiny birds from her system. "Sorry. Go on."

"We want you to write content for us, targeted toward millennials and Gen Z." Pulling his phone from his pocket, he glanced at the screen before returning it. "We plan to start a blog that will be advertised on the home page of the site. We'll be advertising it on Facebook, Amazon and all social media. Essentially it's to be a column about sex and dating as a member of that generation. We're a new, edgy site, and we want edgy content. Your blog stood out because you aren't afraid to go there."

"Are you sure it didn't stand out because I used to date Theo and he has some kind of guilt complex?" Jo winced as the words left her mouth, but even if it was brazen to ask, she wanted—needed—to know.

She wanted this job. She had that hit of adrenaline, cold sweat, sick-with-want kind of feeling in her gut, and that wasn't even factoring in any feelings left over between her and the boss.

Her writing was hers and hers alone. No matter how much she wanted the job, any joy from it would be tainted if Theo had only offered this out of guilt.

John stopped his pacing in front of the window, his face set in serious lines. In the pale light filtering through the thick glass, Jo noted again how classically handsome he was—and again, she felt nothing. When she looked at Theo, though, with his wild dark eyes, the skin that reminded her of caramel, the way he moved his hands when he spoke about something he was passionate about…

Her entire body clenched just thinking about him.

Damn you to hell, Theo Lawrence.

"Jo, when Theo showed me your blog, he didn't tell me anything at all about your history. I had no idea that you two had ever even been in contact, let alone…close." John tapped a finger on the glass. "I agreed that your writing was perfect. And I have to say, I'm a bit jealous—you have the most fascinating dating life. Reading about it almost makes me feel like I'm there."

If only you knew. Jo forced herself to smile, nodding along with John. If he liked her content, then she didn't think there was any reason to let him know that she had experienced precisely nothing that she'd written about on her blog…well, except for this morning's. Lack of real sex, of desire, meant that she'd filled that void in her life another way, with a fascination of all things kinky. She threw in anecdotes about her sisters, too, since they always insisted on sharing every single dirty detail of their relationships, their hookups.

But her own experiences? Her blog hadn't included a single one, because there hadn't been any—not until Theo had come back.

"So that's what you want me to write, then?" Shit…did Theo think she'd done all those things she wrote about? Not that she would be ashamed of it, she just…hadn't. It was weird that he might think she did. "What I write about on my blog?"

"Essentially, yes, with an emphasis on the dating experience posts. But—" He was cut off when a knock sounded on the door. Theo entered the room without waiting for an answer. "As I was going to say, Theo will be in momentarily with a list of ideas for topics."

"And here he is." Theo's words were light, but his gaze was a punch of pure heat when he ignored John and focused in on Jo. "Is John treating you right?"

Something about the way he asked made the question sound deliciously dirty. Jo found herself unconsciously rubbing her thighs together under the shiny surface of the desk.

"Like a lady," she retorted, casting a smile in John's direction. On anyone else the expression might have looked coquettish—on her, Jo imagined it looked pained, but it had the intended effect. Theo narrowed his eyes at his partner.

Like Jo, he'd always had a temper, often fueled by jealousy. Where that had caused them to self-combust when they were younger, now Jo tasted a hint of how that possessiveness could be…well, hot.

Moving her gaze from John to Theo, she instead found it a bit hard to breathe.

What the hell was she supposed to do with this?

John's phone rang, the no-nonsense ringtone slicing through the thick air. Without another word to the pair of them, he answered it, waving goodbye as he exited the office, closing the door firmly behind him.

They were alone, and the heaviness of Theo's gaze made Jo want to break eye contact. The thread of stubbornness that had been wrapped around her since birth refused to let her back down.

He wasn't challenged by the direct stare. If anything, he seemed amused, his lips curling into a faint smirk. Holding eye contact, he closed the distance between them, stopping when he reached the front of the desk.

Jo immediately felt the need to stand, to put them on even ground, but she knew that the movement would show how off balance he made her feel.

Why did this feel so much like war? And why did she want to wave the white flag and throw herself at that rock-solid chest?

"Since you showed up this morning, I'm assuming you've accepted the job." His posture was arrogant, as though it would never occur to him that she would say no. Looking him over, though, Jo noticed him rubbing the pads of his thumb and forefinger together at his side. It was an old tic of his, a way of releasing excess energy when he was feeling more than he wanted to be.

What was he feeling now? Lust? Guilt? What would she do if she knew?

"I haven't accepted it officially, no."

Theo said nothing, just kept watching her with that dark gaze. Damn it, he knew—he knew how much she wanted this job. Refusing it would show him how much he was affecting her.

Still looking at her, he pulled out his tablet, moving his fingers over the screen. "I just emailed you the employment agreement. There's no need to print it—it can be signed electronically. Of course, you'll want to read it all the way through, but I think you'll find that it's an extremely generous offer."

"Theo..." She closed her eyes. Why was she bothering to put up a front at all? He'd always been able to read her better than anyone, and she had no doubt that he knew exactly what she was struggling with right now. She might as well say it. "Look. I want this job. I'm still attracted to you."

She choked on the last part—that she was terrified of falling for him again, only to have him leave. There was vulnerable, and there was *vulnerable.*

"I don't understand why you can't have both."

Jo's chin snapped up. There was no disguising the desire that was thick in his voice, a sound that was imprinted onto her very DNA.

"You can review the agreement in the car." He tossed an inky-black silk scarf onto the desk in front of her, and for the first time since he'd entered the room, she noticed that he was wearing a light peacoat. "You can also look over the list of potential blog topics that I sent. I'm curious which one catches your attention first."

"The car?" Picking up the fabric, she discovered that it was a kerchief, the type an old-time movie star might have once worn to protect her hair. "Where are we going?"

"You agreed to go on a date with me." The cocky smile he shot her made her feel like she was fifteen years old again, all knobby knees and fluttery feelings for the boy next door. "It's date time."

"I agreed to go to dinner with you." She pointedly checked out the clock on the wall. "It's not even eleven in the morning."

"We'll have dinner, too. Maybe more, if you're good." Damn it. The confidence in his voice, in every line of his body, shouldn't have still been so sexy, and yet it was like his words cast out a hook that caught her and reeled her in.

"You know damn well that I've never been good, so I wouldn't get your hopes up." Even as she spoke, she found herself rising, reaching for the cardigan sweater that was part of the ensemble when Meg had dressed her up like a doll this morning.

Theo frowned when she shrugged into it. "Don't you have a heavier coat?"

"I only wear coats when it reaches minus twenty." Jo held up the kerchief thing. "What am I supposed to do with this?"

"Tie your hair back." He gestured with his hands. "Otherwise it'll get in your face."

Puzzled, Jo struggled to arrange the scarf on her

head. Breathing out on a chuckle, Theo rounded the desk, taking it from her hands.

"Like this." Turning her with the press of a hand on her lower back, he stroked his fingers through the sleek, chin-length strands of her hair. Her pulse stilled as he tucked them behind her ears, brushing over the tops of her ears.

A rough breath escaped her as he arranged the silk over her hair. When he tied it in a knot at the base of her skull, he whispered a light touch down the back of her neck, tracing a line to the top of her spine.

Just a simple touch, but she felt it over her entire body. Her breasts swelled, aching, and she arched into his hands.

"There. You're ready." Breaking the connection, Theo stepped back, put some much-needed space between them. Her heart was hammering so hard that she spoke extra loud in order to be heard over it.

"Ready for what?" And she wasn't ready. She wasn't ready at all.

He grinned, then dangled a set of car keys. "Ready for a ride in the convertible."

CHAPTER TEN

"Jo, YOU MIGHT as well relax. We're going to be in the car for a while, and you're going to get a headache if you keep clenching your jaw like that."

Theo had his eyes on the road ahead but was aware of every movement, every breath Jo made in the passenger's seat of the low-slung F-Type Jaguar.

She'd been tense since they'd left the office, navigating through the congested streets of the city and onto the interstate. He could still feel the heat of her skin, branded onto the tips of his fingers from when he'd helped her with the scarf, and he didn't think the tension was because she didn't want to be there. In fact, he knew it—he knew Jo.

He knew that breathy little sigh, the same one she'd made when he was inside her. She was tense for the same reason he was—because she still wanted him. She wanted him, and she was confused about it.

He hoped that what he'd planned for today would help her clear her mind.

"Where are we going?" She'd asked this approximately every ten minutes since they'd left Boston, making him grin. Patience had never been one of her virtues.

"You'll find out when we get there." Luckily for her, he had patience enough for the both of them. "For now, let's go over that list of article ideas. Pull it up and let's see what grabs you."

Huffing out a breath of exasperation, she wriggled her phone out of her pocket. He watched from the corner of his eye, enjoying the view of her thighs and her slim hips, wondering how on earth she'd managed to fit anything into the pocket of pants so tight.

"'Wildest one-night stands,'" she read. He expected her to make some kind of sarcastic remark—in fact, he was looking forward to it—but instead she nodded thoughtfully. "I could work with that."

What?

"What is the main purpose of Crossing Lines, as far as your marketing goes?" She sank her teeth into her lower lip, and he wanted to do that himself. "Is it for casual dating? Relationships? Or is it like that one site...what's it called? Timber?"

"Tinder." He pressed his lips together, trying not to laugh, since he could see that she was being serious. "And it's for all of the above. But the hope is that by having you blog about all kinds of interesting topics relating to sex and love, it will set us up as being more cutting-edge than our peers. More avant-garde, the ones with our finger on the pulse of what the cool kids want."

She nodded, returning to the list.

"'Sugar dating—dating on your terms.'" She cocked her head, curious. "What's that? I know I've read about that, but I'm a little unclear on the details."

"Ever heard the term *sugar daddy*?" She nodded. "There are a number of sites to connect people who are looking for that kind of situation. Sugar daddies—or mommies—who don't have the time or inclination for a relationship will post, seeking an arrangement with a sugar baby, mostly women, but there are some men now. In return for company and, most of the time, sex, the sugar daddies will fulfill wishes on the sugar baby's list—often that's someone to cover the rent, to help with student debt, to fund travel."

"So we could do an article about why it's called dating when, really, it's a form of sex work?" She chewed on her lip as she thought about it, and he fought to keep his eyes on the road against the distraction those pink lips provided.

"That could work," he said, taking a moment to look the other way, away from those sexy lips. Unfortunately, the endless field of grass didn't have much to offer that could hold his attention.

"I don't think we should do this one. It will make readers curious about these arrangement sites, driving them away from yours. We want to write about things that get them excited about exploring what they've read about, eager to meet people...but to meet people on Crossing Lines. Right?"

"I hadn't thought about that," he said, surprised. She was right, of course, and John would have likely said the same thing if he'd reviewed the list before Theo had sent it to Jo. "That's a good point."

Jo tapped a finger to her temple, grinning. "Not just air in here, my friend."

A dart of warmth—not heat, not lust, but warmth—spread in Theo's chest. This was the first genuine smile that Jo had given him since he'd returned. Something twisted in his rib cage, causing a bone-deep ache.

"'Erotic fire cupping. Naked summer pool-hopping. Marijuana lube.'" She continued reviewing the list, commenting as she went. When she was halfway through the list, she paused, letting out a sexy little sound that made his dick sit up and pay attention.

"'Sex with an ex,'" she read, setting her phone down on her thigh. "'Exploring kink with an old flame can be easier than getting dirty with someone you want to keep.'"

He said nothing. He hadn't added it to the list just to broach the topic, at least not consciously. That said, he'd wondered what she'd say about it, if anything.

With other women, he was on sure footing. He was charming, he was cocky, he was bossy and it worked—oh, how it worked.

Jo, though? Jo wasn't like any other woman he'd ever met. She saw through his charm, laughed at his cockiness, and if he was bossy, well, one nudge too many and she'd kick back like a mule. It didn't leave him with many options—at least, not ones he'd used before.

She was silent for a long moment, her thumb rubbing over the screen on her phone. He wasn't prepared when she half turned in her seat, tucking one leg up underneath her.

"What would you think about that?" she asked, curiosity thick in her words.

"What?" His fingers tightened on the steering

wheel. "Like…what do I think about that in general?"

"No." She drew the word out into three syllables. "You know what I mean. Sex. Us."

She'd managed to shock him. He'd thought that she might read that item and tuck it away in that busy brain to think about later. She might even have ignored it entirely, refusing to give him the satisfaction of letting him know that she was thinking about it.

Never in his wildest dreams—and when it came to Jo, he had a lot of dreams—had he imagined that she would come right out and ask him what he thought about them having sex.

"I think I've made it pretty obvious what I want here." He cast her a sidelong look. "That's why we're in this car, right? This is a date."

"It's a date, but I wasn't planning on sleeping with you after it," she replied archly. He made a show of wincing.

"Way to hurt a man where it counts, Jo. Right in the desperate hope."

"You've never been desperate in your life," she snorted, tapping her phone on her knee. She was quiet for a moment, and he had to claw back the urge to demand to know what was running through her head.

"I'm not saying this properly." She swallowed,

tapping her phone faster. "Look. I know that I write about a lot of…stuff. Kinky stuff. And you must think I write about it convincingly, or you wouldn't have offered me this job."

"Right." He drew out the word, his pulse picking up. She'd always been easy for him to read, but right now he truly didn't know what she was thinking.

"You're going to make me spell it out, aren't you?" She huffed out a breath, then scrubbed her hands over her face. "Look. I write about kink because I'm interested in it. But I don't…you know I don't do all of those things, right?"

Her words came out in a rush. A terrible, wild hope began to build up inside him.

"Are you saying that you want to try some of those things?" His attention had been on her since the moment he'd walked into that office, but now it was laser focused.

"Yes." His Jo had never been anything but direct, and right now, by God, he appreciated it. "But I don't… I'm not interested in exploring with most people."

"Are you saying that you're interested in exploring with me?" His hands clenched on the steering wheel.

"That's exactly what I'm saying." Turning, she looked up at him with those wide gray eyes. "But I need you to understand that that doesn't…it doesn't mean that things are the way they were before."

The tiniest dart of pain hooked itself into his chest. He'd known that she wouldn't welcome him back with open arms, but it still hadn't killed the evil that was hope.

He wasn't a man to settle for halves when he wanted the whole—he was, however, a man who'd learned that nothing was sweeter than something you'd worked for.

"So what you're saying is, you want to use me for my body and nothing else?" Her cheeks were flushed, and he knew that it wasn't from the wind as they flew down the interstate. "I'd be a very stupid man not to take you up on that offer, Jo Marchande. I like to think I'm rather clever."

"So you don't need to do stuff like…this." She gestured out the window as the Jag swung onto the exit to the town of Concord. "Planning dates. Being charming. You know."

"Baby, my charm is natural. You should know I've never been without it." He grinned at her, wiggling his eyebrows, and she giggled, a wholly un-Jo-like sound, but one he was pleased to have pulled from her. "As for the date. Just go with it. You might have been here sometime since I left, but I wanted to bring you here anyway."

"Bedford Street." Letting his GPS navigate

them through the town, he finally brought the car to a stop outside a large set of wrought-iron gates. On either side of the entrance were long, low-slung stone walls, worn with age and slicked with moss.

Jo squinted forward, reading the sign.

"Sleepy Hollow Cemetery," she read, her words tinged with confusion. He waited patiently.

Every other woman he'd dated would have been horrified to be taken to a cemetery on a date, and rightly so. But this truly was someplace he'd wanted to take her for well over a decade, and when the confusion on her face gave way to delight, he knew he'd scored a home run.

"Author's Ridge!" Shoving her phone back into the pocket of her pants, she undid her seat belt, then scrambled out of the car. "Let's go!"

High on the success of his idea, Theo followed more slowly, catching up with her as she paused to take a picture of the cemetery entrance. "How have you not been here yet?"

She shrugged, turning to get a shot from the other direction. "Well, I drive, but I don't trust my scooter to go this far. And no one I know is even the slightest bit interested in going to see graves."

"Their loss." He shrugged. He wasn't overly pumped about graveyards as a whole, but knowing how much Jo had wanted to come here made it appealing for him. Plus, he thought as he looked around, sucking in the clean air of the wide space, the freshly budding trees and the scent of spring, there were worse ways to spend an afternoon than outdoors, exploring history.

"Come on!" More animated than she'd been since he'd come back, at least to him, she grabbed a paper map from a box affixed to the gate. "Did you know that Ralph Waldo Emerson gave the dedication speech when the cemetery first opened? *And* that he's buried here?"

Theo chuckled as he followed after her. Watching Jo study the map, her brow furrowed, something settled in his chest, something that he recognized as contentment.

He'd missed this. He'd missed her. And he understood why she was wary when it came to her feelings about him, but once he'd seen her again, he'd known that this was it.

He just had to convince her that this—them—was it, too.

He enjoyed the walk through the cemetery, which reminded him of one of the gorgeous, slightly overgrown gardens that he often saw in Europe. The stones were weathered but well taken care of, and the greenery was lush and wild. It was peaceful, he realized.

One thing he'd never really had in his life was peace. It was the thing that had been lacking among the countless other luxuries he'd once taken for granted.

He caught up with her when she paused, staring with barely concealed excitement at a stone marker. "This is it. This is Author's Ridge."

He didn't entirely understand why she was so excited that she was trembling a bit. He didn't have to understand to respect it, though, so he stayed silent, his arm brushing companionably against hers as they started to weave their way among the graves.

"Henry David Thoreau." She pointed to a simple stone that, rather than being marked with the last name, displayed the first in blocky letters. "Wow."

"What's with the pencils?" Scattered among the bouquets of flowers and votive candles that showed that something noteworthy lay here were pencils—singles, bundles wrapped with ribbon, even whole boxes, the cardboard warped and faded from the sun and the rain.

"Thoreau and his father ran a big pencil company before he was a writer," she murmured, capturing the image with her phone, then consulting the map. "And just over here should be…holy crap. It's Louisa May Alcott."

"*Little Women*, right?" He followed Jo over to where she'd stopped at the base of a plain stone set into the ground. Around it were more flowers as well as a handful of apples and paper—so much paper. Dog-eared books, shiny new copies, torn book covers, what looked like art.

"That's right." Jo's voice was hushed, and he understood that this particular grave was why she'd so badly wanted to come here once upon a time. "I don't even know how many times I've read that book. I still have my first paper copy, the one I had as a kid, but it's so tattered you can't read it anymore. But I feel like… I almost feel like part of myself is in those pages, because they gave me so much growing up. That sounds stupid."

"It doesn't sound stupid at all." A lightbulb went on in his brain. "Was she what inspired you to start writing?"

"Yeah." Jo nodded, then looked up at him with a wry smile. "She wrote a classic American novel, beloved by millions. I have to wonder what she'd think about me writing a sex blog."

He grinned. "If you found so much inspiration in her, then I have to think she was pretty cool. She'd probably say that as long as you were writing what made you happy, it was all good."

The look Jo cast over her shoulder at him then was almost shy, and he felt something in the vicinity of his heart squeeze, just the littlest bit. Turning, she closed the space between them until she had just enough room to place a hand on his chest, the other behind his neck.

"No matter what else happens with us, thank you for this." Drawing up on the tips of her toes—he really had forgotten how small she was—she drew him down for a kiss. It was a sweet brush of the lips, almost chaste, but the bolt of emotion he felt as she sighed against his lips nearly set him back on his heels.

He'd thought he'd loved the girl that she once was, but he saw right now, with clarity, that what he'd felt then paled compared to the potential of what he could feel now.

He looked down into her eyes, where she was watching with curiosity and a hint of wariness. He wanted to pull off the scarf she was still wearing, to grip that sleek hair and plunder her mouth with his tongue, but he figured that was probably inappropriate when standing at the grave of her idol.

Still, the moment seemed to call for something—something to pin it in place, bookmarked for the future.

"You know why I had to go."

"Of course I know." Angling her chin up, she regarded him with those big eyes. "We fought. You realized that we didn't fit. That we never would."

"What?" His fingers squeezed her shoulders as the words hit him like a bat. "You think I left because we fought? Is that seriously what you've thought this entire time?"

The sneaky snake that was guilt coiled in his belly and settled in. He'd thought the reason for his leaving was so obvious, he hadn't left a note. Hadn't emailed. Hadn't said a damn word to anyone, not even his dad.

No one had come after him, either. Years later, that still hurt.

"That wasn't why you left?" Jo pushed lightly on his chest, enough that she could look up at him. "What on earth was your reason, then?"

"I left because you were right." He slid his hands down until he held her by her upper arms, somehow needing the connection.

"I was right?" Her brow furrowed.

"I was throwing my life away. Drinking and partying and wasting money that wasn't even mine." He rubbed his hands up and down her arms, as though to warm her, though he was the one feeling a chill. "I looked at how hard you were working to achieve your goals, you and your sisters. The way I was must have just rubbed it in your face that I was squandering what I had, and what you so badly wanted."

"That's part of it," she admitted, then to his surprise leaned forward and pressed her forehead to his chest, letting out a soft sigh.

"What was the other part?" he asked quietly.

She kept her face buried, and he liked how it felt. Finally she sighed again, then spoke.

"The other part was that I loved you." She shifted position, now pressing her cheek against him. "I loved you, and I believed that you were capable of taking over the world if you wanted to. Instead, you seemed intent on self-destruction. I couldn't just sit by and watch."

Theo opened his mouth to reply but found that he had no idea what to say to that. Most of the decisions that he'd made over the years had been pondered with Jo's voice in his ear. He'd done it with an eye to proving himself to her, even though he wasn't sure if he'd ever see her again.

He had no idea that she'd thought him capable all along.

A drop of rain splashed squarely on his nose, breaking up his thoughts. It was followed by a sprinkling of rain in Jo's hair.

"Shit." Clouds rolled in, thick as soup, and a bolt of lightning lit up the sky and made the hairs on the back of his neck stand up straight as the electricity charged the air around them. "Let's run!"

Jo squealed with laughter as he grabbed her hand, tugging her back in the direction they'd come. They were both soaking by the time they reached the car, which he'd thankfully folded up the top to.

He opened her door, helping her in, before sprinting around to the driver's side. When he was safely enclosed in the dry space, he shook like a dog, cursing as he looked down.

"Since when do you get so worked up about rain?" Peeling off the silk scarf, Jo combed her fingers through her hair, which was sleek with moisture. "I distinctly remember you once streaking down the street in it after a few too many beers with your school friends."

Theo grimaced, unbuttoning his suit jacket. "I'll go streaking anytime you want me to, baby. But I'd prefer not to ruin this suit. I was assured that it was made by blind monks on a hill somewhere, woven out of their blood and tears or some such nonsense. That's the only explanation behind the price."

He tossed his jacket behind his seat, then loosened his tie, unbuttoning the top of his shirt. Moving on to loosening his cuffs, he found Jo watching him with more than a hint of hunger on her face.

He didn't think; he just acted, placing his palm flat on the nape of her neck and hauling her against his chest. She made a muffled moan as he crushed his lips to hers, his tongue immediately tracing the seam of her mouth, demanding that she open for him.

She did, a sigh of surrender on her lips when he slipped his tongue into her mouth and tasted her. The smoky scent of cinnamon that he swore came from her very skin surrounded him, drugging him as he stroked between her lips the way he wanted to taste between her legs.

A crack of thunder so loud that the car vibrated crashed through the air, and they jolted apart, both breathing heavily. When he looked at Jo, saw her lips swollen from his kisses, her cheeks flushed with desire, it took everything he had not to haul her astride him then and there.

He didn't want their first time again to be in a cramped car outside a graveyard. No, what he wanted was to strip her naked, lay her out on his bed and do every single thing he'd ever dreamed of doing to Jo Marchande.

The way she was looking at him right now? He thought he might finally have the chance.

CHAPTER ELEVEN

THE HOUR-LONG RIDE back to Boston was quiet, the only words exchanged as they picked their way through the picnic that Theo had packed. Actually, he'd ordered it from a popular deli downtown, but he didn't see why that made any difference. She was too keyed up to eat more than a handful of grapes and a small wedge of smoked cheddar, and he liked that she seemed worked up.

"Where do you live?" As he turned down their street, he realized how little she still knew of his life in the years between. "I can't imagine you're staying at the house. It's been empty since…well, since your dad died."

"I actually am." He cast a sidelong glance at her in the growing shadows. Warmer weather was approaching, but the nights were still long and the light was already fading. He liked it—the blueberry tones of twilight seemed to wrap them in a little cocoon, where they could stay as long as they liked. "I stayed away for a while because…well, I just couldn't handle going through his things yet. Not when I know what a disappointment I was to him."

"You didn't come to his funeral." There was no judgment in her words.

"I did, actually," he admitted, pulling the Jag into the long driveway that led to the stately mansion. Jo gaped at him as he put it into Park and turned to face her.

"Why didn't I see you there?" A spark of anger licked at her words, and he knew he deserved it.

"I made sure you didn't," he replied simply, shrugging. "I wasn't ready."

"Ready for *what*, for the love of God?" She threw her hands in the air.

"I wasn't yet the person I'd gone away to become." He watched her steadily as she seemed to mull that over. He knew she had questions—she'd always displayed every single thing that she thought on her face without a filter.

"Have you been back in Boston since then?" she asked carefully.

"No." He wanted to reach for her, to touch her, but wasn't sure she'd welcome it right then. "No, I came back just for the funeral. I was in New York then. Had been for a few years. I only moved back to Boston a couple of months ago, when I opened the Crossing Lines office here. I stayed at the Boston Plaza until this week."

"Until you were ready to let me know you were back?" She seemed to chew on that. He held his breath, wondering what she was going to ask next. "Is Crossing Lines that new of a company?"

"Yes and no." He thought back, pulling up the details. "It's been in the works for a few years. I didn't want to use my dad's money for it, so I had to raise funds, which took a while. Then there was the programming, structuring the company. I didn't move the offices to Boston until we were officially open. Some of the staff came with me, which made me happy. I'm trying to instill a certain kind of corporate culture, one that treats its employees right and makes them happy, because I think that happiness will filter down to the users of the site."

"Was Ava one of the employees who moved with you?" Theo studied her face as she asked. He didn't see jealousy, but there was a hint of possessiveness that made him want to drag her into the house and claim her, caveman style.

"She was." He didn't feel guilty about anything he'd done with Ava—he assumed that Jo had had lovers over the years, as well. "But we were never together romantically. It was just sex."

Not even that great of sex, either, but he didn't think that Jo needed any details—at least, any more detail than what she'd already seen with her own eyes.

She nodded, appearing to accept that, but then pinned him with an intense look. "I don't care what you've done when we were apart. But I'm not comfortable with you being with other women while we're...while we're doing whatever we're going to do."

"Say it." He savored the spark that lit her eyes. "Say what you want me to do to you."

"I want you to fuck me." Her voice was quiet, but sure. His girl had always known what she wanted before she reached out and took it. "Only you."

Taking her chin in his hand, he tilted her head so that she was sitting up perfectly straight, his hand on her skin their only point of contact. "You don't want to see what I'd do to any other man who touches you."

"While we're together," she added, expression daring him to argue.

He smiled grimly. "We'll see."

Leaving her frowning over that, he exited the car, circling round the back so that he could open her door for her. He helped her out, hooking his suit jacket—now only slightly damp—over her to protect her from the relentless drizzle that was still coming down.

He led her through the front door, closing it behind them. The door was old, like the rest of the house made of heavy wood. The sound of it closing was satisfying, solid, and Theo again had the sense that they were being wrapped in a cocoon that was all their own.

"Do you want a refresher tour?" he asked quietly, watching as she looked around, those keen writer eyes taking in every detail. "It's been a long time."

She turned her attention from the heavy, dated crystal chandelier overhead to him, and his heart skipped a beat when he saw the decision in her eyes.

"No." She inhaled softly, pulling his suit jacket off and holding it back out to him. "I just want to see your room."

If he touched her, they wouldn't make it to his room. Hanging his jacket carelessly on the post of the banister, he followed her upstairs, stopping her when she tried to turn into his old room.

"I've moved." With a jerk of his chin, he pointed her in the direction of the master suite. "Over here."

Inside the massive room, he slid the dimmer switch on halfway—he wanted to be able to see her, every part of her. Pulling off his tie, he enjoyed watching her explore the space.

"You must have just redone this." She paused to run a finger over the headboard of his bed—a new one he'd had custom built when he'd decided to move into this house. "I can smell paint."

"It was just finished last week, actually." Kicking off his shoes, he undid a few more buttons on his shirt, noting the way her eyes tracked the movement. "Moving into my old room felt like moving into the past. But I thought it would be weird to live in here with my dad's old stuff, which was hugely dated, anyway. So I gutted this room and the master bath. Some of the crew was actually putting the finishing touches on your hotel, so I'm not surprised you didn't notice. They would have blended right in."

She appeared to chew on that as she moved to the window. Bracing her hands on the sill, she peered outside, in the direction of her house, the one that her family had been in for decades, the one he knew she'd worked herself to the bone to make sure they kept.

"You renovated these rooms." She spoke carefully, measuring each word. "Does that mean you plan on staying?"

He was taken aback by the direct question. He

knew his plans for the next few years, but beyond that…he hadn't really thought.

He couldn't help but be honest. This was Jo. He'd never lied to her, and he didn't want to make it a new habit.

"I'm here as long as it makes sense for me to be here, for the company." He took a deep breath. "I've always assumed that sooner or later I'd sell, though. That I'd take the profits from Crossing Lines and go invest in something else. Something bigger."

"Something away from Boston," she said as she stared out the window. He wanted her to turn around so that he could see her face.

"Well…probably," he agreed, raking his hand through his hair. Why did that suddenly not sound as appealing as it once had? Why was he even asking that question? He knew why. Chances were, after this he would move back to New York, or more likely, to LA. His dreams didn't start and end with Crossing Lines. And no matter what happened here between him and Jo, she would never leave Boston. Never leave her family.

He shifted uncomfortably in the silence, suddenly filled with a restlessness that made him edgy. He watched as Jo pushed away from the window, sauntering over to the bed. Her body language said that she didn't care one way or another what his answer to that question had been, and it made a thread of something darkly possessive spark to life inside him.

She perched on the edge of the bed, smoothing a hand over the steel-gray quilt. "This bed is huge. You could have an orgy in it."

"Let's save that for another night." He felt his lips form a lopsided smile as she arched an eyebrow at him, seemingly content with the subject change. "I promised you dinner."

"I'm not hungry." Rising, she crossed to him, stopping a foot away. His stare fixed on her pulse, beating rapidly beneath the glove-thin skin of her throat. He wanted to press his mouth there. Use his teeth to mark her as his own.

"What should we do, then?" Even as he spoke, he undid the last of the buttons on his shirt, letting it hang open. He enjoyed her appreciative glance. He'd always logged long hours in the gym, even as a teen, since he wasn't doing much else. But he'd thickened since then, no longer had any of the gangly limbs associated with puberty. As Jo shed her cardigan, he noted that her body had changed, too, though the differences were subtle. She'd always been petite, nearly skinny in her teens. Now she was curved in all the right places, and though her breasts were still small, they'd plumped up enough to make him think about all the dirty things he wanted to do to them.

"What should we do?" he repeated, taking her by the waist. She shivered as he drew her slowly to him, until the tips of those pretty breasts brushed against the bare skin of his chest.

"I'm cold." He didn't think she meant just physically, though her hands were chilly from the damp, the rain. "I want you to warm me up."

Heat rocketed through Theo's body. He'd been with other women, beautiful women, sexy women. Most of them had been so eager to be with him that he hadn't had to do much to charm them into his bed. He hadn't had to do much to please them there, either, since ultimately what they were after wasn't really him. No, they wanted the idea of him—the maverick rich boy, the one who turned his back on his family fortune and made his own millions. They liked the travel, the luxury, the lifestyle.

With Jo, his money had always been more of a hindrance if it was anything at all, which it often wasn't. The woman who stood before him in what he was pretty sure were clothes belonging to one of her sisters had no interest in money beyond keeping her family comfortable. She wasn't into shopping, hadn't batted an eye at his Jag. So the fact that she was here at all meant that it was because she wanted *him*. Him, Theo.

He'd never had to work so hard to get a woman into his bed. And no other woman heated his blood quite like she did.

He wanted this to be good for her, wanted her to be fully aware of who was inside her when she came on his cock.

"Strip for me." Peeling her cardigan down just enough to expose her delicate shoulders, he pressed a kiss to one then stepped back. He enjoyed the shiver that passed through it, because he knew she was thinking of what was about to happen.

"I said I was cold. How am I supposed to get warm if I take off my clothes?"

But even as she spoke, she was tugging the damp sweater down her arms and off, tossing it to the floor.

"Keep going." Wanting to see if she would buck against the command, he infused it with arrogance. His brave girl merely arched an eyebrow and slithered out of the long shirtdress thing that hid far too much of her tight little body.

"Last time we were together, I don't think you even owned a bra." He nodded at the simple, baby blue cotton that covered her chest. "This is new."

"I was a little smaller then. I didn't need one."

Rosy pink flushed the skin of her torso. "They're still not that big, but it's enough that I'd be giving everyone a show without one."

"I like it." He really did—the simple cotton held up her sweet breasts like an offering. "Take it off."

"You're probably used to seeing women in things a lot sexier than this." Flicking open the front clasp, she held the bra up by cupping her hands around her breasts. "I can get something fancier."

"Don't you dare," he ordered with enough force to make her blink up at him with surprise. "If I wanted to see other women in fancy lingerie, then that's what I'd be doing right now. But I'm here with you, so what does that tell you?"

She stared up at him almost nervously, her tongue flicking out to lick over her lips. She didn't answer.

Before she could inhale even one more time, he'd closed the space between them, threading a hand through her short, sleek hair. She gasped but arched into the touch, letting her bra fall open and down to the floor.

"I want to hear you say it," he commanded, focused on every little detail of her expression. Her pulse had quickened, her eyes were dilated and her lips had parted, making him think about how they would look wrapped around his cock. "Answer my question."

"You're here because you want me." Her voice was quiet, but her words were clear. She knew it, too—there was no point in fighting the connection that had snapped tight between them since the moment they'd met.

"I like hearing that from your mouth." Without letting go of her hair, he tugged at her leggings, yanking them down her thighs, along with a pair of briefs that matched her bra. Sliding his foot between her legs, he pushed down until she was forced to step out of them.

She gasped when he lifted her without warning, hauling her over his shoulder. "What the hell are you doing?"

"I told you to strip and you took your sweet time about it, so I decided to do it for you." Carrying her toward the bathroom, he let his palm roam over the supple planes of her ass. "Since you don't seem to take direction well, I decided that I would just take you where I wanted you, rather than wait for you to get around to it."

"Since I don't take direction well?" Her lips parted in shock as he carried her right into the massive shower that he'd had installed when he redid the bathroom. Flipping her hair out of her eyes after he set her on her feet, he saw her struggle to make sense of that play out over her face.

Her lips parted as if to ask him something, then closed again.

"Ask me," he said as he entered a series of settings on the sleek control panel built into the wall of the shower. Triple rainfalls burst down around them, steam rising hot and quick. He looked back at Jo, was entranced by the droplets of water sliding over her skin.

"Do you expect me to do what you tell me to?" Her voice was tentative. "Are you dominant? Are you into that?"

She didn't sound horrified, only curious, which raised his temperature far past the point of comfort. Shrugging out of his now soaking-wet dress shirt, he tossed it to the floor, his slacks and briefs quickly joining it.

Her stare immediately went to his erection, and even over the thunderous spray of the shower he could hear her soft moan. He'd been hard since they stepped into his bedroom, but with her eyes on his cock, he swelled even more.

"I'm not into hard-core BDSM, if that's what you're asking. I don't expect you to call me sir." He grinned down at her; she snorted in response. He grabbed her wrist, tugged her wet, naked body against his own and gave in to the urge to lick those water droplets from her neck.

"I'd rather hear you say my name when you're coming on my dick," he murmured into her ear, nipping at the lobe when she shuddered. "And like I said. I'm not dominant, but if you let me be bossy, I think you'll find that you enjoy it."

"I'm…not…the…submissive…type." She gasped, rocking into him when he trailed kisses down her neck. He laughed.

"I don't want you to be submissive. I like women who give me hell." Trailing a hand down her spine, he pressed her to him, groaned himself when his erection pressed into the lean planes of her belly.

"That's always been a special talent of mine," she gasped as he ground into her. He was surprised at how tentative she was when her hand slid lower and found him. She stroked his length, cupped his shaft as though she'd never seen a cock before.

Her next words nearly brought him to his knees. "I'm always happy to give you hell. But… I don't think I'd mind if you…told me what to do. I think I'd like to try."

"Hell, Jo." Both of his hands found her hair, smoothing through the wet ribbons of it and dragging her mouth to his. He claimed her lips, tonguing her until she was rocking against him with breathy little sighs. "If you don't like what I'm doing, you just say so in plain English. Or shake your head. Whatever. I'll stop."

She nodded breathlessly, then raised her chin defiantly. "You're talking an awful lot. Got any action to back it up with?"

With a growl that was part laughter, part pure animal lust, he cupped his hands under her ass and lifted her, carrying her to a small seat carved out of the marble wall. Placing her on it, he reached for his discarded pants, pulling his belt free from the loops.

His leather belt, his suit, they were all ruined after today. He didn't give even a single fuck. It was all going to be worth it.

Jo's eyes widened at the sight of the belt. "You're not hitting me with that thing."

Theo snorted, though he couldn't resist slapping it against his palm, just to test her reaction. "Not this time, baby. But something tells me you might like a little spanking."

"You're not—" Her words were stuck in her throat when he grabbed her hands, pressing her palms together. She watched with wide eyes as he wrapped his belt around them, securing her wrists together before sliding a finger underneath to make sure the belt wasn't too tight.

Part of him, the one that was very familiar with her temper, expected her to tell him to fuck right off if he thought he was going to tie her up. But this Jo was older, more mature and had a self-professed interest in all things kinky. This Jo made a low, breathy sound when he lifted her bound wrists and hooked them over one of the showerheads, tethering her in place.

"Oh, I like this." Stepping back, he admired his handiwork. Seated on the small bench, the position of her arms forced her to arch her back, which showed off those pretty tits. Man, he'd missed those. Cupping one in each hand, he circled his thumbs over her nipples, satisfaction coursing through him when they pebbled beneath his touch. "I can do whatever I want with you all trussed up like this, can't I? You can give me lip, but you can't do much about it."

He was testing her. If she gave him even one sign that she wasn't into it, that she was scared, he'd let her go in an instant. Instead, her body rocked forward, trying to get closer to him.

"For heaven's sake, Theo, stop messing around. Come here." Her voice was raw with need.

Letting go of one breast, he tapped a finger against her lips. "You're not the boss here, remember? You'll get my cock when I say so, and not a minute before."

She cursed, and he laughed. Sliding his hands down, he parted her thighs wide enough for him to stand between them. She gasped eagerly when the head of his shaft brushed the soft heat of her cleft, but he had other ideas.

"I wish I had another belt in here to hold you open just like this, but since I don't, we'll just have to make do." He slid a finger through her folds, her knees tightening on either side of his hips against the sudden contact.

"You're soaked." He lifted his fingers up so she could see her own moisture on them, wetter even than the water pouring down around them. When he slid those same fingers into his mouth and licked them clean, her head fell back, watching him through partially lowered lids.

"You're the only person who's ever made me that way." Her focus stayed locked on him, and he understood that she was sharing something important with him. The weight of her words hit him with the impact of a bulldozer.

He didn't deserve this, not after the way he'd left. But then, he'd never claimed to be a good man. He certainly wasn't above taking what she was offering to him.

He thought he just might die if he didn't.

"Are you warming up?" He ran a hand along her inner thigh. She melted beneath his touch, her muscles liquefying like honey in the sun. She continued to regard him with that laser-like focus, as though she was afraid he would disappear if she looked away.

"Keep looking at me like that." Moving his hands to brace them on either side of her face, he leaned in, let his cock press against her slick heat. "It makes me so fucking hard."

"Good." She gasped when he rubbed against her, her thighs clenching around his hips. "That's how I want you."

"Mmm, but this isn't about what you want. I'm bossy, remember?" Dipping his head, he laved his tongue over her nipple. "It's about what I want to give you."

"Damn it, Theo." She tugged at her bindings, cursing when they wouldn't give. "I want to touch you."

"And I want to touch you." Standing, he reached for the detachable showerhead mounted into the wall. "Guess what? I win."

So would she, though, and very soon. Adjusting the nozzle of the showerhead until the water flowed in a steady stream, but not one that would be too hard for her sensitive flesh, he aimed it between her legs. Her gasp when the water made contact sent a stream of pure desire through him.

"Jesus." She writhed on the bench, twisting against her restraints like a wild thing. Her hips bucked, and he wasn't sure if she was trying to lean into the spray or push away. Steam rolled through the shower, and he couldn't tell if the droplets of water on her skin were from the water falling around them or sweat, not even when he laid his tongue to her shoulder for a taste.

"Theo. I can't… I'm going to…" She arched like a bow as he began to move the spray in slow circles between her legs, edging around her clit but not coming in direct contact with it. Her frenzied motions brought her heat into contact with the swollen length of his dick, and he briefly closed his eyes to regain his control.

When he opened them again, he was struck by the visual that was laid out before him. Slim as an arrow, she still curved in all the places that made his mouth go dry. Her milky-white skin was a pretty shade of pink from arousal and heat. Her nipples were cherry red and their tips bunched enticingly, begging for his mouth. Her eyes were still at half-mast, glassy with lust but fixed on the visual of his cock, the water and her parted thighs.

"You surprised me," he said as he ran a finger through her folds again, letting the water beat around the touch. She gasped, groaning when he pulled away again.

"What do you mean?" She ground this out through gritted teeth. He could tell from the look on her face, the increasingly frenzied movements of her body, that the pleasure was rising high and fast inside her. He loved that he could bring her there so quickly.

Grinning wickedly, he returned his hand to her pussy. This time he tucked two fingers inside, savoring the way she clenched around him as he slid through her liquid heat. “You’re completely bare. That’s new.”

“I…like it…that…way.” He found that special place inside her, rubbed over her and watched the way her eyes blurred. “Jesus fuck, Theo. I can’t take it anymore.”

“You will take it, because I say so.” He kept up the pressure inside her but moved the showerhead so that the spray was focused directly on her clit. She cried out, the sound echoing off the glass walls of the shower, her inner walls squeezing him so tightly it hurt.

“Come for me, Jo.” He’d barely said the words when she screamed his name, her body clenching tight, her mouth open as she cried out. She rocked against him once, twice, then shuddered, every muscle melting like candle wax.

His cock actually throbbed with the need to be inside her, to claim her as his. He wasn’t sure that he could keep her here once they were done, though—he thought she might go rabbiting back home to overthink what had just happened. With that in mind, he ground his teeth and called up every ounce of restraint that he possessed, not yet ready to stop playing with her.

She murmured something as he reached up and unhooked her from the showerhead, then undid the belt around her wrists. She was pliant, letting him pull her to her feet, pressing his front to her back.

She unconsciously rocked back against him, pressing her ass against his length. Grabbing his shaft at the base, he stroked it gently between her cheeks. She shuddered when it pressed against the tight rosette, and he grinned.

"Dirty girl." She murmured in agreement. When he rubbed the bar of soap over her breasts, she leaned her head back on his shoulder trustingly, and he stilled for a moment.

She might still be scarred from what he'd done, but some primal part of her, something that they'd just tapped into through their bodies, still trusted him. He would hold on to that and pray that the rest of her followed suit.

When her skin was coated with a creamy lather, he set the soap down and squirted shampoo into his hands. The crisp scent of citrus permeated the steam as he rubbed it into her hair, massaging her scalp, her neck and her shoulders.

Once he'd rinsed her clean, he watched as the sleepiness disappeared from her limbs. Turning in his arms, she cast a very obvious glance down at his red, swollen length. "I think someone is feeling deprived. I'd better take care of him."

She panted out a breath when he yanked her against his chest, hands splaying over her back so that she couldn't move away. Those watchful gray eyes focused in on him like lasers, questioning, and he slowly rubbed his erection back and forth across her soft flesh.

"You don't listen very well, baby." His cock slid between her thighs, and they clenched around its length, making him exhale sharply. "You don't get to make the rules."

CHAPTER TWELVE

SHE WAS GOING to have sex with Theo again. Tonight. Soon. There was no question. After so long with numbness as her constant companion, she was overwhelmed with feeling—like steam building up in a pressure cooker, she needed to let some out before she exploded.

The orgasm that had just exploded through her body hadn't relieved the pressure, not at all. As Theo rubbed his cock against the tender skin of her inner thighs, she wondered if she was going to survive this intact, or if her entire body would self-combust the second he slid inside her.

"Put your arms around me." She did as he commanded, her heart melting a little as he scooped her up in his arms, fireman-style. He snagged a towel the size of a lake as he carried her from the shower to the foot of the bed. When he wrapped her in it, the hem of the plush fabric fell almost to the floor. Content for the moment, she watched as he crossed to the massive fireplace, picked up a remote and set a blazing fire to life with the press of a button.

"That's quite the toy," she commented when he returned to her, rubbing the towel over her hair and then lower. She closed her eyes against the sensation when he scrubbed the fabric over her sensitive nipples and then between her legs, the nubby fabric a tease.

"I like toys." He didn't bother to dry himself off, instead tossing the towel to the ground. She felt his gaze everywhere he looked at her just as much as if he was stroking her with his hands.

What was it going to be like, this time? In the first few years after he'd left, she had a few fumbling encounters, but she always stopped it short of penetration, because why would she go there if it did nothing for her? But now, all she could think about was the one time he'd been inside her, how it had been when he'd slid his arousal right into her very core.

"Please." She didn't want to wait even a minute longer. However stupid it was, it felt like all this time she'd been waiting for him to come back—him, the only person who could make her feel good. Her entire body was restless, riding an edge of need that was almost painful in its intensity.

"Please what, Jo?" Her gaze snapped to his when she heard the need in his voice, equal to her own. How was this happening? How were they here together again? "I need to hear you say it."

Need, not want. That little distinction did something funny to her insides. She reached for him without meaning to, wrapping her arms around his waist, pressing her cheek to his heart.

"I want you," she whispered, listening to the thunder of his pulse, knowing that hers matched. "I want all of you."

"How do you want it?" His hands roamed over her back, tracing the lines of her shoulder blades, the curve of her spine.

She thought of all the filthy things she'd written about, the pictures she'd seen as she researched.

He was giving her a chance to ask for what she wanted. To explore.

Swallowing past the hard, sudden lump in her throat, she gently disentangled herself from his arms. Trying not to feel self-conscious about the fact that every inch of her naked body was on display, she knelt at the edge of the bed, angling herself away from him.

"I want it like this." She was sure that her skin

was on fire, but her voice was sure. "And I don't want you to be gentle."

The sound he made was nearly inhuman, and she felt herself grow impossibly slicker. "You can't be real. I'm imagining this."

"Not this time." Not sure what to do, she leaned forward until her hands rested on the bed, so that she was on all fours. She knew he had a full view of every intimate part of her, and knew damn well that he was looking, but knowing that sent a little thrill through her. Made her feel powerful.

"You asked for it, baby." She heard the rip of foil. Her pulse stuttered, then began to beat again, double time, as she closed her eyes and imagined him rolling the tube of latex over his cock. She nearly looked back over her shoulder, just for the visual of those sure fingers on his own erection.

Next time, she promised herself. This time she didn't want to think, because then the little voice in her head would nag, reminding her of the heartbreak she was opening herself up to here. No, she just wanted to be taken, to have all thoughts shoved from her mind so that the only thing in her existence was Theo and what he was doing to her body.

"What is that?" Something soft danced over the skin of her lower back, and she gasped.

He didn't answer, but a moment later something was placed over her eyes. He smoothed her hair back, then secured what she now knew to be the silk scarf at the back of her head.

"I don't want that busy brain of yours thinking of anything but what I'm doing to you. Understood?" She nodded, her throat suddenly so dry that she couldn't have spoken to save her life.

She didn't have to speak. Like he said, all she had to do was feel. And that's exactly what she did when he pressed the head of his cock to her aching entrance, alighting nerves that hadn't been touched in a very, very long time.

She inhaled sharply when he pushed forward. Or rather, when he tried to. Her body was as tight as it had been when she was a virgin, and it wasn't sure what to do with this intrusion, no matter how good it felt.

"How are you still so tight?" His hands gripped her hips as he stilled, only the head of his cock tucked inside her. "Am I hurting you?"

"Not hurting." Dropping down to her forearms, she tilted her hips, changing the angle. He slid in another inch, and she gasped at the friction. "I just—I haven't—"

"Jesus, Jo." He stopped again, and she felt the tension in the hands that gripped her hips. "Tell me you've been with someone else."

There was no shaming in his words, but she felt

it all the same. "I didn't—I've never wanted to." And she hadn't. Something was just different with her body, her brain.

If she didn't love the person, she wasn't interested in sex.

Oh shit.

She was still in love with Theo. In love again.

This was going to hurt.

"Baby." His voice was full of wonder. "You're a gift."

Then he reached forward, sliding his hand between her legs. Sure fingers found her clit, circling and teasing, and as she melted into the pleasure of his touch, he worked in another inch.

"That's it," he coaxed, circling her swollen nub again and again until she felt that strange tension low in her belly, that aching need for more. "Just relax. We've got all the time in the world."

Her forehead was damp with perspiration, and she pressed it to the soft cotton of his quilt. Her hips were canted, and the higher his fingers brought her, the farther he was able to slide inside her. When he pinched her swollen flesh between his forefinger and thumb, she gasped, feeling something inside her open, and he worked in the final inch. Stilling, she felt his hips resting against the curves of her ass and shifted against the unfamiliar fullness of him inside her.

"How are you doing?" His voice was strained, and she knew that the slow pace had to be killing him. He was doing it all for her. It made her a little weak in the knees.

How could she be afraid of him hurting her when he acted like this? How could she believe that he'd once again be careless with her heart?

"I'm good," she gasped, unable to keep from pushing back against him when his clever fingers worked her higher still. "So good. I think I—"

"Don't you dare come yet." Clenching her waist, he pulled back, and the slow drag of his erection over her swollen tissues had her eyes rolling back in her head. "Don't you do it."

"I don't think I can help it." That wild wave was rising inside her as he worked his way back in, swiveling his hips to get her body to let him in. She gasped when he sheathed himself to the hilt again. "I can't—I think—"

"We're going to go together." His pace quickened slowly, bringing to life nerves that she hadn't even known she had. "Hold on."

She was lost in the world he created for her. Eyes covered, she existed in the seductive dark, her fingers scrabbling to hold on to something and finding nothing, realizing that she had to let herself fall. He gripped her hips, moving in and out of her tight flesh with increasing speed, a relentless onslaught of pleasure that had them both gasping each time he bottomed out inside her.

Her knees gave out, and she fell face-first on the bed. Bracing his weight on his arms, he continued to pump. Beneath her, the cotton rubbed against her damp clit with the friction she needed to fly over the edge. She started to chant his name, trying to wait as he'd told her to, but the rocket inside her was ignited and counting down to launch.

"That's it," his voice rasped in her ear. "I want you to feel this tomorrow. Every time you take a step, every time you sit down, you're going to remember who filled you up. Yes?"

"Yes," she agreed wildly, and then she was flying. He pushed into her one final time, thrusting as he emptied himself once, twice, three times. The smell of salt and sweat hung heavily in the air as her body clenched around him, her muscles shaking as she exploded so brightly that stars danced behind her eyes.

She was aware when he pulled out of her, and when he used the towel to dry the sweat on her brow, but it was as if she was watching someone else. Surely that couldn't be her who felt so sated, so blissful. Surely that couldn't be her half draped over Theo's chest as he tucked them in and promised that he would cook her spaghetti just as soon as they could move.

That dead space inside her was alive, filled with light. And she was scared of going back to the dark.

CHAPTER THIRTEEN

I GET A lot of repeat questions in my in-box. You, my dear readers, have helped me to define some of the most common problems of our generation. The one on my mind today is, can you ever really let an ex back into your life?

Hear me out. We're all familiar with that phenomenon where our memories make things in the past seem better than they actually were. So when an ex comes back into your life, and you're consumed by that flood of emotion that inevitably shows up with it, how can you be rational? Throw sex into the game, and it's like all of your efforts to move on and heal have disappeared like a puff of smoke.

The question you ask me, time and again, is if I think a relationship can be different the second time around. Can a cheater change his stripes?

Can you find common ground when you want different things? Can people grow up, can people change? I don't have the answer to that for you. What I can tell you is what I've discovered for myself this week—even if it's scary, even if it means you might get hurt, aren't you going to be disappointed if you don't try? Now, I'm not talking getting back with someone who didn't treat you well, or taking an abuser back because he asked you nicely. But what if the reason you parted ways with someone ultimately came down to youth and stupidity? What if, as an adult, they're the best thing that ever happened to you? Will you turn them away because you never make the same mistake twice? Or will you let them back in, even knowing that you might get—probably will get—hurt again?

Is the experience worth the pain?

Thoughtfully yours,

Jojo Kink

"Hey." Jo jumped when Theo poked his head into her office. She hurriedly—and not very subtly—closed the screen of her laptop, not wanting him to see the post she was working on. When she'd sat down at her computer that morning, she'd debated which topic on Theo's list to tackle first, but ultimately, when her fingers started to fly over the keyboard, she'd found herself writing about him.

She wasn't ready for him to read it, though. She might not ever be. But it had been cathartic to get her feelings out into words.

"You left before I woke up." He studied her with those dark eyes as he entered the office that had been assigned to her, closing the door behind him. She sat up straighter when she saw the sternness on his face.

"I had to get ready for work." She cocked her head slightly but saw that he knew the truth.

"And?" He crossed his arms over his chest, his muscles pulling at the fabric of his suit. After the up-close and personal look she'd gotten at his muscles a few days earlier, it was extra distracting, because all she wanted to do was rip off his jacket and shirt and run her tongue over the bumps and ridges.

She considered pretending not to know what he was talking about, but he would see right through it. Sighing, she tucked a ribbon of hair behind her ear and leaned back in her desk chair.

"I just needed to think," she admitted, shifting restlessly in the cushioned seat.

"You couldn't think with me there?" His voice was gruff, and she saw that she'd actually wounded him, which hadn't been her intention at all.

"I'm sorry," she blurted out, rubbing her suddenly sweaty palms together. "You're—you're very distracting. I needed to think about you, but I couldn't be around you while I did."

"You needed to think about me, huh?" Crossing the room, he only stopped when he could brush against her knees as he sat. "And what conclusion did you come to?"

Her mouth was dry. She reached for her coffee cup, only to find it was empty. She replaced it on the desk, desperate for something to do with the nervous energy in her hands.

"You might hurt me again," she started, holding up a hand when thunderclouds gathered fast and thick in his eyes. "Just bite back on your temper for a second, okay? You might hurt me. I might hurt you. I feel like I still know you, the real you, but the truth is that I'm missing the details on a huge chunk of your life. I'm terrified that that's going to jump out and bite me on the ass."

"If anyone is going to bite you on the ass, it's going to be me," he promised darkly before gesturing for her to continue. "Go on."

"But..." The words stuck in her throat, nearly choking her before she forced them out. "Nobody ever made me feel the way you do. I don't think anybody else *can*. So... I want to keep exploring whatever this is. Slowly."

He lifted her out of the chair by her elbows. She sucked in a breath when he brushed his lips over hers so softly it felt like butterfly wings. "There's never been anything slow about either of us, Jo. We both jump headfirst, all or nothing. But know that when you fly off that cliff, I'll be right there beside you."

"When did you learn to be so smooth?" She huffed out a laugh, pressing her forehead against him.

"Baby, I've always been smooth." He grinned down at her, then jerked his chin at her laptop. "Now. What were you working on that you so desperately don't want me to see?"

"Nothing." The lie was automatic. Damn it, she wasn't ready for him to read those words yet. "It's nothing. It's not ready. Don't open that."

"You know that just makes me want to look even more, right?" Arching an eyebrow, he reached for the computer. She smacked his hand—and wasn't gentle about it.

"You did not just smack me." His eyes glittered, and she felt something dark come to life inside her.

"You're not going to read that. Not as long as I'm standing here." Stubbornly, she lifted her chin in the air.

"Oh really?" Bending down to her height, he brushed his lips over the shell of her ear. "I've heard that I can be very distracting."

"Damn you," she exhaled, then before she could

overthink it, she snatched up the laptop and darted to the far side of the office. Pressing herself back into the corner, she watched Theo warily as she fought to keep a grip on the computer with her slick hands.

She had no idea what the hell she thought she was doing, but when he grinned, her stomach flipped with a potent combination of nerves and excitement. The sensation only intensified as she watched him remove his suit jacket with excruciating slowness, folding it before placing it on the seat of her chair.

"What the hell are you doing?" Her pulse quickened when he loosened his tie. All the time he watched her with laser focus, and she suddenly understood what a gazelle was faced with when cornered by a lion.

"Seems to me like you want to be chased." He grinned, but there was no humor in the expression, just wicked intent. "Who am I to say no to that?"

"What?" She darted a panicked glance between him and the door, even as wetness surged between her thighs, a fresh ache blooming where she was already sore. "It's nine o'clock in the morning. Your whole staff is out there. *John* is out there!"

"If you're so concerned about where John is, maybe I should invite him in to watch," Theo commented mildly, taking a step closer. "Then you won't have to wonder."

"Oh God." He wouldn't. Would he? The dangerous look he was casting her way told her that she really had no idea what he was capable of in that moment. "The door isn't locked!"

"Guess you better hope no one comes in, then." Without warning, he leaped forward. She squealed and scuttled down the wall away from him, still clasping the laptop to her chest, though she understood it wasn't about the article anymore.

"I don't know why you think you can run." He started toward her again, but this time his steps were slow and deliberate. "Where are you going to go?"

Having lulled her with the steady moments, he sprang, catching her by the front of the silky T-shirt that she'd stolen from Meg's closet that morning. She made a wordless, choking cry when he yanked and it tore right down the front, gaping open to expose the lacy bralette that she'd liberated as well.

"If you run out of the office right now, everyone will know what we're doing." He grinned, running a steady palm down her torso, between her breasts. She was quivering with suppressed sensation. "The new girl fucking the boss. Whatever will they think?"

“No!” The laptop slipped from her hands onto the plush carpet, and she barely noticed as it bounced away. Backing up rapidly, she wasn’t aware that Theo had stopped in his tracks until her ass hit the edge of her desk.

“No?” He searched her face intently, and she realized what she’d said. “Do you want to stop?”

Something delicate inside her snapped. He’d stopped. His cock was so hard that she could see its full outline, straining against the fabric of his pants, and his face was flushed with arousal, just like hers was. They were in the middle of some hot, kinky game that she didn’t fully understand, and he’d just *stopped* because she’d said no, even when she hadn’t really meant it.

How could she not trust this man with her heart?

“No. I mean… I don’t mean no. I mean, I meant it, but not like that.” Sighing with frustration, she scrubbed both hands over her face. “Is this where a safe word comes in?”

“*No* will always work with me. I’ll always check in with you if you say that, okay?” The intensity he spoke with told her that he needed her to understand this. “But if you want to choose a safe word, choose it now. Make sure it’s something you wouldn’t normally say in conversation.”

“Shower,” she blurted immediately, feeling herself flush when he grinned. “That’s my safe word.”

"Shower. Got it." He nodded to emphasize the point, and then he unbuttoned the collar of his shirt. Her eyes fixed on the inch of golden skin it revealed, desperate to press her lips there, to gauge his pulse.

"Run."

She blinked, not sure she'd heard him correctly, but when he moved, a surge of adrenaline had her scrambling back. The corner of the desk bit into her hip as she pushed past her chair, but she didn't feel a thing besides the need to get away.

She knew she wouldn't, not in the end. It didn't stop the urge to move, move, move, move, because once he caught her, she was at his mercy.

"Might as well give up," he taunted, continuing after her with that slow, relentless pace. "You know I'm going to win."

"Not if I can help it." Bracing herself to leap back the way she'd come as soon as he got a little closer, she wasn't prepared for him to anticipate the move. He caught her around the waist, hauling her off her feet as she cried out.

"I don't care if anyone hears you," he informed her as he dragged her back to her desk, splaying her out on its surface, "but you might not like it when someone comes to investigate just why you're being so damn noisy."

"Theo," she begged, and she wasn't sure if she

was asking for him to let her go, or to touch her. Still caught up in the game, she writhed against him, forcing him to pin her arms above her head with one of his hands, to catch her lower body with a thrust of his hips. With the other, he tore at the front of her bralette, treating it to the same fate as her top.

"I told you not to buy anything fancy just for me." Cupping one of her breasts, he squeezed the mound lightly. "I told you I liked what you wore."

"That was Meg's," she spat out, still struggling. The dressy jeans that completed her outfit—also her sister's—caused delicious friction against her clit as she wriggled against where the firm pressure of his hips pinned her down, her legs dangling on either side of his hips.

"Guess I owe Meg some clothes then." He grinned, not sorry at all, as he continued to massage her breast. Her world narrowed to the point of his touch, the pleasure he was pulling out of the swollen tip of her breast. "Gonna tell her what happened to the things you borrowed?"

"Something tells me she'll know." She yelped quietly when he swatted the side of her hip.

"You're awfully mouthy for a captive." Dragging his hand roughly down her torso, he tugged at the waistband of her jeans. "I'd like to give your mouth something else to do, but I don't have enough time for that today. Guess I'll have to hope that a quick fuck will knock that sass out of you for a while."

Her mouth fell open. Never in her life had someone spoken to her like that—not even Theo when he was younger—and it shocked her to her core. It also thrilled her, that part of her that was fascinated by the new, the different.

How he managed it, she wasn't sure, but he managed to work her jeans open with one hand while she was bucking against him. Dragging them and her underwear down over her hips, he worked one of her legs free before wrapping it around his waist.

"Keep on struggling," he told her as he undid his own slacks. She found herself watching avidly as he shoved his boxer briefs down far enough to release his erection. It was thick, and long, and swollen with need, a slick of moisture already making the head shine. She marveled for a moment that she'd managed to fit that inside her. And then she just wanted it inside her again.

"I won't let you do this," she spat, fully immersed in the role she was playing. She pulled against him with renewed vigor, even managing to pull free for a split second, causing him to curse and haul her back to the edge of the desk.

"It's happening, baby." The dark intent in his

words made molten heat pool in her core. Her spine pressed into the flat surface of the desk, her breasts freed by the torn garments on her torso. Her ass was balanced on the edge of the desk, one leg still tangled in her jeans while he held the other tightly to his hip. "I'm going to let go of your hands, but there's no point in trying to get free. I'll just catch you again."

"I have to try," she said breathlessly when he released her arms. She tried to roll, but he caught her, forced her back down with a hand pressed flat on her chest. Dropping the leg he'd clutched to his hip, he lined his shaft up with her wet slit and pushed inside, the intrusion making her eyes fly wide-open.

"Fuck," she groaned, letting her head fall back to the desk. He held still for a moment, letting her adjust to his thickness just inside her, but before she could get too comfortable, he flexed his hips and drove himself home.

A wordless cry escaped her lips, her hands sliding over the slick surface of the desk as she tried to catch hold of something, anything. Finally she settled on his shirt, his tie, but instead of shoving him away as her role demanded, she pulled him down closer until he was bent overtop of her, his chest rubbing against the tips of her breasts with every movement.

"Fuck, that's good." Bracing one hand on the desk above her head, the other again finding her hip, he pulled back until he almost slid out. Her slick channel clenched around him as he drove forward again, his length dragging over sensitive flesh and igniting a level of arousal she'd never felt. "Shit. *Shit.* I'm not wearing a condom."

She growled when he pulled out, wanting him back in. Propping herself up on her elbows, she watched, fascinated, as he fumbled with his wallet, pulling out a condom and tearing into it with his teeth. Within moments he was sheathed, his wallet was on the floor and he was pushing back inside her with renewed urgency.

"How is it possible for you to feel so fucking good?" He worked in and out of her at a slow, steady pace, and she watched with fascination as beads of sweat appeared on his forehead. She was hot, too, aroused to a fever pitch as she felt the pleasure begin to gather in her core like it had the night before.

"You feel good to me, too," she admitted as she watched his cock slide in and out of her parted lips. She'd never thought about watching, but it was just about the hottest thing she'd ever seen. "I feel so much, and I don't know what to do with it."

"You don't have to do anything with it except what I tell you to." He slid back into his role, and

Jo eagerly followed. It was so easy to let go when she pretended that she had no other choice. There was no point in worrying about getting hurt if the decision was being made for her.

"And what are you telling me to do?" She couldn't resist taunting him. Reaching down between them, she grabbed his waist, holding him tightly to her as he thrust deep.

"Mouthy brat." He grinned down at her, but his eyes were starting to glaze over with what she realized meant he was edging close to his own release. Knowing that she was the one to bring him there was heady, a kind of power she could get drunk on.

"That's not an answer." Her hand slid from his waist to dig into the hard planes of his rear, and she wished she could have that view, too—what he looked like from behind as he thrust inside her, the muscles of that truly spectacular ass flexing as he moved.

"You're going to come on my cock, is what you're going to do." He increased his pace, his head falling back. Her vision started to blur as the pressure inside her coiled tighter and tighter, a spring about to snap. "And you're going to do it now."

His hand slid to the place where they were joined, and the first touch of his fingers on her clit sent her flying over the edge. She swallowed her cries as she contracted around him, senses dulled to everything but the bliss that was riding her.

He grunted as he emptied himself in her, and she found herself fascinated by watching as he was lost. Stilling himself above her, he remained as he was, fully inside her, fully connected.

Fully hers. Without thinking, she reached up to brush a lock of his inky hair back from where it stuck to the sweat on his forehead. He opened his eyes, and when he looked down at her, she felt a jolt as she wondered what he was trying to say without actually saying it.

"I still want to read what you wrote." He broke the strange tension of the moment by nodding toward where her laptop lay, discarded on the floor. "I also feel that this is a good time to remind you about respecting company property."

"Jackass." She smacked his chest lightly, struggling to sit up. "And you can read it when it's ready, which it might be if someone hadn't decided to hunt me down in my own damn office."

"Much as I'd love to spend the rest of the day inside you, I should get back to my own office." He pulled out of her slowly, holding on to the condom as he did. "I'm very busy and important, you know."

She rolled her eyes, but inside felt lightness buoying her up. She'd missed this, too, so much it had hurt—this friendship that they'd shared before everything had gone to hell. Because when he'd left, she hadn't just lost her boyfriend and her love, she'd lost the best friend she'd ever had.

"I missed this." There. She'd said it. And though a flicker of surprise crossed his face as he tied off the condom and tossed it in the trash, he nodded in agreement.

"I missed it, too." Stepping back, he slowly zipped himself back into his slacks, straightening his shirt and tightening his tie. Catching her watching, he cast her a cocky grin. "How do I look?"

"Put your jacket on, and no one will know you've spent the last half an hour abusing every human resource code you put in the contract in the first place." Sliding from the desk, she struggled to pull the snug jeans back up over her hips, then looked down at her chest in dismay. "What the hell am I supposed to do about this?"

"You wore a sweater into work this morning. I saw you." He gestured to the back of the door, where a thin cardigan hung. "Just wear it buttoned up."

"With no bra?" But she was already reaching for it. It wasn't like she had much choice.

"Never used to stop you." He smirked at her, then stared avidly as she tucked her now braless breasts beneath the thin sweater. “Just don’t get too close to anyone else. Not that you’d want to after having a taste of this.”

“Go!” She rolled her eyes, then pointed to the door. “My boss is a bit of a tyrant. If you’re not careful, he’ll literally hunt you down just to check on your work.”

“Sounds like my kind of guy.” Opening the door, he cast a look back over his shoulder at her. She couldn’t stop the swelling of her heart as he winked at her like this had all been their dirty little secret. “Dinner tonight?”

“All right,” she replied softly, thrilling to the question even as she knew she was diving off a very high, very dangerous cliff.

But oh, how she was enjoying the fall.

CHAPTER FOURTEEN

THEO FELT LIKE he'd just completed a champion workout. He was riding high on endorphins, body loose, mind sated as he all but staggered back into his office.

Hell. He'd had some good sex before. He'd had some great sex. But what had just happened with Jo was so astronomically amazing that it couldn't even be described.

They'd connected on a physical level when they were younger, for sure. He'd thought he just might die from insisting they wait until she was eighteen.

Now, though? That innocent girl he remembered was kinky as fuck, and he knew he'd never in a million years find someone who inspired the same filthy urges in him. Never find another woman who challenged him, who called him on his shit. Who got excited when he took her to a graveyard on a date, and who really could not have cared less about the number of zeroes in his bank balance.

He was in love with her. Again? Still? It didn't really matter, because the truth was there, written in the way he could still feel her hands on his skin.

He wanted to tell her. Wanted to give her that certainty that he wasn't going anywhere. That he couldn't, not without her.

Loosening his tie that had just been straightened, he sat forward in his desk chair, tapping his keyboard to wake up his computer. He'd take her out for dinner, not someplace fancy, because she wouldn't care about that. Someplace that had meaning for them.

What was the name of that little Brazilian dive they'd frequented when they were in high school? His mom had taken him there when he was little, whenever she'd been craving food from home, since she was the type to burn toast. He'd never gone there with anyone else, not even his dad—not until he'd decided to share it with Jo.

It would be the perfect place to tell her what he felt. He knew she'd catch the significance. Now if only he could remember what the hell it was called, so he could look it up and make sure it was still open.

As he typed Brazilian food restaurant Boston

into his web browser, his cell phone vibrated against his hip. John's name flashed across the screen, and Theo put it on speaker.

"What's up?" When Theo had hired the consultant to help ensure a smooth official launch of Crossing Lines, he'd somehow pictured a rich old white dude. John Brooke was rich, certainly, but he wasn't old and he wasn't white, or anything else that Theo had expected. He was, however, everything that he'd promised, and Theo knew he'd miss him when he'd finished out their contract and moved on to another business. The other man had really thrown his heart and soul into Crossing Lines and was the nearest thing that Theo had to a real friend.

"Ass into my office, Lawrence." There was barely concealed glee in the other man's voice. "I'm about to make all of your fantasies come true."

"In your dreams, Brooke." Theo started walking as he spoke. Ava looked up from her desk, arching an eyebrow at him since he was talking so loudly. He shrugged, striding down the hall to John's office, which would be empty soon enough. "You don't have the right equipment."

"I could have you if I wanted you." John held out a paper cup of coffee as Theo entered the room, grinning mockingly. He leaned back in his chair, smugness written in every line of his body.

"We'll see how I feel about you after you tell me whatever has you grinning like a freaky-ass clown." Settling himself in the chair across the desk, Theo sipped at the coffee, gagging as soon as it touched his tongue. "What the hell is this garbage?"

"I made it myself." John frowned, gesturing at the coffee machine in his office, one that looked like it belonged in Starbucks. "It's an Americano."

"It's swamp water, man." Shuddering, Theo set it down on the desk. "But it's reassuring to know that you're human, after all. Now what's up?"

John took a cautious sip of his own coffee, and Theo watched with amusement as his eyes widened. He swallowed gamely. "It's not that bad."

Theo rolled his eyes; John set the cup on the edge of his desk.

"When you hired me, you told me that your goal was to grow Crossing Lines from a highly valued start-up to a company that could sell for a minimum of fifty million, correct?" Theo nodded. "We estimated three to five years for that growth."

"I know all this, Brooke." Theo waved a hand in his air. "What's the news that makes you look like you're going to come in your pants?"

"I have far too much self-control to ever come

in my pants," the other man replied archly. "Now. What if I told you that I've found a buyer for Crossing Lines already? One willing to pay seventy-five million, not fifty, with the caveat that she take over the company now. Now, not in three to five years! I've never come across this kind of deal, man. You must shit gold."

"Every morning," Theo responded automatically, but his eyes widened as the news sank in. "Seventy-five million? Are you for real?"

"Real as rain, brother." John drummed his fingers on the desk. "She's the sister of some European prince. I guess she met her now-fiancé on Crossing Lines and fell in love with the premise. She's excited to take it in a new direction."

"A new direction?" Theo frowned, rubbing a hand over his chest. "We've barely started going in *this* direction."

John shrugged, his smile wide. "For seventy-five million, I'd say she can take it in whatever direction she wants. And here's the thing. She wants to hire you as the business head of her corporation. Interview other people with start-ups like yours, develop them under her banner."

"Really?" That was what he'd vaguely thought that he'd wind up doing eventually, but years down the line—and for his own corporation, of course. Still, excitement buzzed along his skin. It felt like validation—this was the kind of opportunity that most people only dreamed of, and it was being offered to him because he'd earned it himself. It sounded too good to be true. "I can't even wrap my head around that."

"It's the dream." John cocked his head, studying Theo's expression. "Of course, you'd probably have to leave Boston."

"What?" The airy excitement crashed to the ground, weighed down by reality. It *was* too good to be true. Because leaving Boston was the one thing he couldn't do.

His fingers reached out to grip the edge of the desk, steadying him as his world tilted.

"Well, she's from some little country I've never even heard of," John said slowly, watching Theo closely. "But she did mention something about San Francisco."

San Francisco was a million miles away.

His unease must have shown on Theo's face, because John cocked his head, looking at him with concern. "What's wrong? I thought this was what you wanted. You should be thrilled."

"It's amazing." Theo heard the hollowness in his own words. "I think I just need to let it sink in."

John smiled with relief before rising to his feet. Pitching both his coffee cup and Theo's into the trash, he leaned across the desk to clap Theo on the shoulder. "To hell with this swill. I'm going to go send Ava out for a bottle of scotch. No, I'll go myself, to that place next door. This calls for a celebration."

Theo opened his mouth to tell his colleague that he didn't drink, but the words caught in his throat. He nodded numbly as John rounded the desk and opened the door.

Jo was on the other side.

"Jo!" John was flying so high on the offer that he reached out and caught Jo in a one-arm hug. "Come on in! We'll be celebrating in a minute. Join us."

Jo arched an eyebrow at the uncharacteristic buoyancy in John before casting a vaguely amused smile Theo's way. "What are we celebrating? Must be good. He was bouncing like Tigger."

Theo blinked up at her mechanically. He should have been thrilled. This was everything he'd worked for, everything he'd dreamed of, years ahead of schedule. He'd prove to everyone, and finally to himself, that he was no longer just a trust-fund baby. He was a self-made man.

The only person he cared about proving that to was standing right in front of him.

"There's been an offer to buy the company." His words sounded like they were coming from a great distance, somewhere outside his own body. "A great offer, actually."

Jo's face lit up, and it was like she'd taken a pair of tweezers and started pinching at his heart. "That's amazing! So amazing, Theo. I'm so happy for you."

Theo's arm felt like it weighed as much as an elephant as he lifted it to rub a hand over his face. "Yeah. Plus, it came with a new job offer. One that's hard to turn down."

Jo flew at him, wrapping him in an enthusiastic hug that was completely devoid of any of the shadows of their past. He caught her around the waist, urging her back to her feet instead of hauling her into his lap like he wanted to.

She blinked, clearly startled. Wariness flickered through her eyes. "What's wrong?"

There was no good way to tell her, but he knew that she'd never tolerate him keeping something so monumental from her.

"I wouldn't be able to stay in Boston."

Jo froze. Literally just froze in place, eyes wide, an empty smile pasted on her face. She stared at him for a long moment, and he knew that she could see every ounce of the angst that he was feeling, pouring off him in waves.

"Well, of course you have to go." She clapped her hands together, as if in glee, but her voice was hollow. "This is what you wanted, even if it's a little ahead of schedule!"

"Jo." He couldn't handle it. Her voice was positively perky. The girl he'd known, the woman he knew were many things, but perky wasn't one of them. "What about us?"

"Theo." Her almost manic smile dimmed a few watts but remained pasted on her face. "We've been back together…or whatever this is…for less than a week. I'm glad we got to move past some of that old hurt, and I'm grateful for it. But there's no question that you have to take this!"

"Jo," he said again, this time more urgently. Her eyes widened, but the mask of fake happiness stayed plastered to her face. "Talk to me."

"I actually have to get back to work." She dusted her hands on the thighs of her jeans. "I just had to ask John a question about the article I'm working on, but I can ask him later. I promised him I'd have it in this afternoon, so I really do have to get back to work."

Her movements were choppy, robotic, as if controlled by someone else. And as if he didn't already feel like absolute shit, Theo realized that if he sold the company, there was no guarantee that Jo's job would still exist once the new owner had taken over.

Closing his eyes for a second, he fisted his

hands at his sides as he tried to get ahold of his options. When he opened them again, Jo was half-way through the door, her own hands balled into tight fists, too.

"Jojo." He used her old nickname without thinking. She stiffened, her shoulders hunching up around her ears. "Tell me not to go."

She didn't turn around. Theo held his breath, and he knew that he wanted her to tell him to stay more than he wanted to sell his company.

"This is the best thing that's ever happened to you." She didn't even bother to turn around, instead directing her words back over her shoulder. "And you know what, I'm really not feeling well. I promise I'll get the article in on time, but I think I need to work from home for the afternoon."

"Jo." Rising to his feet, he strode across the office after her, but she sliced a hand through the air, letting him know without a word that she wouldn't tolerate being touched.

"'Bye, Theo." And then she was gone, down the hall and into the elevator. Ava stood as Jo hurried by, clearly picking up on the waves of emotion emanating from the other woman. His assistant looked back down the hall toward him, and the pity on her face told her that she'd intuited what happened.

He didn't know what to say. He didn't know

what to do. He started down the hall after Jo, but Ava shook her head, halting him in his tracks.

"If you go tearing after her, you'll argue and one or both of you will say something that you regret." Shaking her head, she sat back down at her desk. "But honestly, Theo, I don't know what you thought you were doing with her. You're on your way up. You're a star. And she's just the girl from where you started."

Theo looked down at her, wondering how he'd ever found her attractive. How he'd ever even looked at a woman besides Jo. Still, Ava had a point. Jo needed some time to calm down.

And he needed to absorb the fact that the woman he'd planned to tell he loved had told him in no uncertain terms to go ahead and move across the country.

The elevator doors slid open, and Theo felt his heart leap into his throat. He groaned when he saw that the only occupant was John, bearing a bottle of what Theo recognized as a brand of scotch that was both hideously expensive and very old.

"Don't look so thrilled to see me," the other man said drily as he stepped off the elevator. He held up the bottle of scotch, wigging it so that the amber contents sloshed invitingly. "After all, all I've done today is earn you seventy-five million big ones."

Striding forward, John passed the bottle to

Theo, then continued down the hall. “Ava, can you grab us some glasses? Then come join us. It’s time to celebrate!”

Acid churned in Theo’s gut. The last thing he wanted to do was celebrate. His heart was too heavy for that. But if Jo didn’t care whether he stayed or went, then what else was he going to do?

Drawing everything he felt into a tight bundle and shoving it down deep inside, he followed John down the hall. He was about to accept the deal he’d been working toward since…well, since the night of Jo’s eighteenth birthday, when she’d opened his eyes to everything he’d been taking for granted.

So why did it feel like he’d lost it all?

CHAPTER FIFTEEN

THE BOTTLE OF hideously expensive scotch sat on the polished Brazilian wood coffee table. Its legs were carved with whimsical tree frogs and palm fronds, one of the pieces that his mother had once hauled into the house to counteract his father's love of everything stiff and dignified.

He would have given that entire seventy-five million dollars away on the street just to be able to talk to his mom again, right now. His relationship with his dad had deteriorated beyond the point of repair by the time his father had died, but he still believed that if his mom had been able to fight back the cancer that had killed her, they would have still been close. He would have been able to call her right now, to ask her how to fix this gigantic mess.

He couldn't do that. And so he was still eyeing the unopened bottle of scotch, its contents glimmering enticingly in the fading light streaming in through the living room window.

A drink wouldn't help him make Jo love him, but it would sure numb the misery that had weighed down his limbs so much that he wasn't sure he'd ever move again.

He leaned back on the stiff sofa, letting his head rest on the back. Closing his eyes, he fought the desire for the drink that was taunting him. He focused on slowing his breathing, on trying to find some semblance of calm. When a chime sounded, he thought that maybe he'd finally achieved some deeper state of being, though he wasn't entirely sure he believed in stuff like that.

The musical note sounded again, and he sat up stiffly, feeling like he'd been drugged. The doorbell—it was the doorbell. Woodenly, he pushed off the sofa and moved to the front door.

Jo's mother stood on the other side. Well-worn yellow oven mitts covered her hands as she clutched tightly to a large pot.

"Hello, Theodore." She smiled up at him, the fading sunlight catching in the virulently crimson strands of her hair as she held out the pot. He smelled garlic, Italian seasoning and, best of all, spicy sausage.

He knew that smell. "Italian sausage soup?" He'd eaten countless bowls of that soup on the well-worn table in the house next door. His heart contracted, and the warmth he'd been so desperately craving as he stared at the bottle of scotch gathered in his core.

"You know it." She arched an eyebrow, and he saw a hint of Jo's stubbornness play out over her finer features. "Are you going to invite me in, or do I have to be rude and invite myself?"

Choking out a laugh, he stepped back and let her in. She sailed through the door like a steamboat, heading back to the kitchen.

"I'll just get this right on the stove. You'll eat a bowl now, yes?"

He knew Jo's mother—Mamesie—well enough to know that this wasn't a question. She wanted to talk to him, and she'd decided that he could use a meal while she did.

He rubbed his stomach, which had woken up at the tantalizing scent of the comfort food. She wasn't wrong. He couldn't remember if he'd eaten lunch, and he remembered quite well that his breakfast had been derailed by sex with Jo.

Mamesie had already filled a large bowl by the time he entered the kitchen. She'd placed it on the wide marble island with a spoon and had produced a loaf of bread from the tote bag she'd had slung over her shoulder. The yeasty scent of home-baked bread made his stomach rumble as she sawed off a gigantic slice and balanced it on the edge of his bowl.

"You haven't been by to see me since you've been back," she commented mildly as she leaned over the edge of the island, across from where she'd set the soup. He winced as he slid onto one of the bar stools.

"You still don't pull punches, I see." Lifting the spoon, he trailed it through the soup, watching the red droplets as they slid off the metal.

"I'm not done." Hooking her thick-rimmed glasses into the front of her blousy shirt, she cast him a disapproving stare. "I've got one miserable girl at home. She's holed up in her room and won't talk to anyone, not even Beth."

"Shit." Theo dropped his spoon. "It's my fault, Mamesie. I'm so sorry. I didn't mean for any of this to happen."

"Are you the only person in this relationship?" she asked mildly, and he shook his hand, feeling as though she'd slapped his hand. "Then I highly doubt that it's all your fault. So why don't you tell me about it?"

He opened his mouth, then shook his head. "With all due respect, I don't think I should. Jo is your girl."

"Theo." The depth of emotion in Mamesie's voice had him looking up, startled. "Jo is my girl.

But you've been my boy, ever since the day I met you. Don't you know that by now?"

Her words were the balm he'd needed. Swallowing thickly, he forced himself to begin speaking. He found himself telling her everything, right back to the night he'd left—well, everything except the sex. There were some things a mother didn't need to know.

She nodded when he was done, and he set his spoon down. He was surprised to discover that he'd eaten all of the bread and soup, and felt a hell of a lot better for it.

"So let me get this straight." Pushing back from the island, Mamesie fixed him with a cool, pale stare. "You told Jo, before this offer came in, that this exact thing was what you dreamed of accomplishing. Then you told her that your dream had come true. And *then* you told her to be the one to tell you to stay."

"Ah…yes. That would be accurate." When it was all laid out like that, it didn't sound so great. "But I want to stay, if she'll have me."

"Do you think my daughter loves you?" There was no judgment in Mamesie's words, but the question brought Theo up short. He knew how he felt, but Jo's response earlier that day had made him question whether he'd imagined everything between them.

But…he knew he hadn't. Jo might not want to love him, but she did. They'd been apart for a long time, but he still felt he knew her heart.

He nodded.

"So she loves you. And she told you to go pursue your dream, because it's what she thinks will make you happy." Mamesie shook her head. "Gee, I wonder why that is."

Hope was a wild thing, unfurling inside him. "So what do I do?"

Unhooking her glasses again, she placed them squarely on her nose, then peered at him with the withering expression that no one mastered like a mother. "You go get her, you lunkhead. But have another bowl of soup first."

CHAPTER SIXTEEN

"YOU'RE GOING TO have to talk about it sooner or later," Amy commented mildly. Jo peeled a slice of cucumber off her eye and glared balefully down at where her youngest sister was painting her toenails neon pink. "If you don't we're just going to keep torturing you with beauty treatments."

"There's nothing to talk about." Jo removed the second cucumber slice, tossing them both into the trash can as she struggled to sit up. Holding up a foot, she wiggled her newly polished toenails and grimaced.

"Why pink?" she asked Amy, voice sullen. "You have every color of nail polish known to man in your room, so why the hell would you choose pink for me?"

"Pink with sparkles," Amy replied cheerfully, pulling her legs up under her where she sat on Jo's bed. "And I just told you. We're torturing you with spa night until you talk to us."

"There's nothing to talk about." Jo crossed her legs as well, looking down at the floor where Meg was stirring something in a bowl. "What the hell is that?"

"It's a hair mask." Meg smiled beatifically up at her. "Egg yolk and avocado oil. And it's going on your head unless you spill."

"I just said, there's nothing to spill!" Throwing her hands into the air, she accidentally brushed one against her cheek. It came back with a smear of green slime. "Can I wash this off now?"

"Not until it's dry." Beth sat on the floor with Meg, holding a plastic shower cap. "The clay won't have pulled all the crap out of your pores until then."

"Fantastic." Jo sucked in a deep breath. Her sisters had her number—this was a form of torture uniquc to her, and she wasn't enjoying even a second of it. Her room smelled like flowers, the mask on her face itched and her toenails were fucking pink. More than that, she was miserable.

Had it really only been a few days since Theo had crashed back into her life? As far as her heart was concerned, he'd never left. But that was the thing, wasn't it—he was going to leave.

And if she stopped him, what the hell kind of

person would she be? Not one who wanted the best for the person she loved, that was for sure.

Her computer pinged, a notification that she had a new comment on her blog. Normally she loved checking out people's responses to what she'd written, but right now she couldn't imagine ever posting again. She couldn't imagine wanting to know anything about sex ever again, because she'd always associate the act with Theo. He was her match in every sense of the word.

She'd known he would probably go, but the pain was worse than anything she could have imagined.

"Well, then. Since you're still holding out, it's hair treatment time." Meg wiggled a paintbrush in her direction. "Come here!"

The thought of raw egg, cold and slimy on her head, was finally enough to make her crack. Scuttling back into the corner of her bed, out of Meg's reach, she growled at her sisters as a whole. "Fine! Fine! I've been sleeping with Theo. And I fucking fell in love with him again, and he's moving to San Francisco with all of the hippies, and I'm *miserable*! Is that what you wanted to hear?"

"It's what I wanted to hear." Jo shrieked as Theo stuck a leg inside her window, knocking her pen cup off her desk. Clapping a hand to her chest as he hauled himself up so that he was straddling her windowsill, she gaped at him in shock. "What the hell do you think you're doing?"

"The last big discussion we had, you climbed in my bedroom window." With a grunt, he pulled his second leg in through the window, sliding into her room. Offering a disarming grin to her sisters, he nodded. "Hi, girls. Do you mind giving us a minute?"

"Not at all." Balancing the bowl of hair gunk in one hand, Meg rose smoothly to her feet. Smirking at Jo, she waved the paintbrush around. "Should I save this for later?"

Jo bared her teeth, and Meg just laughed. Offering Beth a hand, she hauled her other sister to her feet, then nudged her to the door. "Come on Beth, Amy. You guys can argue over who gets the hair mask."

"Not on your fucking life," they said together, all three jostling their way through Jo's bedroom door. Beth was the only one who looked back over her shoulder, smiling softly at her older sister. "Don't be a total bitch, okay? You know what you want."

Then she was gone, closing the door softly behind her. Jo didn't even take offense to her parting comment, because heaven knew, she was *feeling* bitchy. Bitchy, and prickly, and spoiling for a fight.

"That's a good look for you," Theo commented

mildly as he turned to face her, arms crossed over his chest. Damn it, why did he have to look so good? Dressed in a pair of jeans that were faded in all the right places, with a navy T-shirt that stretched tight over his chest, she had to curl her fingers against the urge to reach out and touch.

Jo looked down at her torn jeans. She was only wearing a cotton sports bra on top, since she still had a thick layer of clay on her face. Her hair was scraped back from her face with a fuzzy headband, and her toes were pink and glittered when she moved.

Well, he'd seen her looking worse. Spreading her hands wide, she shrugged. "This is who I am, Theo. What's the matter? Not fancy enough for your big new job?"

He ignored the hostility in her voice. Instead, he held out a small, tattered package wrapped in faded paper. Hesitantly, she took it, squinting to read the words printed on the wrapping. "Happy birthday? My birthday isn't for months. How quickly they forget."

Never mind Beth's gentle admonishment—she was being bitchy. She couldn't seem to help it. She was furious, not with him for pursuing his dream, but with herself for knowing that she'd never get over him.

"I'm reenacting our last night together, back

then. But backward." He stuffed his hands in his pockets, then rocked back on his heels. He was barefoot. "You climbed in my window. I'm climbing in yours. We had a fight, and I didn't give you your present. We are *not* going to have a fight now, and I'm finally giving that birthday present to you."

"This is the present you were going to give me then?" Shock crashed over her like an ice-cold wave. "You kept it all this time?"

"It was still in the drawer beside the bed in my old room when I moved back here." He grinned mischievously. "Right beside a box of condoms that are most definitely expired."

Jo rolled her eyes but couldn't stop her fingers from trembling. Why was he giving this to her now? Couldn't he just go and leave her and her broken heart alone?

"Open it," he commanded, and before she could think it through, she was tearing open the paper. Inside was a square gift box, and as she lifted the lid, her pulse started to thunder at the base of her throat.

Inside, nestled in a bed of cotton, was a gleaming white-gold pendant. She didn't wear jewelry, never had, but when she held it up closer to her eyes, she immediately understood why Theo had chosen it for her.

"These are made from antique wax seals, ones that were actually once used by someone to seal letters," he informed her, attention focused on her, laser sharp. "Your Louisa May Alcott probably used one. I didn't know that then, but I'm just trying to make you like it more now."

"I do like it," she managed to force out through her dry throat. "But—"

"In case you haven't looked that closely yet, it has two hearts on it," he interrupted, smiling innocently when she glared at him. "They're tied together with a ribbon. And it says *forever.*"

Jo felt her heart crack right open. "Why the hell would you give this to me now?"

"I love you, but sometimes you need to try to see beyond that thick skull of yours." Her head snapped up, but he wasn't done. "I was going to tell you that I loved you this afternoon, before everything went to shit."

When he dropped down to one knee in front of her, Jo gasped. "What—"

"Just let me finish before you yell at me." Grabbing one of her hands, he held tight even when she tried to pull away. "Look. You walked in right after I heard that news. I hadn't even begun to digest it yet, and I needed to tell someone. You were it."

"And I still think you should go." This was

a nightmare, bringing her so close to what she wanted before cruelly tearing it away.

"I don't want to." A cry of anguish tore out of her throat, and when he tried to speak again, she shook her head.

"You can't stay because of me. You'll resent the hell out of me, and I'll wallow in guilt." She swallowed past the sting of incoming tears. "But I…fuck, I'm just going to say it. I love you, too. You can be a cocky asshole, but you're my cocky asshole. I… I'll go with you. If you want me to."

A grin as bright as sunshine spread over his face, and its light chased away some of the dread that crowded after her declaration. She absolutely would go with him, because she needed to be with him. But leaving her family would be one of the hardest things she'd ever done.

"I don't want to go." He growled overtop of her protest. "Hear me out, woman. This deal is amazing, but it's not the deal for me. I'm not ready to turn Crossing Lines over to someone else. I might not ever be. And I don't actually want to move. I've lived in lots of places, but this is the one that feels like home."

"I—what?" Jo gaped down at him as a terrible hope sprang up inside her.

"But I want to stay on one condition." Squeezing her fingers, he looked up at her, and love shone from his eyes. "I'd marry you tomorrow, but something tells me that you'll inform me that that timeline is ridiculous. So I think, in exchange for my selfless decision to stay here in Boston, that you should move in with me."

"Move in with you?" Jo couldn't keep up. Her fingers clenched around the small box that she still held. "Next door?"

"That's the idea. I know you're attached to your family home, but I've discovered that I'm kind of attached to mine, too." He cocked his head, studying her face. "I suppose I could move in here, but I think Ford might try to punch me in such close quarters, and it would be a shame to leave that giant house next door all empty. Just think, you could have an office. You could have a suite of offices."

"You sweet talker, you." Closing her eyes, she shook her head in disbelief. "I don't know what to say. I'm sorry I was such a bitch."

"It's part of your charm." He rose to his feet when she snorted. "I'm serious. I love you, Jo, every last bit of you. I wish I had a ring to put on your finger right now, but today has been a little bit busy. Tomorrow we can go pick a ring."

Unable to hold back the laughter, Jo allowed a tear to spill over. It scalded the tender skin of her cheek, allowing another to trickle down, and before she knew it she was crying full out, burying her clay-covered face in Theo's T-shirt. He didn't even complain, just pressed her against him as though he never wanted to let go.

"I don't need a ring." Her voice cracked, and she cleared her throat. Lifting her head, she grinned up at him as a content she'd never imagined she could feel flooded through her like warm sunshine. "I only need you."

"And I need you. I love you." Dipping his head, he pressed a kiss to her clay-smeared forehead, then wiped the excess off his mouth with a grin. "Come on. Let's go home."

*****

COMING SOON!

We really hope you enjoyed reading this book. If you're looking for more romance, be sure to head to the shops when new books are available on

Thursday 25th July

To see which titles are coming soon, please visit

millsandboon.co.uk/nextmonth